A Time to Heal

To Ross & Veronica
Great friends to
Evie and me

Tom Fiske
8/21/2007

A Time to Heal

by

Thomas Sebastian Fiske

FirstPublish, Inc.
Orlando, Florida

ISBN
1-929925-62-X

Thomas Sebastian Fiske
A Time to Heal

Also by Thomas S. Fiske
Four on the Floor
The Courage Place

FIRSTPUBLISH, INC.
170 Sunport Ln. Suite 900
Orlando, FL 32809
407-240-1414
www.firstpublish.com

Dedicated to the memory of a man who believed in
freedom,
Henry Bruce Vallandingham

¼ Indian

Foreword

A man named Henry Bruce Vallandingham was murdered in public on a main street in a small town in Missouri. It was 1856, a wild time just after the famous (or infamous) John Brown hacked up a half-dozen or more slave owners in the nearby Kansas Territory.

Most murders occur under the cover of darkness, but Henry's murder was at noon, in public, on a busy street. The claim was made by the killer that Henry had been seeing the killer's wife. There was something very odd about this claim.

In order to tell the story, I provided a set of imaginary characters to discover each painful fact, but the historical characters were real people. I included at the beginning of each chapter *actual* advertisements from the newspaper of a small town, which I call Levanger. Most of these are important to the story and I recommend that the reader read them carefully.

A Time to Heal describes actual historical events. The *Grover Genealogy* is real and the names I have taken from it are also real. While the town and its county where the murder took place were made up, the people in the story who associated with Henry Vallandingham did exist. S.H. Woodson can be found in the register of the U.S. Congress. The newspaper ads used actual names of people living in 1856. Lawrence, Kansas, was actually raided, causing the deaths of many people. And there is one more bit of historical significance.

If Henry's surname seems familiar to historians, it is because his first cousin, Clement Laird Vallandigham (slightly different spelling), was the "Copperhead" who dared to stand up to President Lincoln during Lincoln's period of tyrannical behavior toward Northern Democrats during the War Between the States.

Neither cousin was in favor of slavery. They may not have even been acquainted, although Henry's family was aware of the existence of Clement Laird's family.

Lt. Col. George Vallandigham of the Continental Army had a son, Lewis, by what appears to have been an American Indian woman in 1761. Perhaps the first wife died. At any rate, George Vallandigham later married Elizabeth Noble and began a second family, which led to Clement.

Lewis Vallandingham, also a soldier in the Continental Army, was said to have been quite dark-skinned and was employed to spy on Indians. It is quite likely, since his father was tall, blue eyed and light brown haired, that Lewis had an Indian mother. Thus, his son, Henry Vallandingham, would have been one-fourth Indian. He may well have known what it was to be "different" from all the white settlers. Certainly, his father knew. Perhaps it was this background that led to his dislike of slavery.

All that exists of Henry these days is an old portrait, a letter to his daughter, a poem and his grave in Georgetown Cemetery in Scott County, Kentucky. Attempts to blacken Henry's name worked for a while. But research has shown that Henry was a hero, not a villain. His wife knew that. She waited patiently for about forty years, but now lies beside him for all eternity. She knew the truth, and this book is an attempt to set the matter straight.

Acknowledgements

First, many thanks to my wife, Evelyn Shippy Fiske, who read through this manuscript and devoted many hours to the reduction of its errors. Mrs. Barbara Ajello also lent her editing efforts. Second, many thanks to my writer's club at the Church of the Good Shepherd in Arcadia, California, who spent many hours patiently listening as I read each chapter. They offered suggestions to clear up misunderstandings they observed. Third, thanks to the research librarians at the Arcadia Public Library who were able to fill my odd requests for material, no matter what I asked of them. Finally, I want to thank the folks at the LDS Family History Library in eastern Pasadena, California, who also provided much kind direction to my research.

Some of this material appeared in *Heritage Quest Magazine* and in *Northern Kentucky Heritage Magazine* and is used with the generous permission of the publishers.

Chapter One

Recovery room nurses are so damn polite. "Mr. Towles wake up now! Your surgery is over and you are doing just fine. Come on now, we have to leave the recovery room and get you back to your bed soon."

Stokely Towles, known by his friends as "Stoke," heard most of this message as he came out of his anesthesia-induced sleep. The day's events drifted in to fill the space left by a wonderful dream about camping out in the lush forests of early Kentucky, where he was another Daniel Boone with a long rifle, being chased by Indians.

Reality faded in harshly. Earlier in the day he had been running. He had not slowed at the two steps in front of the building where he lived. Somehow, his left foot slipped off the first step. Then his right foot came down hard and at the wrong angle on the second step. He heard and felt his right ankle shatter. It hurt like hell.

A man who was mowing the lawn saw what was happening and went to a neighbor who called paramedics at the local fire station. A big red shiny ambulance dropped Stoke off at the nearest emergency room within ten minutes. There were few customers at the time and

1

medics came to his aid almost immediately. One attendant apologized and asked if she could cut open the legs of his running clothes so they could see them better for X-rays. Thinking of the alternative of pulling his pants off over his obviously broken right ankle, Stoke quickly agreed. After a while a doctor came in with the X-ray plates and showed him how badly the bones were broken.

Telling Stoke it would be best if he would operate and put screws in the pieces of bones to hold them together, the doctor waited for approval. Stoke hated the thought of surgery. He knew his past history of infections and long periods of recovery. He countered with a plan to put the leg into a cast and wait for the bones to heal. The doctor said it would take forever. There was no assurance that the bones would heal correctly. So Stoke gave in.

The progression of people Stoke saw after his accident exhibited an extraordinary interest in his Social Security number. After reciting it forwards and backwards several times, he realized that his inquisitors were only trying to see if he were in shock. They weren't really interested in the number at all. Actually, he was in a state of boredom, not shock. Someone shot a blend of Demerol and Valium into his hip, so his pains slipped away. There was nothing to do or read until a doctor showed up. When the doctor came to Stoke, he asked if it would be all right to put the dislocated ankle back into position. Stoke watched as the doctor pulled and pushed and grunted. Finally it popped back together. The drugs were so effective that Stoke hardly felt any pain.

As time for surgery grew near, a new doctor came in and was introduced as "Doctor Schmidt," who was to be administering anesthesia. Everybody including Stoke shook hands. Even though the situation was serious, he couldn't help but think of a restaurant scene, where a young girl saunters up to a table and says, "Hello, my name is Debbie and I will be your waitress tonight."

Dr. Schmidt seemed to recognize Stoke's name. He frowned a minute and said, "Towles. Are you related to the Towles who is on the board of the hospital?"

"Very closely," Stoke said. "I'm on the board of your hospital but that's kind of unimportant at the moment." Service immediately improved, although he didn't expect it. He thought the staff was very solicitous before they knew he was connected to the hospital.

While he was waiting for surgery, Stoke took a small telephone from his shirt pocket and called his office to let his secretary know where he was. He said he would be unavailable for a few days, which turned out to be a grand understatement. The supervisor of admitting clerks came to get vital information, such as the drugs he was allergic to. She was almost afraid to approach his bed. But finally, the administrative work was done, and he leaned back to wait for a series of events over which he had no control.

So that was why the recovery room nurses were trying to rouse Stoke from his dream of a day in the Kentucky woods. Doctors had screwed his leg bones back together. He was now waking from the operation. Lying on his back with his leg in a heavy cast, his eyes focused on the friendly face hovering above him. It was a pretty face. If his leg didn't hurt so much, he would have liked to engage the face in conversation, while checking out the rest of the person to whom the face was attached. But his leg felt as if it were on fire and he was unable to find a comfortable place to put it. The Demerol had worn off. No matter what position he tried, pain continued to stab at him.

Somehow a nurse and an aide got him off the surgical bed and onto a portable bed. This wasn't easy because Stoke was six feet tall and weighed 180 pounds, without a cast. They wheeled the portable bed out of the post-operative room and into a hall. All he could see was a series of ceilings and lighting fixtures. Then he saw a familiar face. It was a surgeon he knew named John Balyo who had just come out of another surgery room. At least he hoped it was another surgery room since John was a gynecologist.

"Hi, John," Stoke said as he rolled by. The orderly stopped the bed when he saw the doctor.

Dr. Balyo looked down at the face for a minute and said, "Stoke, what are you doing here?" Automatically, he took Stoke's medical chart and scanned it while talking.

Stoke told him, "Did your mother ever tell you, 'Don't run up the steps! You'll fall and break a leg and then don't come running to me?' Well, I ran up the steps. Come up to my room and see me some time."

"Great," said John, "but I don't want to have lunch here. Let's wait until you can go out, okay?" He put the chart back and signaled the orderly to continue with the bed.

With that forbidding evaluation of the food, Stoke and his bed swept into an elevator. The door closed. He went from the second floor to the third floor. There was another long trip down a hall filled to overflowing with strange noises. Then he was rolled into his room. Shifting to his permanent bed was another painful experience. At last he was back where he was to stay for the next five days.

Several nurses introduced themselves while they poked and prodded and took temperatures. He was grateful that they put the thermometers in his mouth. Stoke had a fever, so one of the nurses attached a bottle of medicine to the IV line that was already pumping a clear liquid into his arm.

A different nurse came in with a syringe. This nurse was a man, but he was extremely welcome, and almost as pretty as the women because he was carrying a painkiller. Hospital gown up, quick wipe with cold alcohol and a shot in the hip occurred almost in one motion. Stoke began to relax.

In a kind of a dream state, Stoke faded out of the present and drifted into the past, where he thought about his grandmother and a conversation they had when he was a boy, almost thirty years before.

"Grandma, who was it that was murdered?" the young Stoke asked.

"It was my great-grandfather. I didn't really know him. Who told you about him —-your mother?"

"Yes, she told me. Why did they do it?"

"Maybe," she said wisely, "you are worried that someone will be mad at you, too. But those men all died long ago. They were in a war and it is all settled now. So, please don't worry about it."

"Don't you remember when it happened?" Stoke asked.

"No, I don't. Some time before the Civil War, I think. I'm kind of hazy about the story. In fact, I don't even remember his name! That's silly, but you will be old someday. Then you will understand."

"You mean no one knows who did it?"

"Not anymore. Of course, his wife knew. I'm sure their children knew. His wife moved back home and started her life over. Then the War Between the States came; so many were killed that one death more or less didn't make any difference. It was a terrible time for most American families."

"Mr. Towles, are you all right?" came a loud grating female voice that interrupted the dream.

"No, I seem to have a broken leg," was the reply. "Other than that, I had a good day and met lots of nice people."

"What I meant was, do you need anything?" asked the hospital volunteer aide who came in to pay her respects. She was an elderly lady who had a positive outlook on life that was matched only by her deafness. She said, "May I call your wife or someone to tell them that you are in the hospital?"

"You can call my ex-wife, but I suspect she has enough problems. There's no one else nearby who needs to know." Stoke thought about Susan and her career that took her away from California to New York. She had found a new love, "the great love of her life," until she had to kick him out for romancing her girlfriend. After that there was not a whole lot of conversation between Stoke and Susan.

"What about your office, Mr. Towles?" the aide asked, not willing to give up.

"I've talked with them already. My staff is taking care of things."

"Oh, what do you do?" asked the woman.

"I'm a consultant. My name, by the way, rhymes with what you pay to cross the Golden Gate Bridge—tolls, not towels."

Stoke did some consulting; what he said was true. But that did not say it all. He owned several companies and had not actively consulted for several years, except to help his own managers. His expertise was in management. His clientele had been people in a few very select, very profitable companies, whose owners were grateful for Stoke's help. Their gratitude allowed Stoke to buy struggling divisions which they had "spun off." He rebuilt them and made himself quite wealthy. Such success provided Stoke with powerful enemies, who forced him into more anonymity than most people would seek.

Then he thought there was one person in town who might care: Marilee. Marilee Cho was a nine-year-old Chinese girl who lived on the floor below Stoke's penthouse. She was one of the very few females who ever got past his doors. Most women didn't know where he lived. He discovered after his divorce that too many single women wanted to be his "friend."

Stoke first met Marilee in the lobby of his building. When he was at his California home in Newport Beach, a limousine picked him up at his front door each morning. He began to notice a small girl waiting for her ride in the front lobby where he waited for his ride. She was a very ordinary-looking girl: thin, with black hair that went in all directions. Her eyes were obviously Asian. She was with her mother, a small, delicate Chinese woman in some kind of Asian costume, wearing carefully applied makeup. The mother looked like a porcelain doll.

One morning as Stoke entered the lobby, he saw the girl and her mother in their usual places near the door. Something was on the ground by the girl's foot. It was a small hat from the head of a doll the girl was holding. Stoke knelt and picked up the hat.

"Excuse me, madam," he said, "I believe you dropped this."

"The girl looked at Stoke and said with precise British English, "Thank you, sir."

As she took the hat, Stoke said, "I was speaking to the lady you had in your arms. You and I haven't been introduced, you know."

The mother broke her silence and said, "I can fix that. This is Marilee Cho. May I present Mr…?"

"Stokely Towles, ma'am." With that, he shook Marilee's small hand.

Turning to the mother, Stoke said, "And are you Mrs. Cho?"

"Yes," she said, also in British English, tinged with a slight Mandarin accent. "I am Elizabeth Cho. We seem to be neighbors."

"That seems to be the case. I'm on the top floor."

Stoke noticed that his limousine had driven up. "But I see my ride is here. Perhaps we can talk more tomorrow," he said as the driver got out and looked both up and down the streets. He made an "all clear" hand signal and Stoke went out and climbed in the back seat.

Having broken the ice, Stoke talked more the next day with Marilee and Elizabeth. After a few weeks of these morning "meetings," Stoke and Marilee were pals. Elizabeth was more reserved. But she did mention that her husband had been killed by soldiers in Mainland China two years ago. Then one day, Elizabeth did something completely out of character; she asked a personal favor of Stoke.

"I have to go out for a while this evening. Would it be possible for Marilee to stay with you for a couple of hours? She is very shy and hates to go out with me. If you say no, I will understand. I hate to ask you, but there has been a death in my family!" She looked somewhat stricken.

Stoke answered, "Well, Elizabeth, you have to understand that I'm a bachelor and not used to small girls. I can easily be taken advantage of."

Elizabeth smiled. "Yes, that is a danger. Still, it would help us both a great deal. Can I leave her with you at seven this evening?"

"Sure. But you can't get to my place from yours. It takes a special elevator code." He wrote out some numbers on his business card.

"When you get into the elevator, push these keys and it will let you come up to my floor." Stoke didn't want to make a copy of the code, but he felt that this very self-sufficient Chinese lady had no ulterior motives. He felt had to trust someone, once in a while.

That evening at seven, Stoke had forgotten all about Marilee when a knock came at his door. He looked through the peephole and saw no one. Then he remembered Marilee. She wasn't tall enough to appear in the viewer. He opened the door and there she stood, with some books in one hand and a doll in the other.

"Good evening, madam. How are you?"

"Just fine, Mr. Towles. May I come in?"

"Sure, but where is your mother?" Stoke asked, thinking Elizabeth would bring Marilee herself.

"Mama is getting ready to go. Is that all right?"

"Of course. Why don't you call your mother and tell her you're here?"

"All right," said Marilee as she took off her coat and reached for a telephone. Then she had a short conversation with her mother in Mandarin. After that she spread out her books and began to read on the floor. Stoke went to work on a report he was preparing for the next day.

In about an hour Stoke turned on his television to see the evening news on cable TV. There was a sameness to network TV that caused him to try other sources for his news. He looked down at his side when he felt someone near his hand. It was Marilee. She sidled up to him and took his big hand in hers. She showed him a drawing she had made. It was a sketch of mechanical objects in three dimensions. He was startled; little girls usually drew flat pictures of cute little things. As he pondered the drawing he found that she had worked herself under his arm as he watched the TV. That lasted a few minutes. Then she went back to her books. Stoke wasn't sure he could cope with a very perceptive child who missed her father as much as Marilee did.

Marilee came back to Stoke several times for reassurance and returned to her books each time. After several hours had gone by she had insinuated herself into his lap. She wondered out loud if there were any ice cream in the refrigerator. Stoke didn't know. He usually ate out or had someone bring his meals to him.

Together they explored the kitchen and found some vanilla ice cream. Marilee found two bowls and a big spoon and gave each of them a large helping. They ate it all.

"Well, Marilee, it appears that your mother wasn't able to get back tonight. Would you be willing to leave a message on her answering machine that you'll be staying here until morning?"

Marilee smiled broadly. "Sure, Mr. Towles. Mama wouldn't mind that at all!"

"Would you please call me 'Stoke'? You can call me 'Mr. Towles' when your mother is around."

"Yes sir, Mr. Stoke. But I don't have any pajamas."

Stoke thought a minute and said, "No problem. One of my tee shirts would make a fine nightgown. I'll put it in the bathroom down the hall. That will be yours for the night."

In a few minutes, Marilee was back, looking quite small in Stoke's big shirt. "That is some outfit," he said as he appraised Marilee's bedtime costume. The tee shirt hung off her shoulder and the sleeves went past her elbows. She looked like a waif from an Asian version of "Tobacco Road."

"You can have the bedroom down the hall just past the bathroom. Good night, Marilee."

Marilee said nothing. She just stood there and looked at him. Stoke looked back, expecting something to happen. Nothing did. Then he had a flash of inspiration.

"It's dark back there, isn't it?"

Marilee nodded her head, but did not take her eyes off Stoke.

"I can understand. Let's go back there together. A girl could fall over something in the dark." He walked down the hall and Marilee followed. Stoke turned on a small nightlight. He tucked Marilee under the covers, her doll clutched tightly in her arms.

Marilee said, "My mother says that people sleep best in the dark."

Stoke responded, "I'm sure that your mom knows what's best at her house. But in my house, people who haven't been here before need small lights so they can find their way around in the dark." Marilee held her arms out to Stoke. He leaned toward her and kissed her good night. She hugged him. The capture of Stokely Towles was complete. And not a shot was fired.

"Well, how in the world did you manage to fall and break your leg?" the deaf hospital aide continued.

"I was just lucky. The steps had their eye on both legs and a hip," Stoke said loudly, "but I outwitted them and came away with only one bad ankle and a few bruises." It was obvious that she wanted to hear more, so Stoke told the entire tale with just the right amount of embellishment. Little did he know that he would be telling the same story over and over to everyone who walked into his room. The accident seemed to have caught the attention of the entire staff.

The aide left a copy of the hospital menu for dinner. Stoke noticed right away that they offered wine with the evening meal, so he signed up for a "house" red. Roast beef, peas and apple pie were also offered. Stoke ordered everything.

When the meal came, he understood what Dr. Balyo was talking about. There was no wine, the food tasted something like cardboard, and it was cold. Stoke's surgeon was a strong religious leader in the area and didn't want his patients to have any wine. Since the good doctor couldn't remove wine from the menus, he had it removed from the "acceptable" list of foods his patients could eat.

As evening came, a few friends dropped in, followed by managers from his businesses. They asked the inevitable question and got the story about his broken bones. Stoke had already decided people liked to hear stories of morbid activities, but he didn't know they were so fascinated by genuinely dumb incidents like falling up steps. His employees tended to put him on a pedestal, so he used the accident to let them know he was just an ordinary mortal.

Reviewing his situation, Stoke knew he had been lucky. He usually healed quickly; he had a good doctor and a good hospital. And there was no great urgency to get back to work. Best of all, the prognosis for complete recovery was good.

Yes, there were some plates and screws in his leg. They might have to come out sometime, but for the present no more surgery was scheduled. He was in good physical and mental shape. *People break their legs all the time and survive quite well,* Stoke mused to himself. But he had not experienced much pain in his life; he was about to get a graduate course in that subject.

During the night, Stoke got Demerol regularly. He would sleep a while, then move slightly and wake up in agony. He would look up into the face of the night nurse who would be adjusting something that fit the tube in his arm. She was a marvel of motion economy, never needing to do the same thing twice. They would talk a bit. Then she would scurry away to the next room. Stoke would drift back into sleep where he would meet with his grandmother once again. The story of the murder would be repeated, but it never got as far as names and places.

The next four days in the hospital were marked by steady improvement. His temperature went down to normal, his blood pressure remained steady and his pain slowly diminished. He told the nurses to stop the pain medicine. Deciding which hip to inject and feeling the needles was getting to be as onerous as the surgery. His leg swelled in its cast, so his surgeon obligingly sawed the cast open to allow more room.

Everybody who came into Stoke's room, from the hospital administrator to the janitors and window washers, wanted to know what had happened. By this time Stoke's story about his broken leg was highly polished and stylized. His humor and good nature made many friends among the staff.

Finally the day came for Stoke to go home. Early that morning a therapist came in with a wheelchair. He showed Stoke how to get in and out of the contrivance without falling on his face. This process was easy for a man with sturdy arms and shoulders, so Stoke handled it well.

With the help of his friend Frank Kendall, Stoke got out to a waiting car and started home. It felt good to leave the hospital but Stoke felt strangely vulnerable. When he put his legs on the floor of the car, blood pressure surged to his toes and made everything ache below his knees.

On the way, which was a short distance across Newport Beach, Stoke watched Frank trying to be very careful not to jar him with sudden stops, or turn too quickly. Frank was a tall, good-looking guy about thirty-five years old. With his crisp curly hair he was the kind of man women go ape over.

Unfortunately for the ladies, Frank was gay. He and Stoke had been friends for five years, when Frank was a labor lawyer and Stoke was a management consultant. They joined forces to end a crippling strike at a client company. They had made a good team professionally. The men's different sexual preferences were mutually ignored as their friendship grew over the years.

By trial and error, Frank got Stoke got out of the car and into his wheelchair. He pushed the chair up to the front door of Stoke's building. Turning the chair backwards, Frank pulled Stoke up the "killer steps" where he had fallen five days before. The elevator took them quickly to the top floor.

Once inside, Stoke wheeled himself over to his favorite recliner chair and swung into it. He looked around his living room, happy to be home with familiar surroundings once more. His home was filled with real antiques and good reproductions of Queen Anne style furniture, which some people called "genteel early American." It was a bright room filled with warm wood tones. Blue predominated among the colors of materials on the couches and chairs. There were some sterling silver plates and pitchers on the tables.

Suddenly Stoke said, "I need to get back into the chair and make a run for the head, Frank. Would you roll the chair over here?" A former Navy pilot, Stoke still used some Navy terms.

Frank got the wheelchair. Stoke gently put himself in it. Then he wheeled it to the bathroom door and stopped. "Damn! This chair is almost too wide for the door!" He made a mental note to check on the sizes of the doors in the various businesses he owned.

It took a while, but Stoke gradually worked his way in to the bathroom. It was a painful process. There was no way for him to close the door.

Relieved in several ways, Stoke worked his way back into his recliner chair in the living room. The trip had taken fifteen minutes. He had scratched paint off the woodwork. He was weak from exertion. He almost wished he were back in the hospital.

Frank said, "Will you be all right if I go out for a while? I'll get some food and something to drink. Here's the TV control, by the way. Have fun with daytime TV."

With that, Frank left. Stoke felt very, very alone for the first time in his life. He called Marilee's apartment and left a message on her answering machine to drop by when she got home from school.

Chapter Two

DISSOLUTION

The partnership heretofore existing under the
Name and style of J. & R. Hale, is this day dissolved by mutual consent. All persons indebted
either by note or account, are requested to call
and settle immediately, as they *must have money*

J. & R. Hale

The undersigned will continue the lumber
business at the old stand, and will keep on
hand an assortment of the

Best Lumber that can be bought

And will be glad to accommodate all old friends.

ROBERT HALE

A faucet was dripping in the kitchen. Each drop sounded like a drumbeat. Stoke pointed the remote at his TV and pushed a button. A picture of Montel someone came up. He seemed to be discussing something inane like the agony of a castrated man trying to find appropriate padding for his jockstrap. He tried another channel. More junk. He found a Dodger baseball game. The Dodgers were losing. He flicked from one channel to another, then turned the TV off in disgust.

Next he turned on his sound equipment. Not wanting to get up, he just played the CD which he had been listening to before he went to the hospital. It was a piano concerto by Beethoven. Number four, he recalled. As the magnificent music swelled throughout the room, Stoke put his head back, closed his eyes and drifted off into a light sleep.

"Grandma, why did someone shoot that man?"

"I don't know, child. People have lots of reasons to be mad at each other. Why don't you do some research when you get older? I bet there is a good story in it. But be careful—we always assume he was a good man. It might be that he was a criminal and then maybe you would wish you had forgotten the whole thing."

In harsh contrast to Grandma's soft southern drawl, the telephone rang loudly to wake Stoke from his daydream.

"Yeah?" Stoke said as the phone came near his mouth. He was more than a little irritated.

"Stoke?" said a woman on the other end of the line.

"Oh, hi, Sandy," Stoke said as he recognized the voice.

"Stoke, I just heard about your accident. How *are* you?" Sandy said, showing concern in her voice.

Sandy was an attractive woman who had had an on-again, off-again relationship with Stoke since he and Susan divorced three years before. He thought about her: tall and blond, with a slender but very feminine shape. Sandy was quite independent, with no immediate plans to settle down. She genuinely liked Stoke, but was not sure about the depth of her love for him. They had fun together and that kept her coming back for more.

"Oh, I'm great from the waist up," Stoke said, "but below the waist there have been some alterations."

"What a shame," Sandy sympathized. "May I come over and split a Coke or something with you while I inspect the damage?"

"Actually, Sandy, I don't want anyone seeing me like this. How about waiting until I get healthier?"

"If I do, I might forget about what goes on from the waist down. Would you want that?"

"Well, if you put it that way," he said, "I guess I could do with better company than Montel."

"I'm on my way." And with that, Sandy hung up.

The telephone rang three more times. Salespeople wanted Stoke to buy a new roof, answer a survey and accept a gift. He declined all three generous offers, then forwarded his calls to an answering service.

Stoke really did not want Sandy to see him so helpless. He was always a *provider* of assistance to people, not a user. He hadn't been dependent on anyone since he was a child. It made him feel quite uncomfortable. Besides, since he went to the hospital five days ago, he hadn't been able to wash his hair. He needed a haircut and his hair was stuck together in one oily, matted hunk.

Somehow he got back into his wheelchair and scooted off to the bathroom, where he leaned over the sink and gathered enough water to wash his hair. He managed to blow it dry before Sandy arrived. He was beginning to feel better, but the experience was tiring.

Just as he eased himself back into his recliner, he heard Sandy at the door. She breezed into his living room followed by a very pleasant perfume and a breath of fresh air from the outside. While carrying a bag of groceries, she leaned over and kissed him firmly on the mouth.

Standing in front of Stoke for a minute, Sandy looked him up and down carefully. She was a pretty woman, wearing a light tan business suit that caressed her form in just the right places. As usual, she looked very trim and every hair was in its correct position.

She broke out in a giggle and said, "So Superman has an Achilles heel after all. You've lost weight, you look pale and you have that huge white cement thing on your leg."

"I need a second opinion."

"All right, your hair looks funny."

"I can have my barber come in and fix that. You should know that I've been in "mint" condition for most of my life. The mint is slightly limp these days, but that won't last."

"Enough excuses! Let's get to the food. I stopped by Trader Joe's to get some goodies you'll like. That's what took me so long. Now tell me what happened and what they've done to you."

Stoke grinned and looked at her. "Did Frank ask you to come over or did you decide to become a caterer on your own?"

"You didn't answer my question, but Frank did leave a message on the answering machine. He was going to get some food, but called me to see if I wanted to bring it over. I just got back from a trade show in

Dallas. Now whether you are hungry or not, I am. Am I going to make an omelet at my place or yours?"

Stoke considered this question for two, maybe three seconds. "Yes, I would love to have an omelet. And a glass of wine would go well with it. The hospital had wine on its menu, but someone drank mine before it got to my room, or something, because I never saw any."

"I thought about that," she said. "I found a very good Chardonnay, but it's not very cold. Do you still want it now?"

"Is a bear Catholic?"

"All right, let me get you a corkscrew," Sandy said as she went off to the kitchen. "Which glasses shall we use?"

"Two straws, please," Stoke responded from his chair.

Sandy came back into the room with two glasses instead and a corkscrew. She handed the corkscrew to Stoke and put the glasses near his chair. "You sound as thirsty as a wino in the Sahara."

"Remember that St. Paul said, 'Take a little wine for thy stomach's sake.' We must defer to the Scriptures in these matters."

"Yes, but I'm sure he meant 'a little' as opposed to 'a lot,'" she interpreted.

"Please, just make an omelet that will match the quality of the wine," Stoke requested.

"Hah!" Sandy replied. "My omelet will make your wine pale by comparison. So what happened to you?"

"Chardonnay is already pale. And how about our discussing the state of my health over the food?"

"That's a deal!" Sandy said, as she picked up her bag of groceries and turned toward the kitchen. Stoke plunged the corkscrew into the cork. He withdrew it from the bottle slowly and poured wine in each glass. There was a clanging and banging coming from the kitchen where Sandy was getting plates ready for the omelets.

Stoke inhaled the odor of the wine. Then he tasted it. And sighed. Maybe he could go on living after all. He didn't drink a lot, but when he did, he wanted it to be worth his while.

After about twenty minutes Sandy appeared with two plates in her hands. She was holding them with hot pads. She set the plates down on a table and put a magazine in Stoke's lap so the heat would not incinerate him. Then she pulled up a chair and sat down gracefully with a plate in her lap.

"Right, Studley, now what happened? Was it an outraged husband or did you try to rape one of those East German female track stars?"

Some stories are the unvarnished truth. However, varnish always adds a bit of luster, so Stoke varnished his story some. Especially the part where he was running up the steps chasing two scantily clad young ladies and miscalculated the stairs. Then he told her about his five days in the hospital and promised never to do it again.

Sandy sat quietly through this explanation as she thoughtfully ate her omelet. At the end of the explanation, Stoke noticed a tear in her eye. He thought he had upset her.

But then Sandy broke out laughing with a mouthful of omelet that threatened to go all over the room. She tried to be dainty and cover her mouth with her napkin. She almost carried it off. Nevertheless, some landed in her lap. On the fine linen suit.

Stoke watched all this with some indignation at first, but then saw how funny it really was. He broke out with the first good laugh he had experienced in weeks. They sat looking and laughing at each other for several minutes.

Stoke said, "All that on a half glass of wine? Think of what we could do on a half bottle!"

"I'm sorry," Sandy replied, still trying to repress a giggle, "but that's the funniest story I've ever heard. And I know that you've never had to chase women. They like you. If you'd cut off that damn bushy mustache, they'd like you even better."

"I've had five days to polish my story," Stoke said, "and I was hoping for a tad more sympathy, especially from you! And the mustache stays."

"How does my competition like the mustache?" Sandy had heard all about Marilee from Stoke.

"Marilee has never had the effrontery to complain," he replied. "Of course, you're closer to it than she is."

"Well, I should hope so! Let's call a truce, Stoke. Besides, if Marilee is smart enough not to say anything about it, I guess I should do the same."

"Deal," Stoke said as he shifted his leg to find a comfortable spot.

"Do you want a pillow for your leg?"

"Yeah. I could use something."

"Do you have any pain pills?" Sandy asked with some concern in her voice.

"Yes, but I would rather wait it out. I hate pain pills."

"Don't be so noble. If it hurts, take them," Sandy told him emphatically.

"They screw up my insides. And I am *not* being noble, just wise in the long run."

"Well then, Stoke, do you have any books? I can read to you for a while."

"That would be great! I have a new mystery by James Martin. You'd like him. It's in the bedroom."

Sandy brought in a book she found beside Stoke's bed. It had a bookmark about one-third of the way through. She opened it and began to read. As she read, Stoke's eyes began to close. He drifted off to sleep. Sandy noticed that Stoke was not listening, so she quit reading and put the book beside his chair. She picked up the dishes and put them in the dishwasher. Then she took a stack of books over to his chair where he could reach them.

She wrote a note saying she would be back in a few hours to see if she could help with dinner. Then she quietly slipped out the front door.

Stoke was dreaming. "Grandma, don't you know what the man's name was?"

"Oh, I think it was Henry or something like that. But I don't know as much about my ancestors as I should. That's why I thought it would be a good project for you to investigate, one of these days."

Startled by a new ache, Stoke woke up. The heavy cast had pulled his leg into an uncomfortable angle and was straining a tendon in his knee. As his eyes opened, he saw that Sandy was gone. He read her note. Then he reached for the books that she had left for him. On top was a small, thin book he had hardly noticed before. Its title was *Genealogy of the Grover Family*. Before he could open it, there was a faint rap at the door. He pushed a button beside his chair and the door was unlocked. Marilee came in.

"Stoke, you're back!" Marilee ran to him and hugged his neck. With a sigh she let go, then stood back and examined the cast on his leg. "Does your leg hurt a lot?"

"Sometimes, Marilee. But it's good to see you again. Now I'll probably forget about the leg."

Marilee looked at him gravely for a minute. "Your hair looks funny. But I think the mustache is fine."

"You've been talking to Sandy, haven't you?"

"I saw her in the lobby. She wanted me to talk to you about your 'damn mustache.' But my mother doesn't want me to use that word."

"Mustache?" asked Stoke.

Marilee giggled. "She doesn't want me to say 'damn.'"

"I hate it when my critics get together," Stoke moaned.

Marilee put herself in charge of Stoke's home. He couldn't very well get up and do things for himself, so she was able to wait on her hero. She got him water and crackers and medicine and magazines, just to be doing something. Her wages consisted of a small hug and a pat on the back, which were worth millions to her.

They talked, and Marilee said she might have to leave someday. She said she heard her mother on the telephone with her uncle, arguing about going back to Hong Kong. Marilee cried some. She said she didn't know how to speak much Mandarin and she didn't want to leave California.

This problem called for severe measures, so Stoke had Marilee raid the refrigerator for ice cream. It took two bowls before Marilee was sufficiently comforted. But the treatment didn't work for Stoke. He was uncomfortable at the thought of her leaving.

Something else was bothering Stoke. His dreams seemed to conflict with stories he had heard in his childhood. Now that he thought about it, he seemed to recall that his ancestor was killed in a feud. It was one of those Missouri gun battles over nothing really important. They started and then lasted until there were no more males to continue the battle. He was embarrassed that his family could be involved in such a stupid thing. Still, there were those dreams...

Painfully climbing into his wheelchair, he decided to look at some old papers of his mother's that could possibly tell whether the dreams or the recollection were correct. He propelled himself to a closet and

found an old shoebox that contained letters and other old papers his
mother kept. He remembered looking at them briefly when he was a
boy, until his mother protectively took them and put them away. He
lost his curiosity after that. Somewhere in the box he thought there
was a news clipping that might help.

A small stack of letters was in the box, tied with a red ribbon. They
smelled of lavender, a fragrance left over from a sachet that once
belonged to an old lady in years past. Gently lifting off the ribbon,
Stoke sorted through the old documents until he found a yellowed
newspaper clipping. He read,

WALKER KILLED

James M. Walker was shot and killed yesterday in front of the Owen
County Court house by two men in what was described as a continuing
feud between two families of Owen County, the Walkers and the
Smoots…

The rest of the undated article was missing. *So it was a feud after all!*
he thought. Triumphantly, he put the letters back into the stack and
replaced the ribbon, but he kept the newspaper clipping to put with
his genealogy book. He stuffed the box back into the closet and
wheeled himself back to where Marilee was busily playing a game with
the TV.

* * * * *

It was late in the afternoon when Marilee went home. Stoke
returned his attention to the thin genealogy book, which he was looking at when Marilee had come in. On the inside page was a photograph of an old woman, ostensibly the person who wrote it. Her name
was Martha Ann Grover. *Probably some old gal with a lot of money and
nothing else to do but write a family history,* Stoke thought. *A waste of
time. Self-aggrandizement.*

The book was printed about 1904 in Lexington, Kentucky. He
flipped through the yellowing leaves for a while, just laughing at the
funny names: Thankful Smith, Ebenezer Grover, Diantha Welch, and

Vesta Armstrong. *Wow!* he said to himself, *and I thought 'Stokely Towles' was bad!*

As he got to the end, he saw a familiar name: Alice Walker Pryor. *Hell, there's my grandmother! What is she doing in this book?* He looked at the number above her name and the Italics written there: "Children of Stella Walker and Robert Pryor, her husband. "My great-grandparents!" Stoke said out loud. I never knew much about them.

Slowly Stoke traced the family line back until he found that Martha Ann Grover was his great-great-great-grandmother. Coming back down the family line, Stoke noticed that the Grovers had a child born in 1861, the year of the Civil War. His name was Jefferson Davis Grover. "No doubt about which side of the War these folks were on," he said out loud.

He put the book down to stretch his sore leg. As he did so, the next page flipped over. Stoke picked up the book again and saw this entry:

No. 50 Alice Porter Grover, b. Sept. 8th, 1847; married
1st, James M. Walker, May 4th, 1866; married
2nd, Dr. Jas. D. Munday, Dec. 12th, 1877; married
3rd, H. P. Montgomery, Jan. 1st 1889.

Something about this entry struck a familiar chord. *Who was this Alice? She was Jefferson Davis Grover's sister, all right, but was my grandmother named for her? How come she married three times? Did she wear out three husbands? Too bad I didn't get this information before Mom and Dad died. Maybe they wouldn't have known, anyway. And who was James M. Walker? Is he the man who was killed in the article I just read?*

He traced the line from Alice Porter Grover Walker to the next generation and then found out who Alice was: she was his great-great-grandmother. *Then that's where my great-grandmother, Stella Walker, got her last name! So this book is really about my family*, he thought to himself. *And James M. Walker was my great-great-grandfather. But in my dream the man was named Henry and he died before the Civil War.*

He reasoned, *Assuming James Walker was about twenty-one when he married Alice in 1866, that means he probably was born in 1845. The Civil War began in 1861, so he would have been sixteen then. He could easily have been the man in the article. Good heavens! He would have been in his early thirties when he died, because his wife remarried in*

1877, and he was probably dead a while before then. That's younger than I am! It's looking more like he's the one who died in the feud. But in my dream the man was named Henry and he died before the Civil War.*

Then he wondered about the author of the book, Martha Ann Grover. She almost had to be listed somewhere in it, he realized. So he looked again and traced her back. *Well,* Stoke said to himself, *if the man I'm looking for is named Henry, maybe I should be looking for a Henry Grover. That might be the name of the man I dreamed about.*

Proud of himself for solving "The Mystery," Stoke put down the Grover book and picked up a real mystery, the one Sandy had been reading aloud. He read until he had finished it. Then he heard a noise at his front door. He pushed his opener button, letting in Frank and Sandy.

"We decided to invade your privacy together, in case you were in a bad mood or something," Sandy called out. Both of them walked into the living room and exchanged greetings.

"That's nice of you both to visit the neighborhood cripple," Stoke said.

"Is that what you are?" asked Frank.

"Yep," Stoke said, "and I have a lot of hospital bills to prove it. So let's have the proper amount of sympathy."

"Anybody want wine?" Sandy asked. "It beats the heck out of sympathy."

Frank said he didn't want any wine. He was watching his weight again. Stoke said he would like some. Since Sandy was the only drinker who wasn't lame, she had to prepare it.

"Do you need anything?" Frank asked. "I can run some errands for you."

Sandy sipped her wine. Stoke said, "I can't afford your fees."

Frank responded, "I'll put it on account and get you later."

"Then would you be able to go to the library tomorrow? I want to look up an address," Stoke asked.

"Sure," said Frank. "Anything at all."

"I'm curious about something. Sandy left a pile of books for me to look at when she left, the last time she was here. One of them was a family history I've never read before. I don't even know how it got on my shelf. I must have brought it from my mother's home when she

---

* *The Courage Place* by Thomas S. Fiske

died. Here it is," Stoke said, as he picked up the book and showed it to both Frank and Sandy. Sandy said she remembered putting it by his chair.

"There's a list of many of my ancestors in the book. And I found a project I could work on while my bones are knitting. But I'll need some outside help."

"So what can I do?" asked Frank.

"Would you please get me the address of a historical society in central Kentucky? I'll bet the research librarian could look it up for you. I want to write them and see if they have any information about my ancestors."

"You got it," said Frank.

"What about histories of the area?" asked Sandy. "There might be some local histories that could tell you what was going on."

"I don't think the local library would have them," Stoke said.

"Yes, but if you knew the correct titles, you might be able to get your library to borrow them from some other library, say, in Kentucky."

"That's right. I didn't think of that. Would you look in my desk and pull out that old map of Kentucky?"

Sandy rummaged around in the desk drawer and pulled out a ripped-up road map that had the title "Kentucky-Tennessee" written on it. She handed it to Stoke in two pieces.

"What's this project?" asked Frank.

"I want to know what happened to one of my ancestors, like who murdered him and why?"

"Hell, that's no mystery… He was playing around and some husband shot him. A lot of men would like to go that way," Frank told him. Then he added quickly, "Not all of us, you understand, but a lot would enjoy that trip."

"Yeah, right," said Stoke. "But on my mother's side there were a lot of fairly strict Baptists. 'Fooling around' doesn't sound like them." He looked at the old map. "The book said these people were from Owen County. Would you see what you could find about Owen? Also, there was a mention of Scott County. Henry County is in the same general location, so you might see if there is anything on it as well."

Frank wrote the names down and put the list in his pocket.

"Is anybody hungry?" asked Sandy. "I brought some more food."

"So did I," said Frank. "And I'm one hell of a good cook."

"Why, Mr. Kendall," Sandy said with wildly blinking eyes, "you would make some girl a wonderful husband someday."

"I'm not cut out for that sort of thing," Frank told her with a smirk. "But I can whip up something really good. Tonight I'm going to make a great meatloaf with a salad and rolls to die for."

"Anything sounds fine to me if I don't have to fix it," said Stoke.

"I second that notion," added Sandy. "Maybe I can help."

"That's entirely possible. But for now, why not visit with Blue Shield's disaster while I get started?"

Sandy hunted around and found a new book to read to Stoke. It was by Stuart Kaminsky, who wrote Russian police detective stories. Stoke enjoyed Sandy's theatrical Russian accent, but the Grover family history still churned in the back of his mind.

Dinner came before an hour had passed. Sandy and Stoke were surprised.

"How could you prepare and bake a meatloaf in half an hour?" she asked.

"Simple, my little friend, who is obviously an amateur in the kitchen: I made it last night and heated it up a few minutes ago. Anyway, it was more like forty-five minutes."

They hungrily focused on the contents of their forks until the food was all gone. "Beats the hell out of hospital food!" Stoke summarized.

"I think it has to be better than most restaurants," Sandy countered.

Frank said they would have to be more positive if he were to cook again. After they had finished off the food, Sandy offered to clean up the kitchen. There were no refusals. Frank had left it in good shape; about all Sandy had to do was put dishes in the dishwasher. Then she joined Frank and Stoke who were discussing the merits and demerits of the Dodgers. The conversation was a bit short on the side of merits.

When the conversation dragged. Frank said he had to get home. Both he and Sandy wanted to know if Stoke were able to get to bed, and if he had handy whatever he needed. They made sure he had a telephone, a book, medicine, water, a bedpan and a towel next to the bed. Then they piled pillows at the foot of the bed so Stoke could prop his legs up.

Wearily, Stoke moved himself over to the wheelchair and headed for the bathroom. He washed and got into bed where Sandy had put his pajamas. But he was too weak to put them on. He turned out the lamp and lay in the dark, hurting too much to sleep. It was about dawn that he finally drifted off.

He dreamed of a scene in which a tall man was walking down a street in what seemed to be a Western town. It was a hot, sunny day. The man had a long, double-barreled shotgun at his side. His dark pants were stuffed in his boots. His shirt was loose fitting, not quite modern, but not out-of-date, either. He wore a wide brimmed hat. The sun was directly overhead. The streets were crowded with people who were going about their daily tasks. As the man walked past a large tree of some sort, Stoke heard the click of hammers being cocked. He tried to shout a warning, but no sound came from his mouth. A blast rang out from beside the tree where the armed man stood. A well-dressed man walking toward the tree grasped at his stomach and fell, bleeding on the dirt of the street.

Stoke became aware of motion as several men came running out of stores. They stopped, eyeing the man with the shotgun. He had fired once and it was a double-barreled shotgun. They did not want to be next. Many other men around the town square began to shout and he heard a voice say, "They finally got the bastard!"

Suddenly, Stoke noticed that everyone went silent. The shooter calmly pointed his shotgun to the ground and walked toward the sheriff's office. Stoke felt drained.

It was ten in the morning when he opened his eyes. Sunlight was streaming in his bedroom window and the room was getting hot. He blinked a few times, tried to move his leg and remembered why he was having trouble.

His first goal was to get to the bathroom. He didn't want to fight with the wheelchair, but saw no other way. He lay on his back for a few minutes, thinking how wonderful it would be to take a hot bath in a real bathtub! However, the cast on his leg would not permit that, nor would the raw surgical wounds on his ankle. Painfully, he managed to shift himself into the chair without falling.

He spent the morning just moving around his home, trying to get into and out of furniture. His knees hurt and his legs threatened to sue him several times, but gradually he learned to get around by himself.

Stoke lumbered out to his deck, which overlooked the Pacific Ocean. It was a grand vista to the edge of the world on most days, but this day he was feeling glum and hardly noticed. He pulled himself out of his wheelchair and plopped down in one of the chaises, leaning back so he could feel the warmth of the sun on his face and arms. His leg hurt and his body felt sluggish, but it was good to be in his favorite spot in the universe.

Suddenly, Stoke felt pressure on his stomach. The neighborhood scrub jay had crash-landed on his midsection, looking for a handout. A scrub jay is about the size of a robin, maybe a bit larger, and is blue with white trim. It has a large head and greatly resembles blue jays of the eastern part of the U.S. Males are aggressive, friendly birds, sometimes comical. Female jays also take handouts, but they are usually shyer around people, and hang back, settling for leftovers. This male had adopted Stoke as one of his main sources of supply. Stoke did not train the bird; the bird trained him.

Stoke named the jay "Oliver," for the little boy in Dickens' novel, *Oliver Twist*, who held out his food bowl and wanted "more." Jays often store each morsel of their food in a tree or flowerpot. They come back for more because they are still hungry.

Stoke look at the bird for a minute. "Oliver, you turkey, I guess we'll have to get some peanuts." Oliver responded with a quiet, gentle song of anticipation. He hopped aside while Stoke got himself back into the wheel chair. The sliding glass doors that led out to the deck were still open. Stoke wheeled himself in, followed by Oliver. This odd couple went to a metal container on a table in the middle of the room. Oliver knew it well. He flew to it and stood at attention on the tabletop. He didn't like the table because it was slick. He could not walk around on it very well, but peanuts were serious business.

Stoke opened the container as Oliver looked on. He took out a handful of peanuts in their shells. Then he put one out so Oliver could clamp his beak on it. Oliver looked at the peanut by turning his head to the side. Then he turned his head back and took Stoke's finger by mistake. It was a gentle mistake and no damage was done. Stoke did not flinch as Oliver looked again and, this time, got the peanut in his beak.

Oliver flew out the door. Stoke followed him in his wheelchair and once again positioned himself in his chaise, waiting for Oliver to hide his treasure and return for the next peanut. He could have laid them out on the rail of his deck, but Oliver made it obvious some time ago that he preferred to be hand fed. Stoke much preferred this kind of comedy to the forced laughter sit-coms on his TV set.

Worn out by the bird-feeding activity, he climbed into his wheelchair and scooted off to the kitchen to make some lunch. Sandy had tossed out the milk and other products that had passed into eternity while he was in the hospital. She had brought in fresh milk, lunchmeat, lettuce and other vegetables.

Just then there was a knock at his door. Stoke rode his wheelchair out to the entrance hall by the front door. "Who is it?" he said through the door.

"Marilee Cho!" came the high-pitched answer.

Stoke opened the door. Marilee made one huge bound and caught Stoke around the neck and kissed his cheek. Stoke wasn't quite ready for that move, but he managed to keep from turning the wheelchair over.

"Wow, Marilee! I'm glad to see you, too. Would you please come back to the kitchen with me? I'm getting ready to eat a sandwich for lunch."

"Neato, Stoke. What are we having?"

"Whatever you're making, except for peanut butter and jelly."

"What kind of stuff do you have?"

"Rye bread, ham, Swiss cheese, lettuce and all kinds of good things that you probably don't like. And beer. Do you want a beer, Marilee?"

"No, thanks. I hate the stuff. But I'll take a Pepsi. In the can."

Marilee made sandwiches for Stoke and herself and poured two soft drinks. She pushed his wheelchair over to the breakfast table just like a little mother would have done. They both ate. Then he took some pills that had the warning on them "TAKE WITH FOOD." Marilee cleaned up afterwards. Then she fired up one of the TV games he had bought for her and she entertained herself. Every fifteen minutes or so she would return to his side to see if he needed anything.

Stoke wheeled himself to the deck of his penthouse and sat in the warm summer sun for an hour, looking out over the Pacific Ocean. He sensed his bones knitting together. His stomach reacted to the pills, making him glad he really did "Take with food." The sun and the smell of salt air made up for a lot of the unpleasantness of his condition.

In the house he heard Marilee cut loose with a heavy belly laugh. He thought how seldom he heard such uninhibited laughter these days. And how seldom his walls echoed with the laughter of children. The sound gave him a warm, comfortable feeling. It was strange music for a man who had never liked kids at all.

Chapter Three

About six in the evening, the telephone rang. Marilee had gone home. It was Frank Kendall. He had information from the library and thought he might come by to see what Stoke had prepared for dinner. Stoke told Frank to hurry on over, but stop by the deli to pick up something that would go with a glass of water.

Forty-five minutes later, Frank appeared at the door with a sack of food that smelled wonderful. He got some plates and doled out hero sandwiches and kosher dills and other garlic-endowed products.

"You didn't have a date tonight, did you?" Frank asked in acknowledgment of the garlic.

"Only you, or perhaps Marilee."

"That's a relief. For a minute there I was afraid I'd made a dumb mistake and screwed up your social life," Frank said with a large grin.

"It seems that I'm the guy with a bad case of Dumb," Stoke replied. "Who else falls up steps?"

"Look at it as an art form," mused Frank as he crunched down on one of the pickles.

"Yes, but what could I possibly do for an encore?"

"You ever been to the top of the Empire State Building?"

"No," said Stoke.

"If you go, better stay away from the edge for a while."

There was silence except for the munching. When dinner was over, Frank picked up the dishes. They discussed the purchase of a company that Stoke would fold into his growing conglomerate.

Then Frank pulled out a sheet of notes he had made at the local library. "I found some info at the reference desk. I thought you might want to see what I got."

"Thanks. I'm really interested."

"Fine. There's a Kentucky Historical Association in Frankfort, Kentucky. It's one of the largest. Then I found there were a couple of local history books that might help. One is about Henry County. I guess the place was named for Patrick Henry. The other was about Owen County. I don't know who Owen was. I didn't see anything for Scott County."

"Great, Frank. Would you ask the librarian to try to borrow those two for me? I'll write a letter to the Historical Association tomorrow."

"How are you going to mail the letter?" asked Frank. "You're going to have a problem reaching the mailbox, and you're certainly in no position to drive to the post office. If you scratch out a note tonight, I'll ask my secretary to type it up and send it out tomorrow."

"Thanks, but I have a small office here. I'll just FAX a note to my secretary's office and she can fake my signature. Or I can just use email. Let's see what I need to ask."

Frank handed Stoke the genealogy and sat back while he thumbed through its pages. After about fifteen minutes, Stoke said, "You know what? I don't know what to ask. I'm going to have to research this project some more."

"That's fine. I'll go ahead and order the two histories. It may take months to get them, you know. And if you think of anything, I'll be at the office or you can give my secretary the information."

Frank got up to leave and said, "Will you need anything before I go?"

"No thanks, Frank. I didn't make up my bed, so it's ready. I can handle the pills and other stuff. You've been a good friend, you know, and I appreciate it."

"Hell," Frank said, "we make beautiful money together. I need to get you back on your feet so I don't go broke."

"You were doing quite well before we met, you know."

"Yeah, well, I got lazy and forgot how to work," Frank replied as he went out the door.

After Frank Kendall left, Stoke settled in his chair and thought about his next move. "Next moves" required a lot of thought. *Will it be TV or my mystery or my genealogy?* he wondered. He picked up the TV guide from the *L.A. Times.* There were game shows and sit-coms and old movies. There were no baseball games. Football season hadn't started yet. There were no science shows or English mysteries on public TV.

I guess that leaves my book or my genealogy, he thought. With that he picked up his mystery story and read until bedtime.

Sleep came fairly soon. Just before he woke his dream returned, and he was talking to his grandmother once again.

"Grandma, how can I find out about the man who was murdered? I don't know where to look."

"He was Henry Van something, Stokely."

"Wasn't he, uh, I thought he was Henry Grover," Stoke questioned.

"You're on the wrong track", his grandmother replied.

Stoke began stirring. His eyes opened at the daylight in his room. *Darn!* He thought, *I sure hate to start a day with something unfinished. Grandma said the man who was killed was 'Henry Van' something, but I thought I'd solved the mystery and the man's name was Henry Grover!* Stoke lay still with his eyes closed, trying to remember if he really had such a conversation with an old lady when he was a small boy. He thought maybe he had talked with her. He seemed to recall that she was sick and his family was visiting her in some old house. But he couldn't be sure.

After lunch, Stoke settled in his recliner and watched a baseball game on cable TV. Atlanta was playing New York. Atlanta was winning. Baseball wasn't as exciting as professional football, but it was a lot more interesting than the banal talk shows that littered the airwaves.

As he watched in his detached fashion, he noticed the fans making a "wave" by raising their arms, one after another around the park, so their motion did really look like a wave. They seemed to do this late in a game. Stoke thought it was because they were so bored; they had to do something to stay awake. Baseball tended to put him to sleep and he thought it might make the fans sleepy, too.

Not having any great interest in either team, Stoke turned the TV off. Then he looked around for a book to read because he had finished his mystery the night before. People had given him several interesting books since he had gone to the hospital. But somehow his hand found the little Grover genealogy. As he picked it up, he recalled his mental note to find out more about Henry Grover. But there was no Henry Grover listed. Besides, his grandmother said he was a "Henry Van something." That was another family to be concerned about. It was all getting too complicated.

Stoke looked at more pages in the small genealogy book. There was a section about a man named Asa P. Grover. It was a grand tribute to the man. He was husband of the author, Martha Ann Grover. Stoke read the tribute to Asa. *She really must have loved and admired him*, Stoke thought as he read on. *One doesn't often find that quality in a wife these days.* He found himself thinking about his own divorce.

"Aha!" Stoke said out loud when he came to the maiden name of Martha Ann Grover; it was Vallandingham. *That's close to "Van something,"* he thought. He read, "They were residents of Owen County until the last twelve years of Mr. Grover's life, when they moved to Scott County."

Then Stoke wrote a letter to the Kentucky Historical Association, asking about Vallandingham people in Owen and Scott counties. He faxed it to his office and sat back to wait for the reply.

Friends visited Stoke and brought all kinds of good things to eat and drink over the next few weeks. Strangely, he did not put on weight. Sandy was there occasionally to help and Frank also dropped by. Marilee came in after school. She did many simple tasks for Stoke that he had taken for granted before the accident. Now these things were major operations.

He found that he had come to depend on Marilee a great deal. She was in heaven because she had become important to him. She even talked her mother into letting her stay with him several Friday nights, just so she could be there if he needed anything.

It was Frank who took Stoke to the doctor to get the metal clamps removed from his legs where his surgery scars were healing. The doctor had to take off the cast. He replaced it with a removable, three-piece plastic model. This meant Stoke was making good progress and was healing on schedule.

Soon Stoke graduated to crutches and hobbling around his house. Frank returned the hated wheelchair to its home. For the first time in weeks, Stoke was able to take a bath and soak all he wanted. He looked like a prune when he got out of the tub, but he had never felt so good. It was a small pleasure to most people and a chore for small boys, but Stoke loved every minute of the soaking.

With the flexible cast and crutches came another new freedom; he was able to drive his car. Part of the time he was able to get around without crutches. Sandy called them his "sympathy sticks" because he always obtained sympathy when he used them. She said that often, but in reality, they were defensive weapons. Stoke used them to keep people and dogs away from his sore leg.

Acting on advice that Sandy had gotten from friends, Stoke looked in the telephone directory for Mormon churches. He examined each location to see if that particular church had a family history library listed. He found one in Costa Mesa, not too far from his home. So he hobbled into his car and drove over to see what it contained.

Going north on the 55 Freeway, Stoke noticed how clear the air was. He could see the distant mountains and tall buildings in most directions. Stoke located the family history library in the back of the church. Mormons were interested in genealogical research for religious purposes. They set aside rooms in strategic locations where the public could access computers with historical information in them. These computers offered much of the information that was contained in the main files in Salt Lake City.

The libraries also offered microfilm readers, and a way to order films from a catalog, so that a researcher could review many items not in the computer, such as U.S. Census Bureau films and passenger lists of people who arrived daily on American shores.

Some of the libraries had shelves of books that grateful researchers had contributed. That was a key to the Mormon operation. They didn't charge people who came in (unless they ordered films), but they suggested that researchers share what they found with the Mormons.

The workers at the library were very helpful. Older men and women, who were not all Mormons, staffed it. They were just people very interested in their family lines, people who liked solving mysteries. They suggested that Stoke begin his search with federal censuses that the government had taken every ten years since 1790.

Early federal census takers walked from house to house, interviewing folks and writing down the names of heads of houses. Often the home country of a person was listed as well. Census takers would list other people by numbers in certain age groups. Women were seldom listed, except by age. Then in 1850, census forms were revised to show names of all people at an address, instead of numbers in age groupings. More and more questions were asked about literacy in English, numbers of years in school, and occupation. Censuses were great storehouses of information.

The 1890 census burned and not much is known about it. But the other censuses are available through 1920. Those taken after 1920, he was told, will be released over time according to the census rule that those who give information to the census taker are guaranteed that it will not be made public for seventy-five years.

Stoke didn't find what he wanted to know about Owen and Scott Counties. After all, he was in Southern California. Looking at a catalog of available filmstrips, Stoke ordered several on federal census records from Kentucky for 1840, 1850 and 1860, which covered a lot of time before the Civil War. Henry was supposed to have been killed before the Civil War, and that was a good place to start. They should contain the names of people who lived in and around the Owen and

Scott County areas. He also ordered some films of pages from Owen County courthouse records during the same period. It would take two weeks to get them.

So far, he had heard nothing from the Historical Association. Neither of the two books Frank had ordered had come in to the public library. This was not too much of a problem, since Stoke began going back to work and running his businesses full time.

Two weeks after his trip to the family history library, Stoke got a call saying his films had come in. He wasted no time in getting there. Holding two crutches, five filmstrips, a pad and a pencil, Stoke hobbled to the back room with great anticipation. His search was formally on.

He fumbled with the viewer mechanism for a few minutes until he figured out how it worked. The first film dealt with the census of Owen County in 1850. There was no index. Names were entered in the order the census-taker walked as he went from house to house. Stoke realized he was going to have to read every handwritten name on the census until he found the right one, *if it were really there*! Mentally he was going through the steps of hiring a research student at a local university, when a friendly voice asked if she could help. He explained the problem. The owner of the voice, a pleasant older lady, went to a shelf where she selected several books. They were indexes of names for Kentucky censuses. All names that appeared on the census for 1850 had been entered into a computer and sorted for alphabetical order, then printed into a book. The county location for each person was included. Someone had already done the work!

Ignoring his filmstrip, Stoke opened the 1850 Census Index and hunted for two names. One was Vallandingham and the other was Walker. He found the Walkers, mother and father and several children, including James, who was born in 1843. James was too young to have been a man killed before the Civil War, as the dreams suggested. He just wanted to be sure.

Next, he looked at the Vallandinghams. Sure enough, there was a Henry Bruce Vallandingham who was born around 1808. His wife was named Armilda. Now this man was old enough to be the person he was looking for. After several hours of backbreaking and difficult reading that would bring tears to the eyes of a strong man, he found no one named Martha Ann Vallandingham. Then he remembered that she was married to a man named Grover by 1850.

Looking at the 1840 index, Stoke found Henry as head of a household. Then he went to the filmstrip, where he found Henry had a female child living with him. All he could tell was that she was around ten years old. Only the names of heads of houses were used in 1840.

Continuing to look, he found that Henry was not in the 1860 census.

But he found Armilda, Henry's wife. She was living with the Grovers... I *wonder if something had happened to Henry during the period between 1850 and 1860? If he really were the one who died before the Civil War, which officially began in 1861, he probably wouldn't have been on the 1860 census. Or he could have been in another state and on another census. Then was my grandmother pointing to this Henry? Maybe so. Perhaps this Henry is the guy grandmother was talking about. He had what was almost a 'Van' last name, and he could have died before the Civil War.*

Flushed with success, Stoke read on for two more hours from court documents. He found nothing else except more legal dealings of Asa Grover who was a lawyer. It was getting late and his back hurt, so he turned off the reader and put away the films. Perhaps tomorrow, he thought.

It was three days later that Stoke was able to go back to the reader and the filmstrips. They provided no more help, but an aide in the library pointed out the possibility of a forum on the Internet that talked about the Vallandingham name. She gave him the address of a genealogy group that sponsored the forums for different name interests.

When Stoke went back to his house, he fired up his computer, got on the Internet and called up the address. There he found a long list of surnames that included Vanlandingham, but not Vallandingham.

Just for fun, he accessed the Vanlandinghams and left a question with the readers about their relationship to the Vallandinghams. Several people responded quickly that it was all one family, that the people called Vallandingham changed their names about 1750 in Virginia. The name continued to be subject to variations ever since. Some were even known as Flannigan.

One of the correspondents on the Vanlandingham forum, a man named Lou Vanlandingham, wrote that he had been researching the family for forty years. He was writing a book on the descendants of a Michael Vanlandingham, and was willing to trade some of his background information for the results of Stoke's research. Stoke said he was welcome to whatever came up as long as it made the family look good. Lou wrote back that he thought that was possible since none of them was involved in politics. Stoke decided that this crusty individual was probably full of information and should be consulted frequently.

Stoke returned to the library once more the next day. The microfilm reading room at the family history library was kind of spooky. It was kept dark, so people could see their microfilmed materials on their screens. Stoke was the only one there so the light from his reader cast an eerie glow about the room. The air-cooling fan hummed noisily; it was the only sound other than Stoke's breathing. It was almost as though the one speck of light in the room focused his attention, not only on the words of microfilms, but also on the truth about his ancestor.

One thing that became evident was the business of the Vallandingham family in Owen County. They were all farmers or married to farmers except one: Henry seemed to have tried everything except farming. It was as though he wasn't content to turn the soil. Stoke recalled a saying about people like Henry in the South, "His hand don't fit a plow!"

Stoke saw that Henry had operated a tavern, had tried law enforcement, had tried political office and just about everything available. He seemed to have been a restless man.

Another hour of eye-straining research didn't produce anything, so he put away his materials, thanked the people in the library and hobbled back to his car. As he drove back to Newport, his mind was puzzling about the few skimpy facts he had found. They made sense, but they just didn't add up to the kind of life that leads to murder.

Stoke had not done much research since he had finished his Master's degree in Business Administration at Case Western Reserve University in Cleveland. Still, he remembered how to make notes and organize them. And today he had a computer. He had ordered a computer program that would keep track of his genealogy "finds." It hadn't come yet, but he was in no hurry. He hadn't collected enough information to need a program. But he saw that it wouldn't be long before he had too much information to carry around in his head. He'd made lots of notes, but these were becoming burdensome.

He parked his car in the garage under his building, out of the hot California sun, and slowly worked his way back into his house, being careful about the "killer steps" on which he'd broken his legs two months before.

When he got to his living room, he settled down with a glass of lemonade (made from the fresh lemons he took from his tree on the patio that morning). He reviewed the notes. Then he found the box of old family papers he had stowed away in his closet. With them was a huge old Bible he had completely forgotten about.

He laid these items aside for a moment so he could go back to his computer and the Vanlandingham forum. There was a message addressed to him from Lou. It said someone had told Lou about a man named Vallandingham, who was murdered in Levanger, Missouri. The year of the murder, he recalled, was 1856. Lou said he would try to find the article and send it to Stoke. Stoke thought about this for a while and wondered if there was a connection. He thought better of it because *his* Vallandingham lived in Owen County, Kentucky.

Opening the box of old family papers, Stoke found all kinds of curiosities—tintypes of unknown people, some photographs, a few letters and some materials typed on an old-fashioned typewriter. There was also the old Bible. At the bottom of the box, off by itself, was a folded piece of tan parchment about two inches square. Idly, Stoke opened it up, and saw it was a letter handsomely written in an old-fashioned hand. It was difficult to decipher at first, but this is what he read:

Fenanger, Missouri, May 15, 1856

Dear Daughter,
     I sit down this morning to write to you for I have neglected answering yours but as your mother wrote I thought that would answer for that time. We are both well and hope these lines may find you and your

mother the same. I have nothing of importance to write. On the 8th of this month I purchased my partners interest in the St. Charles and your mother occupies the upper part so it looks a little more like living to have her convenient and we are getting along more pleasant that I did when I had a partner. Times are very dull but I hope by industry and economy to make money. I always could make it but never had the tact of saving.

Your mother is getting more dressmaking to doe than she probably can doe. She sticks very close to business. She bought her some finery but she will not take time to make it up while she can get work from others. She is so fond of cash.

I bought her a fine bonnet fine enough for a bride and a silk dress and high heel gaters, kid slipers and velvet slipers and would have bought you a fine silk hat if I knew I would have had a chance to send it to you, but when Mr. W. Roberts came by, he said room was gone.

There was a large house selling out at auction, but the difficulty is this: I have nothing fine enough to wear to walk with the Old Lady.

I had considerable fun coming home last fall. I told the clerks of the boats that we traveled on that I was just married and wanted the bridal chamber and all the ladies looked on her as a bride. She was quite bashful. She looks as well as you ever saw her. I think she has bin heavier than I ever saw her last winter and is well pleased with this country and her greatest desire is to live close to you and family as you are the only child. The Cansas excitement is very high yet and is likely to be higher.

Tell Alice I think she treats me very mean for not writing for I know she can. The other two are excusable. I don't know when Wm Roberts left as I should have wrote by him. I must close as I have several business letters to write. Accept a father's love for your self, husband and children. Write often.

H.B. Vallandingham

P.S.: Tell Aunt Alsy howdy.

What a surprise! Stoke read and reread the letter. Henry had been in Missouri after all. Quickly he got back on the Internet and sent out all kinds of requests to Missouri universities and historical societies, asking them where Fenanger was. He typed his translation of the letter into the computer and sent it by email to Lou Vanlandingham, who lived in Ardmore, Oklahoma.

Then Stoke had to get back to his businesses. He tore himself away from his computer, turning his attention to business. He was able to make calls and get progress reports, and soon was back into the rhythm of his daily operations, while still at home. Yet in the back of his mind, he couldn't let go of Henry.

The next day he began to get replies from his emails to historical societies and universities. They all said one thing: "There is no Fenanger and there has never been a Fenanger in Missouri."

But Lou had more information. He emailed that he had gotten a copy of the story about the murdered man named Vallandingham. However, there was no first name given. He said the man had been fooling around with someone's wife and had collected a shotgun blast to the stomach. Then Lou added, "He sure wasn't a Vanlandingham because they were too smart to get caught! It had to have been a Vallandingham." He also added the date of the news story: July 20, 1856.

Remembering Lou's earlier message, Stoke looked around on the Internet for a Levanger, Missouri, which was in Crittenden County according to the atlas on his desk. Then he located an email address for its historical society. He fired off an email asking if the folks there knew about this killing in 1856. Then he went to bed, greatly puzzled about all he had learned. He sincerely hoped that his ancestor had not been caught fooling around. Certainly, it seemed that the man who wrote the loving letter to his daughter, and who seemed so attached to his wife, would not have done such a thing. It seemed out of character.

When Stoke got up the next day, he checked in with his business managers first and then ate. He felt like he was making good progress with his broken leg. It seemed to be a bit stronger each time he got up. Of course, being on it for a while sometimes made him wish he hadn't thrown away his pain pills, but that was to be expected.

Eventually Stoke got around to his computer again. There was one email directed to him from the Historical Association in Kentucky. It said:

Dear Mr. Towles:

   We do not have any direct information on a man named Henry Vallandingham from Owen County, Kentucky. However, his name appears in the censuses and courthouse records from time to time. I suggest that you look into these records, which are indexed.

Sincerely,
Mary Anne Early, Researcher

Stoke quickly emailed back to Ms Early that there was a possibility Henry had ventured to Fenanger or Levenger, Missouri, in 1856, and asked if she had any connections in either of those places, or if she knew of any reason for Kentucky people to migrate to that part of Missouri.

And what was even better was that he got an email from the historical society in Levenger, Missouri, recommending a book about the history of Crittenden County. He forwarded this one to his secretary and asked her to get hold of a copy. He wondered what she must be thinking about his sanity.

Then he went through his bills and business mail, writing checks and entering appointments in his appointment book. As he looked at the array of days, he suddenly became aware that he hadn't taken Sandy out for a while. So he called her at work.

She was in her office, which was unusual. Often they had to play "telephone tag" for a few hours before they got together, even though both had portable phones close by. After he got through to Sandy and talked with her for a minute to "catch up," Stoke asked if she were able to go to dinner that evening.

"Formal dining?" Sandy asked. "I'll need time to change my clothes."

"No," Stoke said, "let's go to the Bouzy Rouge in Newport."

"Sounds good to me," Sandy said with enthusiasm.

Stoke said he would pick her up at her apartment at seven. Then he hung up the telephone. It rang again. It was Stoke's answering service. The voice at the other end of the phone listed several calls that indicated problems at one of his businesses. So Stoke took down the names and numbers. Then he made his afternoon calls, making appointments for the next day. But his mind was on dinner that night.

At seven, Stoke drove up in front of Sandy's apartment in Laguna Beach. It was in a three-story building erected in the twenties, but was kept clean and well painted. It had withstood many earthquakes. As he got out of the car, Sandy was coming out the door.

"I didn't want you to have to fight those crutches," she said, "so I got ready early and waited near the door."

"You're really thoughtful and I appreciate it, but I didn't bring the crutches with me tonight. I'm trying to wean myself away from them."

"You mean I'll have to fight you off with only my bare hands?" Sandy said with a grin.

"That's about it," said Stoke, "but not until I eat. Anyway, that's hardly been a problem, has it?"

"No, but I'm looking forward to better days," she said as they started out for the restaurant. In just about twenty minutes they got to downtown Newport. In another five minutes they had parked and were walking into the restaurant. It was a French restaurant with a nice reputation. They had been there before and had a sassy waitress with a good sense of humor.

"Do you want to eat inside or outside?" asked Stoke. There was a kind of porch in front of the restaurant next to the water of the marina, with about fifteen tables and small trees and plants. People could sit there with some shade during the hot days and with heaters during the cool evenings. Sparrows assisted with the housekeeping, picking up bits of food from tables, chairs and the floor. This was one of the more romantic spots in the restaurant.

"Let's eat out," Sandy said without any hesitation.

After a few minutes of waiting, the hostess took them to a table. Asked if they wanted anything to drink, they chose a bottle of wine. When it came, Stoke raised his glass to make a toast.

"Here's to better days," he said with a slight leer.

"Hear, hear!" said Sandy as they both took a sip.

They talked about Sandy's day and a problem with her boss. Sandy was a manager in an insurance company. Her boss was a vice-president who was a great technician, but a poor manager. Stoke advised her to anticipate his needs and to look for cycles in the business, such as year-end closing, so she could prepare herself with any information he might require. He also suggested that Sandy keep a record of what she was doing on her own projects. "A manager needs to know better than anyone else where she stands on her assignments," he lectured.

Promising to think his ideas over, Sandy asked about Stoke's past several days. Stoke talked a bit about his activities at work. Then he told Sandy about his research on the Vallandingham investigation. But he didn't mention the dreams.

When he finished, Sandy said, "Why you old romantic! I think you're getting really involved with this ancestor worship!"

They laughed, and Stoke said thoughtfully, "I want to go back there this summer and check some things out for myself. I saw a book at a research library that said there might even be old newspapers on file at some of the places I want to see. One of them might have the story on Henry."

Then he looked directly at Sandy and asked, "How about going with me this summer for a couple of weeks?"

"Two *hours* in one of those small towns would be enough for me," Sandy replied. "Two *weeks* would just about put me in a straight jacket."

"But I'm going to an old part of the country," Stoke returned. "Civil War battles were fought nearby. It's right on the Missouri River where Lewis and Clark traveled in 1804!"

"I don't think so," Sandy said. "Thank you, but no."

"I guess this is a bad time to ask if you've thought more about our social merger," Stoke said evenly.

"Stoke, we've talked about this. And I'm not ready to give you an answer. We have a good thing going. I don't feel there is a need for a big change in our lives now. I like you, I enjoy your company, but I'm not sure I want to settle down with anybody."

"All right," Stoke said, "I just thought I'd let you know that I still want first option in case you change your mind."

"You still have it, and thank you."

They were quiet for a few minutes. Then the waitress returned for their orders. Sandy ordered a large salad and an extra plate. Stoke ordered a Les Miz sandwich, consisting of about everything in the kitchen. It was their custom to share foods they liked on the extra plate. Many patrons of the restaurant did the same thing so the waitresses were used to it.

"Did I ruin your evening?" Sandy asked. "I bet you don't usually get turned down twice in a night."

"When you ask a lot of women, you get slapped a lot. But you also score more often than the average bear," Stoke told her with a grin. "Besides, I can always fall back on my research if I get bored."

"Stoke, do you ever get your back up? I mean, when do you *really* get angry?"

"It's not now, if that's what you mean," he told her. "I work very hard at *not* getting angry. That way I win a lot more battles. It took me a long time to learn that tactic."

Their food came and they ate in silence, enjoying each bite. Sparrows began to drop by in search of crumbs. One fat brown and white bird landed on the tabletop by their hands. Others landed on empty chairs at the tables or scooted around their feet.

As the day grew into night, sparrows punched their time cards "out" and went home to their nests to rest and get ready for the next day's feast.

Their waitress came by and asked them if they wanted dessert. They declined and the waitress sized up the situation quickly. "Right. No use ruining a good buzz, is there?" They laughed, and after paying the check and leaving a handsome tip, Stoke asked Sandy if she were ready to go.

"I'm ready," she said. "Are you going to be able to walk to your car easily?"

"Yes, my leg is stronger now. It seems I'm ready for bed. I thought I'd be ready for more strenuous activity by this time."

"Well, don't push it," Sandy said. "We can wait for the heavy-duty stuff later on."

"You don't mind?" Stoke said.

"Of course, I mind, but I'm not going to worry about it," Sandy told him. "Now let's get on home."

Stoke dropped her off at her apartment and then turned around for home. He had been rebuffed. He *was* concerned about it. But he decided to be philosophical about Sandy's lack of enthusiasm for marriage. It took her a while to do something, but once she made up her mind, she would be extremely committed. And this next time, he wanted to have an extremely committed wife.

Chapter Four

ENGLISH, DIKEMAN & CO.,
(Successors to D. T. Card,)
Manufacturers and Dealers in
CARRIAGES, HARNESS AND SADDLES,
CARRIAGE MATERIALS, &c.,
Corner of Fourth and Vine Sts.,
St. Louis, MO.

The day after Stoke's date with Sandy, he got a call from Marilee's mother. Elizabeth asked if she and Marilee could visit for a few minutes. Stoke said, "Please do." He was bored and needed some kind of diversion.

A half-hour later, there was a timid knock at the door. Stoke knew it wasn't Marilee, who was no longer timid, so it had to be Elizabeth. He looked through the peephole in the door and saw a young Chinese woman. She seemed harmless, so he opened the door.

There stood Marilee with a pretty young woman in a peasant blouse and fitted blue jeans. She had long black hair down her back. She wore almost no make-up. She was exotic-looking, with just the right shade of red lipstick to go with her slightly orange colored skin. Stoke didn't recognize her.

"Mr. Towles, you remember me?" said the woman.

"Elizabeth?" Stoke said somewhat curiously. "You look very different. I thought you were Elizabeth's younger sister!"

"Thank you. I can see that we are going to get along well. I have to wear traditional Chinese clothing when I go to work. I run a rather large, conservative business and my customers expect me to fill a certain role. So does my family. But they cannot see me now."

"I suspect it would be me they wouldn't like," Stoke replied. "Hi, Marilee, come on in." Stoke ushered them in.

Elizabeth examined his living room with great care. Then she said, "I am happy that your leg is improving. Marilee has kept me informed about you. I did not come before because I was very busy with my business and with my uncle's estate."

"There was no need, Elizabeth. You lent me Marilee and she was a big help these past few weeks."

"That is good. I was hoping you would come down to dinner with us one of these days, Mr. Towles."

"I would be happy to have dinner with you."

"We could go out to dinner, but my family watches over me, and they would unhappy to see me at dinner with a non-Chinese man. Even though I run a big business, they want to watch over me as if I were a small girl."

"Elizabeth, that would be fine. And perhaps you and Marilee could come to dinner with me sometime. I can have my driver pick us up in the garage downstairs in one of his limousines with the dark windows. We could go just about any place without attracting attention."

"Yes, we would like that, wouldn't we, Marilee?"

"Oh, boy!" came the reply. "It sure beats Chinese food!"

Stoke grinned. "How about staying for a few minutes and having a glass of wine while you're here? Marilee, would you please get the tray and some glasses?"

Marilee trotted off to the kitchen while Elizabeth allowed herself to be escorted into Stoke's den. "It's very British, isn't it?" Elizabeth asked after looking at the furnishings.

"Yes, but it's also early American," Stoke replied. "There were many homes decorated this way on the East coast two hundred years ago in the larger cities."

"Very nice," Elizabeth said as she tried to take it all in. She looked in vain for a photograph of a woman or some other evidence of a woman's hand. "Where is the famous TV with all the games that Marilee talks about all the time?"

Stoke took Elizabeth on a quick tour of the den, living room, dining and eating areas, being careful to show her where Marilee stayed and where she played. "The TV has educational game attachments on it. I researched them carefully before I let Marilee use them," Stoke assured Elizabeth.

Marilee brought in the tray and drank a soft drink while Stoke poured a white wine for Elizabeth and himself. "Why don't we go out on the terrace to look at the city?"

All three sat in comfortable patio chairs and looked at the shoreline with its twinkling lights while they sipped their drinks. The air was warm, heavy with the odor of orange tree blossoms from the small fruit trees in tubs on his deck. Marilee went inside to try her luck at one of the games on the TV.

"I really appreciate your help with Marilee," Elizabeth began. "She had been in a sort of depression since her father died and I took over the business. I guess I was, too, but there was so much to do that the work saved me from having really serious problems."

"Marilee helped me out of my rut, Elizabeth. That and the interruption of a broken leg. I didn't realize how dull life had become."

"She has been good for both of us then."

Elizabeth and Stoke talked for two hours about nothing in particular. He felt she was just a lonely person, hemmed in on all sides by family and business and culture, elements that were beginning to chafe a great deal. He felt sorry for her and admired her at the same time for her successes.

After a while Elizabeth stood and thanked Stoke for letting her get away from the rat race for a few minutes. She called Marilee and they went downstairs to their home. But not until she had made a dinner date for the three of them at her house in two days.

The two days passed quickly. Stoke was pleased to get an email from Ms Early at the Historical Society in Kentucky. She said she wasn't aware of any reason for people to migrate to Missouri in 1856, except that it was the time when small militias were being formed over the question of slavery in the Kansas Territory. Then she added this:

We do know of someone who is doing research in the Levanger, Mo., area. She asked us to give her name and address to interested people who might be able to trade information. You may wish to write to her at this address:

Ms Ariadne Edwards
11023 Wilson Way NE
Washington, DC 20211

With the clear image of a blind alley in his mind, Stoke wrote a letter to Ms Edwards. He told her of his search for information about Henry Vallandingham, the possible connection to a murder, and mentioned the possibility of an outraged husband. He offered to share what he found.

Stoke found himself at Marilee's door. Marilee pulled at his hand to get him into the living room. The decor was modern, with a blend of Asian and American furniture. There were pictures of storks or cranes on several walls. Stoke couldn't tell which.

Elizabeth came from the kitchen to greet Stoke. This time she was wearing more formal clothes—-tailored slacks and a purple silk blouse. It looked good against her dark skin. The outfit made her look small and vulnerable, although Stoke suspected that she was really made of iron.

"I was, uh, we were hoping you could make it tonight," Elizabeth said while offering her hand to Stoke. Stoke mumbled something about not missing it for the world and sat where Marilee guided him.

"I was admiring the pictures of the birds on your wall," Stoke said.

"They represent good luck for Chinese," Elizabeth told him.

"Maybe I should stand near them," Stoke replied as Elizabeth handed him a glass of wine.

"You're not Chinese, but you seem to be doing well as it is," she said.

"Not if you listen to my associates. I got pretty far behind while I was in the hospital. Now I'm trying to catch up."

"What is it you do, if I may ask?" said Elizabeth.

"Sure. I tell people I'm a consultant, but actually, I run several companies. I have a few small interests in other companies as well."

"Then you're not a gangster?" Elizabeth asked.

"No. I may act like a gangster, but my interests are all legitimate. There are some people who don't like me, and others who want to waste my time on screwball ideas. There are lots of newspaper reporters at times, so I have to maintain some security precautions. Would you invite just any gangster into your home for dinner?"

"No, not just any gangster. I am a discriminating woman. And I didn't really think you were. It is the care you take with the signals to your driver and all that… How do you always manage to get the same limousine driver each morning?"

"I own the company," Stoke said. "The driver is specially trained and has to give me first call on his services. Or he can work for someone else. The reason I'm careful is that I'm trying to avoid newspaper reporters. They can be a pain sometimes."

"Owning the company is nice leverage. Are you ready to eat? The food is about ready."

They walked into the dining room. Its table was a thick sheet of clear glass, sitting on a highly polished and lacquered section of a tree trunk. The dishes were of a Chinese design and were carefully matched both in color and in shape. Each table setting had both silverware and chopsticks.

Dinner was excellent. There was Peking duck, some vegetables and the inevitable rice. Stoke was able to handle the chopsticks well, but he was not as proficient as Marilee and her mother.

"This is delicious, Elizabeth. How did you find time to cook it all?"

"The rice was no problem. I did that. But you missed the delivery person for the rest of the food as you came in. I must confess that I had that sent to me."

"How did you get it here at just the right temperature and the right time?" Stoke asked.

"Same kind of leverage you have. The restaurant belongs to me."

They finished off large quantities of food. Then Stoke gave up on his last plateful.

"I can't eat any more, Elizabeth. Marilee, what about you?"

"Nope. But we haven't eaten so well since Christmas."

"Marilee!" Elizabeth said with some shock. "What will Mr. Towles think?"

"I'll think that you two poor, hungry waifs will need to go out to dinner next week, and I am just the person to lead you to a nice Turkish restaurant."

"What is Turkish food like?" asked Elizabeth, somewhat concerned.

"Have you ever eaten camel meat?"

"No!" Elizabeth said, "and it doesn't sound a bit good!"

"Well, I haven't tried any camel either. Perhaps we should try some Southern cooking."

"Southern where?"

"Southern America. Grits, kale, ham and hush puppies. In the right restaurant it can be a wonderful meal."

"That sounds great," Marilee chimed in, "except for the dog meat. When do we go?"

"What dog meat? I didn't say anything about dog meat!"

"Then what are hush puppies?" Marilee asked.

"It's a kind of fried corn meal that people used to feed dogs. They get quiet while they eat it," Stoke explained. "Nowadays people save it for themselves because it's so tasty."

"And you don't even know what grits are," said her mother, "so how do you know they sound great?"

"She trusts me," interjected Stoke, "and you should, too. Let me know when you have time. I am going to be in town all next week," Stoke told them. He left it for them to figure out what grits were.

The rest of the evening was very satisfying as Stoke and Elizabeth talked about movies they had seen, plays they had been to and books they had read. Stoke noticed that Elizabeth was very much aware of cultural events in the area, more so than he was.

Almost anticipating Stoke's question, Elizabeth said, "Normally, we do not spend all our time out of the house. But for the past two years since my husband's death, Marilee and I have seen just about everything in town to keep us busy."

"There's not much going on at my place, either. I've been too busy to relax. But this summer I may take a trip to the Midwest to dig up victed on the second count. On the day of his hanging he confessed to many crimes and to being a member of the Ku Klux Klan. He named names of other gang members, some from the most prominent families in the area. Some, but not all, were supposed to have been in the Klan.

Strangely, the period including 1874, when Walker was killed, was one in which the man said he was inactive. Stoke filed the "prominent family" reference in the back of his mind under "H" for Hype. The convicted man must have been quite a talker because the book said that thirty-eight pages of his story were compiled and sent to the Library of Congress. It was just another false trail.

So that was it. Many weeks of waiting for the book and all he got was a paragraph or two on a related subject that had no connection.

It was a week later when Stoke got a letter from Washington, DC. Ms Ariadne Edwards had responded to his request. It was a neat, crisp, typewritten letter. From the signature, Stoke could see that she was not old. From the maturity of the ideas in the letter, he could see that she was not a youngster either. The letter said:

Dear Mr. Towles:

Thank you for your recent letter. I am still working on my book about an ancestor who lived in the western Missouri area before the Civil War. My ancestor was Bill Simkins. He was my great-great grand-father.

Bill Simkins was notorious in the area for being a gang leader. He operated mostly in Crittenden County, but occasionally took his gang across the State line into Kansas. You will recall that this was before the Civil War, when the fight over slavery was beginning to heat up. There were great political pressures on both side of the slavery question.

No, I have not found anyone named Henry Vallandingham of Owen County, Kentucky, in my research. However, I will certainly tell you if I find out anything about him. And if you find references to Bill, you might let me know.

Sincerely,
Ariadne Edwards

"Oh, well, I tried," thought Stoke resignedly. He filed her letter with the other documents he had been finding. It was a small stack of papers to show for his two months of effort. He was seriously thinking about hiring a real genealogist.

One evening as he worked at his desk, his telephone rang. Hardly anyone knew his telephone number, so Stoke was startled.

"Hello."

"Stoke, this is Elizabeth Cho. I need some help. May I come up to see you for a few minutes?"

"Sure, Elizabeth. I need a break. Come ahead."

A few minutes later Elizabeth knocked on his door. Stoke let her in and looked around for Marilee. "Where's your daughter?"

"Marilee is at her uncle's. Am I still welcome?"

"Well, Elizabeth, we've had a chaperon for a month. I may not know how to act without one."

"Just try very hard."

"Come on in then. Would you like to sit out on the deck or in the living room?" It was one of those very pleasant nights in Southern California when the air was warm and the breezes were calm.

Elizabeth chose the deck. Stoke turned on his CD player to a collection of Mozart compositions, then switched the output to speakers on his deck. He took with him a bottle of a fine white wine and two glasses as he headed for the open air with this exotic young woman.

They sat almost opposite each other and talked about the weather as Stoke opened the bottle and poured the wine. Mozart quietly surrounded them and provided insulation from the rest of the world. Brilliant stars twinkled at them over the surface of the ocean. The sound of the surf was faint but audible in the background.

"Stoke, I have a management problem. May I ask you about it?"

"Sure."

Elizabeth described how one of her managers was failing to meet company goals. These were goals no one had trouble with in the past. Elizabeth was on the verge of firing the manager, but didn't know if that was the right thing to do.

Stoke, becoming more and more aware of Elizabeth's presence, had a hard time focusing on her problem. He couldn't imagine Elizabeth being indecisive about anything or anyone. He asked a few probing questions about Elizabeth's plans for this manager, and then suggested that firing might not be wise as long as additional training could help.

They had another glass of wine and discussed the types of training available. Stoke was really getting serious about Elizabeth's problem until she stood and walked over to his chair. Gracefully, she sat down in Stoke's lap.

"Let's forget about management," she said. "I really was lonely and just wanted to see you."

Startled, Stoke raised his glass to Elizabeth's, tapped the two together and said, "Here's to loneliness!"

Then Stoke said, "Boy, am I dumb sometimes! I don't always know what's happening, do I?"

He put his wineglass down and placed his mouth on hers. His hand was behind her head so she couldn't pull back. But she had no intention of escaping. Her arms wound their way around his neck and held him tightly.

Coming up for air a few minutes later, Elizabeth said, "You are very old-fashioned, you know. I am not. Did you know I have been watched over for two years? I have never had a moment to myself in that time."

"You're not by yourself now."

"That's not what I meant. The nice thing about good neighbors is that you can visit without interference from your family. They are prejudiced, you know. Are you prejudiced against Chinese?"

"I'm never prejudiced against pretty girls. I may have trouble with ugly men of any persuasion, though."

They kissed long and deeply. Elizabeth seemed almost desperate as she clung to Stoke. Their temperatures increased and they breathed much more heavily. He could feel her soft body try to melt into him. After a few minutes Stoke was almost out of breath when he said softly, "Your place or mine?"

"It takes too long to get to my place," Elizabeth murmured.

Stoke put his hands under Elizabeth's legs and lifted her up to his chest. Then he stood.

"Watch out for your leg!" she warned.

some family history. It'll be the first vacation I've allowed myself in five years."

"Are you involved in ancestor worship? I thought that was an Asian custom," Elizabeth asked with a trace of a grin. Her teeth were small and perfect. Stoke admired them long after she got serious again.

Stoke told her about his passion to solve a mystery in his family's history. It was important to him to discover what had really happened to Henry Vallandingham. Henry's death was a loose end and he didn't like loose ends. He didn't mention the dreams.

Eventually conversation slowed and Stoke realized it was time to leave. He thanked Elizabeth and Marilee for a fine evening. Then Marilee, brazen nine-year-old hussy that she was, reached up and kissed Stoke good night.

Elizabeth watched the kiss and said, "I guess it is a Southern custom." With that remark, she also kissed Stoke, firmly on the mouth.

"I knew it would help to stand by those pictures of your good luck birds," Stoke said with a grin. "When we go out next week, how about bringing one of them with us?"

It was three weeks (and several dinners with Elizabeth and Marilee) later when Frank met Stoke in a courtroom with a battered book he had gotten from the library. It was one of those he had ordered for Stoke, a local history of Owen County. Its name was *Sweet Owen*.

After a pretrial hearing that arose from his latest merger, Stoke put the book in his briefcase and drove home with it. He had not done much work on the Vallandinghams because he had run out of information to guide him.

The Owen County book promised to be a helpful source of information. After his dinner, he settled down with a cup of coffee, a pad of paper and the book. The book mentioned a woman named Vallandingham who had been postmistress of a village for a long time, but that was the only mention of that name. He found a story about a hanging in his search for more information about James Walker, the other person in the family he thought had been murdered.

The story said a man was accused of being (1) gang member and (2) a man who shot and killed his brother-in-law. He was tried and con-

"That's the last thing on my mind," he told her as he walked to his bedroom.

Gently, Stoke placed Elizabeth on his bed. She stretched out as she kicked her shoes onto the floor. Stoke sat down beside her and stroked her hair. He looked into her eyes and reached for the buttons of her blouse. First one, then another button came loose.

Elizabeth moved his hands away and said, "This could take all night, at the speed you're going!" She deftly undid the rest of the buttons and sat up to get her blouse off.

"Anybody that good with buttons should work on my shirt," Stoke said huskily. Elizabeth proved to be a wizard with Stoke's buttons as well.

"I'm not so good with zippers," she said.

With restrained anxiety, they helped each other undress. Stoke looked at Elizabeth's perfect skin and small breasts, thoroughly enjoying each moment.

"I'm not big like American women," Elizabeth said as she watched Stoke's eyes caress her all over.

"I suspect you are the most beautiful Elizabeth Cho in the world," Stoke whispered. He kissed her mouth and her body with great care. Time seemed to stop for them both. Outside, noises quieted. There were only two people in the world. He slid his hands under her once more, picking her up and placing her on his lap. He ran his hands over her small body a few more minutes and said, "I can't wait much longer."

"You are a big man, Stoke. And it has been two years for me, so go slowly, will you?" It was not a command, only a request.

Stoke did go slowly. He was so careful that Elizabeth became impatient. Her small body drew him inside her much faster than she thought possible.

The first time was less than perfect, so they tried twice more to get it just right. It took most of the night.

The next day the book about Crittenden County arrived. A local person who was proud of his homeland had written this book. There was a great deal of information about the people, including industry of the region by decade. Stoke didn't recognize any names but he saw that one of their big industries was the manufacture of rope. *That meant large crops of hemp*, he thought. He also saw that Levanger was a port city on the Missouri River. It provided several schools and denominations of churches and had a population of about 3,000 around the 1850's.

Stoke continued reading the book in its 1855-1862 period. About 1857, he found the story of a hanging. The star of the story was one Bill Simkins, who was called a desperado and leader of a bad gang that operated in a several county area. He was caught, tried, convicted, and hanged off a bridge in the area. "The bridge is still called Simkins Bridge," the book said.

I wonder if Ms Ariadne knows about this book, Stoke mused. *I might tell her one of these days.*

Then Stoke recalled his box of papers and the Bible he had begun looking at several weeks before. His cleaning lady had put them away and he had forgotten about them.

A half-hour later, he found the box. There were several documents about James Walker, but only one about the Vallandingham family. It was a typewritten copy of a newspaper story about the breaking up of the home of a family in Lisbon, Ohio. The spelling of the name was quite close to Henry's: Vallandigham with no second 'n'. It mentioned the given name, Clement. There was a comment at the bottom of the note that said, "doubtless this was a brother of Lewis, since he had a brother, Clement." Stoke realized that, if true, this Clement was an uncle of the Henry he was looking for. Then he looked in the margin of the note where it said that the son of Clement was also named Clement, and he was the man called "The Copperhead," the congressman who had defied Lincoln during the Civil War. Stoke filed this information away as a project for one of his employees on a rainy day. With that, he put his stack of documents back in the box without reading all of them and put the box back on the shelf.

Not having answers didn't seem so bad as long as Elizabeth was able to take Stoke's mind off his problems with her desire and loneliness. There was urgency to their lovemaking because Marilee would be returning in a day or so. They realized they would have to return to the real world of appearing to be sober, dispassionate adults.

Several days later, while reviewing the organization of a small company he owned, Stoke dashed off a note to Ms Ariadne Edwards about finding Bill Simkins in his new book. He again expressed a willingness to share any information he might find. As an afterthought, he wrote that he might take some time off to visit the Crittenden County area late in the summer or early in the fall.

With his leg improving steadily, Stoke returned to most of his old routines. Except that he did not run up steps anymore. He walked as much as his leg allowed.

Occasionally, his ankle would swell and ache. The first time that occurred, he went to his surgeon's office to ask why it was happening. The doctor took X-rays and had blood tests run. Stoke was one of the few patients he really enjoyed. Stoke didn't complain much and he followed the doctor's instructions. He also laughed at his own predicament. The doctor stood in front of the X-ray reader and mused over the bones and plates and screws so obvious in the print. "I've never taken plates out before," he said quietly to himself.

"I'm not anxious for more surgery," Stoke said rather nervously. "Maybe I just over-did my exercises."

"Perhaps," said the doctor, "but we may have to go in and take out those screws."

"How will you know it's necessary?" Stoke asked.

"When they move, you can see them out of place in the X-ray, or sometimes you can feel them," said the surgeon.

"Is that the case now?"

"No," the Doctor said. "You can see that there's been a great deal of healing and the screws are right where I left them."

"Then, when I get a screw loose, I'll tell you," Stoke told him.

The doctor roared at this remark and said, "That's a deal. We'll wait until you get a screw loose." Then he wrote a prescription for the swelling and sent Stoke on his way.

Stoke rested on Saturday and Sunday, with his foot up in the air. Frank Kendall came by to cheer him up and to watch the baseball games on TV. A few other friends came by and offered to help, but Stoke really didn't need anything except a trip to Missouri.

By Monday the swelling had gone down, due to the pills or the rest or both. Relieved, Stoke went back to his office. He was spending more and more time there. Soon he was completely back into his old groove and seldom thought about his leg. It bothered him some, but he managed to keep the aggravation pushed to the back of his mind.

One Monday evening, Stoke found he had a letter from Ms Ariadne. That is how he thought of her anyway. She responded to his note and said she might also make a trip to Missouri, so perhaps they could keep in touch a little longer to see if their paths were going to cross.

He was beginning to wonder if Ms Ariadne's ancestor might have killed his ancestor, Henry. He wasn't sure so he didn't want to say anything. Anyway, he didn't think she had anything more to add to his research.

In the next mail he got a letter from Lou Vanlandingham. In it was a copy of an old newspaper clipping. It looked like an old style font that was used a long time ago. A hand-written note said that it was from the *Levanger-American Citizen* of July 20, 1856.

Vallandingham Shooting

Levanger American Citizen
July 23, 1856 P. 3, column 1

Shot.—On Friday last, about noon, Frederick Myers deliberately shot a man by the name of Vallandingham, in one of our most public streets. So far as we are informed, no one saw the shooting, but Myers immediately went to an officer and gave himself up, confessing the shooting, and the intention to kill. Vallandingham received the contents of a heavily charged shotgun in the abdomen, and expired in a few minutes.

Myers charged the deceased with illicit intercourse with his wife, and we are informed had in his possession a number of letters from Vallandingham to her, from which his guilt was unquestionable. That Vallandingham was a villain of a deep and malignant die, is not doubted. He was the keeper of one of those fashionable places which in polite parlance are called Restaurants, and in the short space that has elapsed since his death, we have heard enough of his villainy to have sent him to the penitentiary for life

But notwithstanding his villainy, was Myers justifiable in laying in wait to take away his life? We know nothing about the domestic relations of either of the parties, and would be slow in condemning an injured husband for inflicting the severest punishment, even the penalty of death, upon the betrayer of his wife; yet there is a time, a place and a manner in which even the crime of seduction should be punished. In providing a punishment for seduction, the law has ever been lame, and from the difficulty in proving such offences, it would be extremely difficult to provide a remedy.

The case underwent an investigation before Justices Veitch and Letton, and after a patient hearing the prisoner was discharged, and the decision was loudly applauded by the crowd of spectators.

The opinion of the Court, we understand, was delivered in writing, and was substantially that the killing was either done in heat of passion, or in self-defence. It is certainly a novel decision, and public sentiment is so much divided that it is more than probable that the case will undergo another investigation by the Grand Jury at the next term of the Circuit Court.

From all we have heard it would be difficult to make it a case of self-defence and what lapse of time is necessary for passion to subside must depend in some measure upon the wrongs received, the temper of the injured party, and the manner of killing. Had Vallandingham been killed on Myers' premises, had he been killed immediately on the discovery of the wrong, every honorable man would have justified the killing; but passion acts without deliberation. It seeks no privacy, and allows no time for plans or preparation.

In all such matters the law should have its due course, and if a jury should convict contrary to public opinion, the Executive of the State is the only tribunal to interpose its clemency.

Disappointed that the first name was not given, Stoke read the article anyway and made notes. He wondered why there was no first name and what it was that this man did that was so bad. "We have heard enough of his villainy to send him to the penitentiary for life," the writer said. He also wondered about the "novel decision" that allowed the killer to go free. It didn't sound right. Also, Stoke noted the sentence that read, in part, "and public sentiment is so much divided." Stoke couldn't help but wonder why public opinion would be so divided over the shooting of an adulterer. *There's more to this than meets the eye,* he told himself. *But it may not be my problem since I don't even know who this guy was.*

On the back of the copy, Lou noted that he had written to the Crittenden County courthouse to see if there were any records on the settling of the estate of a man named Vallandingham on or about July 20, 1856. If nothing else, Lou was thorough.

Stoke forgot about the entire matter until the end of July, when he got another letter from Ariadne Edwards. She said she was going to Missouri the first of July. That was about the time Stoke had selected, but he wasn't sure he wanted to tell Ms Ariadne. That might result in an invitation that would take up his research time. On the other hand, she seemed to be fairly well along with her book and might know how to do better research than he did, so she could be an asset.

He faxed a note to his secretary to see if he had that time available. Then he added, "If I have no avoidable obligations, please make a note to get a jet for about two weeks as close as you can to July 1. I will be landing at Kansas City Airport and will be needing a car."

Ariadne Edwards wrote back by email that she was definitely going to be at Levanger around July 1, and that Stoke should bring his notes. She said she would be staying at a Best Western motel outside town. She gave him the phone number at the motel and asked him to call her when he arrived. That was that for three more weeks.

In the meantime, Stoke wrapped up important merger work and notified associates that he would be gone for a few days. He asked Frank to move for postponements in two court cases. Then he took Elizabeth and Marilee out to dinner. He told them about the meeting with Ms Ariadne and what he hoped to accomplish. Elizabeth said she knew they both would miss him. Marilee cried, but gladly exchanged her tears for an ice cream cone.

Several "captains of industry" had gotten together with Stoke three years ago to set up a small airline for chartered flights. It was really mostly for their own use, but they sold enough time to outsiders to satisfy the IRS. Stoke knew the pilots on a first name basis and they traded piloting responsibilities when Stoke was bored. He was licensed to fly the two-engine jet that was taking him to Kansas City.

Since it was a relatively short flight, there was no need to refuel. It was a clear day as his plane dipped its wing on its final run onto the runway. As the plane pulled into its berth, a large black Mercedes pulled up near it. The driver got out and waited patiently for the doors to open so he could stow Stoke's luggage in the trunk.

"I won't be needing a driver, just a map," Stoke told the man. "What if I drop you off someplace and keep the car?"

The driver smiled. It was fine with him. He was getting paid anyway. Stoke took him to his destination, and with some help in directions, drove the one hour trip to Levanger, Missouri. It was a warm, humid day, but the weather was clear and bright. He thought it was a good omen, as omens go.

Settlers pushing west about 1818 had founded Levanger in Crittenden County. There was also, he knew, a Crittenden County in western Kentucky. *Perhaps*, he thought to himself, *some of those Missouri settlers were from Kentucky*. As he arrived he noted that it had old city problems in that its streets were engineered by cattle. That is, cows determined the paths that later became roads. But a creative preservation committee, he found later, had required that many of the older buildings be maintained. The town had not changed much in its appearance.

Arriving at his motel on the outskirts of town before dusk, he unpacked his bag and went to the desk to ask about restaurants. It was the same motel where Ariadne was staying. He didn't know anyone in the town, so he would not be spending an evening with friends who wanted to marry him off to half a dozen eligible females of assorted ages. He was one of those rare individuals who was happy with his own company. The desk recommended a nice restaurant where a meal of red-eye ham and green beans and grits filled him up completely.

After he returned to his motel, Stoke called the desk to get Ariadne's room number, so he could make an appointment for lunch the next day. She was settled in for the evening, but seemed pleased to talk with him. They made a date to meet early the next day on the main street at the town's only traffic light. Stoke described himself as six feet tall, 180 pounds and walking with a slight limp. He added that he had blue eyes, reddish hair and a mustache, and was 41 years old. He said he would be wearing brown slacks and a tan sport shirt, and he would be carrying a briefcase.

"What do they call you?" Stoke asked.

"Ari. What about you?"

"Stoke. I was named for an early Virginia ancestor."

"Was his name Stoke?"

"No. It was Stokely Towles. His mother was a Stokely and his father was a Towles."

"Well, I'm a bit different from you," Ari said. "I have dark hair. I'm younger than you and reach all the way up to five foot-four. I'll be carrying a manila folder." She didn't give her weight. Stoke imagined the worst, but could tell she had a clear sparkling voice with a hint of the South, and a good sense of humor.

Then he went to bed. It was two hours later in Levanger than it was in Newport, so he had a little trouble getting to sleep. Once again he had vivid dreams of a man being ambushed on a main street when the sun was directly overhead.

Chapter Five

President Pierce's Check Shirt.— Some of our contemporaries are amusing themselves with the check shirt which Mr. President Pierce is reported to have worn on his late visit to Virginia Springs. We think nothing could have been more appropriate as illustrating his checkered administration. Furthermore, check hides dirt, and is thus a good article for a shirt on a dusty journey. Consequently, while other people may endorse the foreign and financial policy of Mr. Pierce, we prefer the approval of his check shirt...

When Stoke had left California, the scenery looked like a sepia tone movie; everything had been tan—bushes, trees, grass and most houses. Missouri looked more like a color movie. Rolling hills were covered with deep green trees and bushes. Grass had a bluish cast to it. Cardinals, robins, redwing blackbirds and blue jays yelled at him from along the roadside. Large brick and frame houses sat back from the road at the ends of long winding driveways. Architectural details hinted that some of these southern homes were almost two hundred years old. White wood fences lined pastures where sturdy cattle and horses grazed.

Right at noon, Stoke parked his car in Levanger on the main street. It was easy to find. There didn't appear to be two main streets in this small town. (There was probably only one horse!) Bright sunlight heated the moist air. His shirt was damp. It stuck to the seat back of his car. That almost never happened in California, where the air was much dryer and where automobile air conditioning seemed to work better.

Ahead of him about twenty yards was the town's only traffic light. It was suspended in the middle of an intersection by wires and looked as though it was at least one hundred years old, although the town didn't need a traffic light a hundred years before. There was only horse-and-buggy traffic then.

He walked to the intersection and looked around at several people who seemed to belong. Some of them wore blue jeans and sport shirts, but most were nicely clothed in dress shirts and neckties. Stoke noticed the town was like so many he had seen as a boy in Kentucky. Everything looked old, but not worn down. He thought there must be some money in the area to keep up the place.

"Mr. Towles?" said a woman's voice at his side.

Stoke looked down. There stood a young woman with dark hair. In her hand was a manila folder.

"Ari?"

"That's me," she said, sticking out a small hand in Stoke's direction. Stoke took the hand in his and shook it lightly but warmly. He liked what he saw. The hand was attached to a pretty young woman dressed in well-tailored slacks and a simple but expensive white blouse. She had pale skin, very black, glossy hair and startling blue eyes. Her hair was arranged in an elegant pageboy style. Worse, Stoke was perspiring while Ari seemed cool and dry. He felt like a big slob, standing by this small, neat person.

"I'm happy to meet you at last," she said. "Your letters seemed so interesting."

"Yes, it is nice," murmured Stoke. "This meeting has been a long time coming," he said, somehow forgetting that he didn't want to have it at all. Beauty was making a hypocrite of him.

"Listen, can we go in the store behind you and get a soft drink or something? Maybe we can compare plans for the day and see if our paths are going to cross," Ari said.

"I've developed a terrible thirst," Stoke told her as they turned around and entered the drugstore.

The store's only concession to modern times was air conditioning. Inside, its appearance was something out of the twenties or earlier, Stoke estimated. There was quite a bit of ornate ironwork holding up shelves. Along one side was a white marble-topped soda fountain. Chairs and tables with curved wire feet stood in front of it. The tables had white marble surfaces and the chairs had round wooden seats.

They went to the fountain and ordered Cokes, which were made up on the spot. Stoke put his hands on the top of the soda fountain. It was deliciously cool to the touch. A clerk, today's version of a soda jerk, a young man about eighteen years old, put some ice in a glass and poured in an exact amount of syrup from a tap. Then he inundated the mixture in soda water. He handed Stoke the two completed drinks and charged him a dollar each. The price was another concession to modern times.

Ari had already picked out a table for them; it was the most secluded one in the place. Stoke put the glasses on the table and sat down across from her. Men in the store were turning around to inspect this pretty customer who looked so cool on a hot day.

"Did you having any problems finding this place?" Stoke asked.

"Actually, I got here early. It was no problem at all. How about you?"

Stoke replied, "I seemed to know the way without actually studying maps. I had no trouble at all."

There was an awkward silence.

"What are you going to do first?" Stoke asked.

Ari fiddled with the paper covering on her straw. Then she put the straw in her glass and drew in a large gulp of drink. She looked up. "I want to see some of the tombstones at the cemeteries in the area. Then there is an old man I'd like to find here in town. He's about ninety, and he's heard about the gangs from his father, who was around them a lot."

"Do you think he was part of the gangs?"

"Who, the old man?"

"No, I mean the father of the old man," said Stoke.

"Oh, I don't know enough about him yet. I'm going to reserve judgment until we talk. Now can I ask about your plans?"

Stoke hesitated. He was looking at Ari's left hand for wedding or engagement rings. There weren't any. "Yes, I also want to visit some of the farms and look at tombstones. But first, I want to visit the courthouse to see if there are any records on the estate of a man who died here in 1856. He might be a relative.

"How're you going to find your way around?" asked Ari.

"I wrote the U.S. Geological Service and asked for a map of the area. It shows hills and prominent buildings and all roads."

"Good idea. I wish I had thought of that."

"No sweat, Ari. Let's make a copy of mine on a photocopier, if we can find one close by. Then you can locate just about anything in the county."

"That would be great. I could really save some time."

"Now," Stoke said as he looked around the store, "where is a copier?"

"There's one down at the Hy Vee Grocery," said the young man who had come out from behind the counter. He had been listening to their conversation with some interest. He was pointing west, up the street.

"Well, that's settled," Stoke said with a grin. "Next, he'll be telling me where all the Levanger hookers hang out."

"They're south of town," the boy said with smirk, "about three miles out on Highway 24."

"You must be kidding," Stoke said.

"I am," the boy replied. "This town isn't large enough to support a hooker, so there's a circuit rider who drives through every other Wednesday."

"All right," Stoke told the boy. "I'm sorry. I wasn't making fun of your town. In a sense, it's my town too, because some of my ancestors may have lived here at one time. I think they're buried here."

"Okay," said the boy. "It's just that a lot of travelers make fun of us. I get tired of defending the place."

"Levanger has the best fountain Coke I've ever tasted. You can tell them that," Ari said.

"Thank you," the boy said, and went back to the white marble fountain, which he scrubbed as Ari and Stoke talked.

Ari said to Stoke, "I noticed one more thing. Did you see that plant out front?"

"No, I don't notice geraniums and those kinds of things that grow green. What about it?"

"It was hemp," Ari said.

"Well, this was a hemp-growing, rope-making area at one time," Stoke recited from memory.

"As long as it's used for rope, I guess it's okay," Ari said. "I guess you're not familiar with similar plants used for smoking?"

Stoke thought a minute and said, "Oh, you must be talking about pot! No, I must confess that smoking is not my thing and neither is dope. I'm a little slow on the uptake at times. I wouldn't know a pot plant from an iris."

Ari seemed relieved. Stoke thought he had said the right thing. But the clerk at the counter was listening to them much more closely.

Ari said, "Hemp must grow like weeds around here because it is kind of a weed. I don't use it either, but I've been trained to recognize it when I see it." Then anxious to change the subject, Ari said, "There's a historical society in town. Did you know about it?"

"I suspected there must be one."

Ari said, "I talked on the phone with the vice-president of the society. She said she wanted to help me. Maybe you'd like to come along?"

"That would be nice," he told her, "if you'd share your sources with me. I'm afraid I don't have much to share at this point."

As they walked to the store to copy Stoke's map, Ari said, "Stoke, there is one thing I want to mention to you. It's about Bill Simkins."

"What's that?"

"Do you think my ancestor killed the man you're looking for? I know he was the leader of a gang and was hanged from a local bridge."

"Ari, I just don't know. I read about him in a book about Crittenden County. It could be that he was in charge of the gang that did the killing, or it could be that there was no connection at all.

She said, "I just hope we find that Old Bill didn't kill him. But even if he did, or if his gang did, you need to recognize how tough times were before the Civil War. A lot of the industry in western Missouri was devoted to building up a supply of guns and ammunition so the pro-slavery folks could drive out the anti-slavery folks, and vice-versa."

"I suppose times were tough, but not everybody became a robber, Ari."

"Well, let's find out. That's a major point I would like to prove one way or another before I go back to Washington."

By this time, they had gotten to Stoke's car for the map and then entered the grocery. They found a copier off in a corner. Stoke supplied the map and some dimes while Ari copied the map one section at a time. He stood back and watched her work. He found the scenery interesting, but the main character fascinating.

When Ari had all the copies she wanted, she gave Stoke his map and suggested that they walk back to his car together. When they got there, Stoke stood by the car door and wondered how to tell Ari that he wanted to see her again, without being too obvious.

"Um, do you think we might meet back in town for dinner? Afterwards, maybe we could talk to the historical society person."

"That sounds good, Stoke, if you'll let me pay half of the bill. Of course, there would have to be a place around here that serves a nice meal. I trust that you aren't talking about McDonald's?"

"No, but a Taco Bell would be refreshing."

"What's that?"

"In California, it's a Mexican McDonalds."

"I don't know if you're serious or not, Stoke."

"I'm not serious. But I did hear there are a few nice restaurants around Levanger. Why not make use of them? We have to come back here anyway."

"I'll meet you back here at six o'clock. Is that agreeable?"

"That's fine, Ari, and if you don't need a car, why don't we drive over together?"

Ari thought it over and said and agreed. They went their separate ways.

Stoke said, "Hello" to an older man in the street. Then he added, "I'm new in town. Can you tell me where the courthouse is?" The man spat out some tobacco he didn't seem to want any longer. Then he said, "It's down this street." He was pointing east.

Stoke said, "Thank you. I'm looking for information about the death of an ancestor. He may have been shot down near here in 1856. His name was Vallandingham. Do you know if any one by that name lives here?"

The man thought a minute. "You might ask in the courthouse. Don't know of anyone by that name. 'Course, I'm a stranger here, too."

Stoke looked at the sign the man had been using for support. It said that Main Street was the origin of the Santa Fe Trail.

Laughing, Stoke walked over one block until he came to the court-house. It was an imposing, Classic Revival two-story building with four columns in front. The building was obviously old. Stoke thought it was probably built just after the county was formed. The walls were about eighteen or twenty inches thick. It was all white. As he got closer, Stoke noticed a cannon ball embedded in the first column he came to.

Woodwork was worn and had been painted many times in the past one hundred and forty years. He wandered from office to office, where he found gracious, friendly people willing to talk with him. A lady in the records department suggested that Stoke visit the newspaper office across the street before he left town. While he waited to get his hands on the 1856 Will Book, the county judge walked in. He sat and talked with Stoke for a few minutes but did not know any Vallandinghams.

Stoke wandered upstairs into a large courtroom. No one else was present. The judge's desk sat in the middle of the front area. There was a door off to the right side. A handwritten sign on it said, "Grand Jury Room." Stoke wandered through the doorway and found a bathroom and several record rooms. Then he went to the back of the courtroom and stood, reflecting on the hearings that must have been held there. He wondered if the killer in the Vallandingham shooting had stood in this room, and had been let go from there.

He felt a tap on his shoulder and saw that the records clerk was motioning for him to come to her office. He followed her to the giant desk where a huge old book was laid out, pages open. She pointed to the first of two entries.

He read:

Records of Wills Bonds Letters H Book A   341

Know all men by these presents that Mr. Alexander Noble as principal and A. E. H. Edgar and C. B. Bayley as security of the County of Crittenden and the State of Missouri, are held and firmly bound unto the State of Missouri in the sum of Fifteen Hundred Dollars for the payment of which will and truly be made. We bind Ourselves, our Heirs, Executives and Administrators, jointly and severally, firmly by these presents, sealed with our seals and dated this 21st day of July A. D. 1856.

The condition of the above bond is that if Alexander Noble, Administrator of the Estate of H. B. Vallandingham, deceased, shall faithfully administer said Estate for pay deliver all money and property of said Estate and perform all things touching said Administration required by Law or the Order or Decree of any Court having jurisdiction, then the above bond to be paid, otherwise to remain if full force.

Alexander Noble (Seal)
A.E.H. Edgar (Seal)
C. B. Bayley (Seal)

The State of Missouri, County of Crittenden

To all persons to whom these presents shall come, Greetings. Know Ye That whereas H. B. Vallandingham of the County of Crittenden died interstate as it is Said having at the time of his death property in this State which may be lost, destroyed or demolished in value if speedy care be not taken of the same, to the end therefore that said property may be collected, pursued and disposed of according to the Law, I hereby appoint Alexander Noble administrator of all and singular the Goods and Chattels and Credits which time of the deceased H. B. Vallandingham at the time of his death with full power and authority secure and dispose of said property according to the Law, and Collect all monies due said deceased and in general to do and perform all other acts and things which are or hereafter may be required of him by Law.

In testimony Whereof I Edward Stratton Judge of the Probate Court in and for the County of Crittenden aforesaid have hereunto signed my name and offered affixed the seal of said Court at office this 21st day of July AD 1856.

Edward Stratton, Judge

The foregoing Bond & Letters of Administration was recorded by me on this 24th day of July AD 1856

Edward Stratton, Judge

H. B. Vallandingham! Stoke felt his knees go weak. Henry Bruce Vallandingham was the right man, but how did he get to Levanger? Quickly, he opened his briefcase and searched for a copy of the letter that Henry had written to his daughter. He could not find it. He asked if he could make a photocopy of the pages of the probate records. The records clerk saw the stricken look in Stoke's eyes and took pity on him. She showed him the corner of the room where there was a copier and helped him make his copies.

Then Stoke took his cell phone from his briefcase and called his office. It was early there, but his secretary was on the job. He told her he was going to stay a few more days than he'd planned.

Next Stoke went to the newspaper office across the street and asked for 1856 copies of the paper. He didn't really expect to find them, but he had to ask. The boss of the outfit, probably the editor, said, "Mister, you could have them if we had them, but we don't. Have them, that is. I don't even know the name of the paper in those days. But I will tell you one thing; the University of Missouri has a very nice collection of newspapers papers on microfilm. If you were to contact them . . ."

Stoke nodded and thanked the man. Then he asked if there were a library in town.

"That's one thing we've got," the editor told him. "You'll find it back on Main Street. I hope it isn't closed, though." Everything was close by, so Stoke quickly found himself in the library. He asked the librarian if he could see copies of the Levanger historical book collection. She was a young woman who appeared very efficient.

"What year do you want to see?" she asked him.

"Let me start with 1856," he replied, thinking this investigation was going to be easier than he imagined.

"Oh, those were exciting times," she told him. "People generally think the War Between the States began in 1861, when the South fired on Ft. Sumter, but it really began in Kansas in 1855"

"Oh, what makes you say that?" Stoke asked her.

"That was the year shooting started, and it wasn't long afterward that John Brown hacked up his first victims. There were six or seven in all. I don't remember if they got all the parts put back together so they could really tell."

Stoke's smile disappeared. "I found that one of my ancestors was killed on Levanger's streets around the twentieth of July in 1856. I suppose you don't have any stories about it, do you?

"Let's see," she said, as she began looking through old books. "Did you say 1856?"

He nodded, and added, "His name was Henry B. Vallandingham."

She kept on looking through first one volume and then another. "Nope, I don't have anything about it in my records. Why was he killed?"

Stoke told her about the newspaper clipping. He explained that it said Henry had been seeing the wife of another man in town, and the man killed him for that reason. "The newspaper writer said the whole thing was peculiar and that the killer was let off because of a 'novel decision,'" he added.

She looked at him for a minute and said, "Let me give you some advice. Your ancestor may very well have been fooling around with some guy's wife. But he might not. There were two main reasons that were given in those days for killing people. One was 'There was a feud going on,' and the other was, 'He was playing around with someone's wife.' You need to understand that juries were comfortable with those two reasons, and they let people off because of them. They were the standard excuses for killing someone, and they often worked. I suggest that before accepting such an alibi you investigate the background first."

Stoke smiled and said she had been a big help. He added, "You've really given me something to think about." After asking for instructions for finding the local graveyard, Cave Hill Cemetery, Stoke left the library deeply in thought.

The graveyard office was closed. But anyone could walk in and look at the stones. The cemetery was well kept, with mowed lawns and few weeds. It was a fairly large site so Stoke realized it was going to take a while to find what he wanted. He walked back in time as he went from the recent burials in front to the older ones in back. When he got to the area where 1856 graves would have been, he didn't find any. Then he remembered from his own experience that people were often buried on their farms in those days. Yet he saw a gravestone from 1843, and another from 1850. The limestone markers were becoming hard to read. But nothing looked like a marker with a Vallandingham name on it.

Giving up on the cemetery for a while, Stoke returned to his motel room so he could shut out the world and think about what he had found that day. Intuitively, he knew that his dreams and the murder of Henry were somehow connected. It was a relief to know there was some basis to them. Stoke did not feel haunted but he did think there was something odd about his dreams. He decided that old memories of things his grandmother told him had been dredged up after his leg accident.

Done in Early American style, the motel room was clean and neat. It had a queen-size bed. Its one redeeming feature was a large bath. Stoke sorted out his belongings in his methodical way that came from years of traveling.

He showered and changed clothes and put on shoes that were not mud-covered. It stayed warm at night in Levanger, so he did not bother with a jacket.

Recalling he had been unable to find the copy of Henry's letter from 1856, Stoke looked through his briefcase once more. Then he remembered he had put a manila folder of information in his suitcase. Digging it out, he found the letter inside. He stared at the word "Fenanger" until the black print on the page began to blur. So he put it aside for later when Ari might be willing to have a look at it.

Soon it was time to pick up her and take her to dinner.

* * * * *

It was a little after six when Stoke called Ari. "This is Stoke and I'm losing weight rapidly. Care to eat?"

She was within ten minutes of being ready, so Stoke said he would be in the lobby area waiting for her. He gathered up his papers and went to the lobby to look at them once more. While he was waiting, he thought more about Henry being intestate, and the man named Alexander Noble who had handled Henry's estate. He realized that women could not legally do such work, so a male family friend or a lawyer usually did it for them. He also noticed that Henry, who was born in 1807, according to a federal census, was forty-nine years old when he died in 1856.

"Hi," Ari said, looking refreshed and quite pretty in a colorful summer dress that had a scoop neck and a full skirt. She was carrying a large purse and a notebook.

"Hi, yourself. I was hoping we could find a place nearby that won't take too long preparing the food, and its name doesn't start with MC."

"Are you still hankering for tacos?" Ari asked.

"Right now I could eat a pig fried in gasoline!"

"We're going to meet our local tour guide at a Mexican-American restaurant at 7:30. Is that all right with you?" she asked. "I don't know anything about the place. It was recommended to me."

"Deal," said Stoke. He thought Mexican food might be a novelty to Ari, and it could be an icebreaker.

They went out to his car and he helped Ari in on her side. He noticed that she smelled good. There was a trace of some kind of perfume like Musk, but she also smelled as if she had just stepped out of the shower. He approved, but thought "essence of apple pie" would have been even better.

The restaurant was only a mile south of the motel. As they drove into the parking lot, Ari said, " You don't suppose this place is like Taco Bell, do you?"

"It looks like it's several steps up from Mr. Taco and his Bell. May be good Mexican food. I thought I could give you a guided tour."

A few minutes later they were greeted by a pretty black hostess. They went through the usual routine of how many there were in their party and were taken to a table in a fairly crowded room. Men in the restaurant stared at Ari. They stopped eating and with food in their mouths watched her walk across the room. Ari was oblivious to them. But Stoke noticed and felt good that his "date" got so much attention.

"She didn't look like a Mexican," said Ari about the hostess when they were left alone.

"Probably all the available Mexicans are cooking the food," Stoke answered. "The taste has to be genuine or the restaurant will be just like every other place in town."

Greens and reds and yellows decorated the room from floor to ceiling. It was a warehouse of colors and delicious smells, a large place with round, wooden tables, and chairs with cane seats, huddled closely together in as many places as one could put them. A mariachi band of five men visited each table and serenaded the guests in Spanish, whether the diners wanted music or not. Stoke wondered if the singers said "You-all" when they weren't singing, as many Missouri people did. Each table had on it an empty tequila bottle and a glass chimney that contained a lighted candle.

"What should I order?" asked Ari.

"Start with a margarita," suggested Stoke. "I suppose you know what that is."

"Oh, I've tasted them from time to time."

A waitress came to their table to take their orders for drinks. She left, and Stoke took some papers from his pocket. "Can I tell you about my day?"

"If you'll allow equal time for my story."

A few minutes later the margaritas arrived. "Here's to ancestor worship!" Stoke toasted.

Ari raised her glass and said, "I'll drink to that, but it's more like ancestor curiosity."

"Are your ancestors as curious as mine?"

"That depends on how you mean 'curious,'" Ari countered.

"I suspect they may be curious about us and we may find them a curious people in the sense of being slightly eccentric."

"Do you always have difficulty with straight answers?" asked Ari.

"Yes, when I can get a laugh."

"Oh. Do you find something eccentric about your ancestors? Mine seem about average."

"Ari, where did your father's people come from, with the name Edwards?"

"They came from Virginia. Why?"

"I'm related to some Kentucky Edwards, people who came from Virginia. I guess I'm trying to tell you that some of my folks may *be* some of your folks."

"You mean, we're. . ."

"Possibly distant cousins, not brother and sister. Maybe close enough to shake hands, but not too close to worry about sharing the same motel."

"You're making it up, Stoke."

"No, I'm not! My mother has some information that we were descended from a Uriah Edwards of Wales, who went to Virginia in 1712. Then his descendants went to Kentucky about 1788. Aren't you willing to trust my sainted mother? It was Mom who taught me not to go to motels with strange women, you know. But she never said anything about family."

"I don't know about your crazy mother, but I haven't checked out my Edwards family line yet. Can it wait until I research my book on the Simkins clan?"

"Yeah, it can wait. I might not want to be related to you if you don't like Mexican food. Kinship would be a moot point. So, what did you find today, Ari?"

She opened her notebook and scanned its first page. There were several pages filled in, so Stoke figured that she was a good observer who didn't miss much. He realized he would have to be careful not to be his usual outrageous self.

"Hang on to your hat. I'm going to put on my glasses. I hate them!" she said. Then Stoke realized why Ari didn't notice the men in the restaurant who were staring at her; she was nearsighted.

"Since we're scholars on a scholarly quest, I can't see what the problem is," he gallantly told her.

Ari put on her glasses, which Stoke thought did not make her less attractive. *But, of course, I may be prejudiced toward family,* he rationalized.

Ari ignored him. "Here goes. I talked to the old man whose dad knew about the gangs. He's about ninety-two years old, but his mind seemed clear. He said there were several gangs in those days. They were in the eastern part of Crittenden County. He also said the Kansas City newspapers carried on about the gang activity in the region, but the local paper claimed there wasn't any such thing."

"Maybe we could look at copies of the Kansas City papers at the local historical association," Stoke interjected.

"That's fine," said Ari, not willing to be sidetracked. "And then I found the Simkins family farm. There was an old graveyard out back, but I was unable to read many of the inscriptions on the stones."

"I found a few of those," Stoke added. "The native rock seems to be limestone, which isn't very durable."

"The old man didn't seem to know your Vallandingham ancestor, Stoke. He did know about some Kentucky people, but he thought they came from there really early, long before 1856."

"Yes, I read about some of them. By the way, I appreciate your looking into my line while you were at it."

"Well, I was there and I thought I might save you some steps if I could rule out one location. Did you find any Simkins while you were looking?"

"I can definitely rule out that name on stones I saw at Cave Hill Cemetery."

The candle at their table went out. Stoke fumbled for a match. He didn't have one. He looked at Ari, who shrugged. Stoke looked at the table beside them. Seated there were four good-looking young men in their twenties. Well-groomed and slender, they were having a good time telling jokes and talking about getting together later that evening. They were not the slightest bit interested in Ari.

Stoke leaned toward the man nearest him and said, "I'm sorry to bother you, but our lamp went out and we don't have a match. Do any of you have a match or a lighter?"

"Yeah, sure," said the closest man as he reached into his neatly pressed jeans pocket and pulled out a gold lighter. "Hold it over here." The other men watched as he lit the candle.

As the flame grew, Stoke said seriously, "Thanks. It's a lot better, you know, to light one of these things than it is to curse the darkness."

The men laughed. One said, "That's very good, you know. You should write that down." More laughter.

"I would, but it's too damn dark at our table to write anything," Stoke added. Much more laughter. Then Stoke turned back to Ari, who was enjoying the entire performance. "One of life's better moments," he remarked as he put the candle back into place.

"Yes, it is," she said somewhat dreamily. But that look passed and she glanced down at her notes. "Well, Stoke, may I continue? I don't have anyone at home to tell about these things and I get excited about my research at times."

"Uh, what do you mean when you say no one to tell these things to at home? Don't you have a husband or 'significant other' to talk to?"

"That's not something I usually talk about, Stoke, but since you're family, I can say I was engaged once, but my fiancée was killed in the line of duty."

"That's terrible, Ari! What kind of duty?"

"He was with the FBI, and was killed by a bullet from one of his own people in a raid on some drug dealers. It was three years ago." Ari told her story matter-of-factly. She seemed to be past the grieving period that often accompanies such tragedy.

"Well, since you told me, I can tell you that I'm divorced and live alone."

"I know that."

"How in the hell did you know *that*?" he asked with astonishment.

"You've done work for defense contractors. That means the FBI has a file with your name on it. I still have contacts in the Agency. When we began corresponding about meeting here, I asked them to tell me what they knew about you. Please don't be angry. A girl has to be careful, you know."

"What else do you know?" asked Stoke with some exasperation in his voice.

"I know what your address is, and that you are a pretty good consultant who owns several companies. You also sing in a men's choral group. But you're a better consultant than you are singer. And *you* told me that on occasion you break your legs."

"Damn!" said Stoke. "The part about my singing is true. I had hoped that no one east of the Rockies knew about it, though."

He added, "I wondered why a pretty girl like you would be willing to meet a stranger in a place like this, just to do research on her ancestors. Are you part of the FBI?"

"Thank you for the compliment, and, no, I am not part of the FBI. I'm a manager in the Department of Transportation," she said a bit hotly.

"It wasn't a compliment, just a statement of fact. I'm not coming on to you. Please don't take me wrong."

"All right, I won't." And then to change the subject, she asked, "Did you find anything that would tie your Vallandingham in with my ancestor?"

"No. But I did find other things; I found a probate document that said the man murdered in Levanger was my ancestor, unfortunately."

"Then it was a good day," she said.

"There's more. I found that the town librarian has a small collection of books about the area that you might want to look at. And I would really appreciate it if you would look at an old letter I have."

"Did you bring it with you?"

"Yes," Stoke said. "Maybe we could look at it after dinner."

"Good. I hope we find something. It would be a relief if I didn't have to go on apologizing for Bill, not knowing whether he did something worth apologizing for!" Ari seemed really concerned.

To ease some of Ari's cares, Stoke changed the subject. "I think you should understand that it's not exactly what I *know* that brought me here. Ever since I was in the hospital, I've been having weird dreams in which I'm talking with my grandmother. She tells me a story about a man who was shot and I conjure up what the killing looked like. I get to ask her questions and she answers them, but I really never get enough information. I could see the shooting as it was happening, but I couldn't warn him. It was so real, it was scary. It feels really nuts."

"Maybe you are nuts, but not because of dreams. Did you ever actually talk with your grandmother or is this dream a complete fabrication?"

"I may have talked with her when I was about five. I can't be sure. My grandmother died a few years after I was born, I think, and she couldn't have talked with me a great deal. But if I did have this conversation with someone, it probably would have been with my grandmother. Whatever else happened, I know I've never seen someone getting shot, and I've never been here before."

"So you don't actually know if you were dreaming or if you were recalling the information she gave you. Did your dreams give any clues about when it happened?"

"From my dreams, I can't tell when it happened, but I know it wasn't recently. There weren't any cars, so I knew it was before 1900. And the streets weren't paved. All I know is that my grandmother said it was before the Civil War."

"Well, ole Bill Simkins had quit his gang work before 1856, since he was in jail then. Unless he was tied in with someone else, he couldn't have been part of a plot to kill your Henry.

"I'm not sure of anything. The dream stuff is too flaky to be relied on," Stoke said.

"Yes, but it's interesting, especially if it all turns out to be true, don't you think?"

"Sure. I know Henry died the way the dreams said he did. That's one thing."

Not waiting for his dinner, Stoke picked up his manila folder. He opened it, flipped a few pages and showed it to Ari. "Here's a letter from Henry before he died. It says he was in Fenanger, Missouri. I've contacted a lot of people who ought to know, and they say there never was a Fenanger. Now look at his letter. Didn't he write *Fenanger*?"

Ari looked at the copy of the letter a long time. Then she said, "I don't know. Look at the *F*. It's older script and very nicely done. But part of it seems to be missing, as if the pen skipped a spot. If that's true, perhaps it curved around and was really an *L*. Then it would say *Lenanger*. And the first *n* could be a *v*. In that case, you have Levanger, Missouri, not Fenanger, Missouri."

"That's it!" Stoke shouted, and all the diners around him looked up, startled. "You're right, Ari. That's what he wrote. He was here, he lived here, and his wife was here when he was murdered."

"Ari spoke softly as if to get Stoke to quiet down by example. "Obviously he wrote the letter to his daughter… there's a lot of personal information in it. But look at this statement: 'The Cansas excitement is very high yet and is likely to be higher.' Do you know what he means?"

"Yes, I do. I got a history lesson today on that very subject. Kansas is not very far away. And he misspelled the name of the territory. If Kansas came into the Union as a free state, then Southern interests would be harmed. Two senators and a few congressmen would most likely be added to Congress as anti-slavery voters. But if Kansas came into the Union as a slave state, there would be more slavery votes and more balance in Congress. People in western Missouri, including Levanger, were desperate to get Kansas into the Union as a slave state. They were willing to go to war over slavery five years before the War actually broke out. In fact, there were some skirmishes in Kansas and quite a few people were killed."

"Ari thought for a few moments and said, "Maybe that's why Bill Simkins gave up his gang. There was too much else going on and he couldn't compete. Or maybe he joined with the slavery people in their battles. You're lucky to have dreams, Stoke. I have to do research."

"It's this dream stuff I don't understand, Ari. Sometimes I feel like I'm in a movie, totally under the control of a director. And I don't know who the director is or what he or she wants. But I feel I'm supposed to be doing something or learning something."

"That's an amazing dream mechanism," she said. "Do you believe that dreams have any real power?"

"No, I don't. And I don't believe in ghosts, either. I don't believe in stray emotional or mental powers just lying around for years, waiting for people to become trapped in them. That's movie stuff."

"Stoke, I don't know. But I can tell you that there were ghost stories long before there were movies."

"That's true," he agreed. "I know it's crazy, but I have the feeling we all have lots of dreams like I'm having. They float around in our heads, but we're not aware of them until something drastic happens, and we have to be quiet for an extended period. I broke my leg. The dreams started during those hours when I was totally alone and unable to do anything but focus on them."

Stoke was interrupted by the waitress, who asked if they were ready to order dinner. He halted his dream discussion long enough to ask Ari if she could find her way among the tamales and enchiladas. The answer was negative, so Stoke suggested a "Combinacion Plate" of several items, which she could try. He did the same. Then he returned to the dream topic.

Stoke felt he could talk with Ari; for some reason he was at ease with her. "What do you think about dreams, Ari?"

"I've had no personal experiences with strong dreams like you're talking about, but I've heard of them. The scientific part of me rejects any importance at all, but I will admit there's a lingering doubt."

Dinner salads arrived. They nibbled on lettuce as they talked.

"What about Freud?" Stoke responded. "He was big on dreams, you know."

"I think at times Freud was an artist rather than a scientist. Really, I'm not qualified to comment. I have only a passing interest in psychology. I seldom hear much about him these days. Perhaps it's because very little of his work was ever proven or tested scientifically."

"I suppose that could be true," mused Stoke. "I guess I'm a little afraid of my dreams, and I really don't enjoy talking about them to people who I don't know well. My close friends know that I'm fairly stable. I would prefer that you think I'm stable, Ari, and this dream stuff is a passing fancy."

"Don't let it bother you, Stoke. I'm not going to let it bother me, unless I start having the dreams, too."

"Perhaps you'd like to star in one of my dreams?"

"Thank you, no. I don't seem to be old enough. Your 'stars' are well over a hundred and fifty years old."

Dinner arrived. They ordered a second round of margaritas and then Stoke explained the food on Ari's plate. The refried beans with melted cheese were a stumbling block, but she tasted them anyway. Then she tried a taco and an enchilada. Her approval was immediate. Stoke tried to explain about his chili relleño and told Ari just to cut off a chunk and try it. She liked that, too.

Ari looked up from her plate. "This stuff is good. Will it bite back later?"

"Not if you don't eat tons of it."

"Have I eaten tons of it yet?"

"Not by my standards. Are you full?"

Ari chewed a bit, stopped, and considered how tight her belt was. "No, but maybe I'd better quit while I'm ahead."

Dinner didn't seem to take long. They took bites between Stoke's explanations of what the food was and Ari's opinions of it. They giggled conspiratorially over each item until they had tasted it all. Ari had a cup of coffee. The men at the next table had already gone; the crowd at the restaurant was thinning out. He couldn't believe that an hour and a half had passed. He was totally unaware of the time.

They were interrupted by a woman, who asked if Ari were looking for her. She said, "My name is May Havens. I understand you're doing some research in Levanger."

Ari looked up. "Of course. Please sit down. We were hoping you would be able to make it. This is Mr. Towles."

Stoke stood and said, "Pleased to meet you. Why not call me Stoke?"

Ari added, "And please call me Ari."

"And I'm May," May contributed.

Stoke liked her open manner. May was in her thirties, a small well-dressed, attractive woman who had a straw purse that hit the floor with a clunk as she sat down with them. He thought of a comic's remark, "He who steals my purse deserves a hernia," as he sat down.

Ari told May, "Stoke and I met through the mail. He's investigating a murder that took place here on Levanger's streets in 1856."

May turned her attention to Stoke as he laid out the barest details of his investigation. May was fascinated, but said she had never heard of the murder or the man's name. She said the major historical attraction of Levanger was its Civil War Battle, which was enacted every year or two.

Then Ari explained *her* research. May listened closely and suggested that they get together the next day to look around the town and its library and other resources, so they didn't miss any possible details. May was a lively, active person who knew many features of the life of the county as well as the city. They couldn't have found a more interested and interesting person to guide them. May agreed to meet them at ten the following day and then she left.

Outside the restaurant, Stoke said, "A meal like this should be walked off. What if we leave the car at the motel and go for a stroll before turning in for the night? We can finish our conversation and make some plans for tomorrow."

Ari looked relieved because she really didn't know how to end the evening gracefully. And she needed looser clothes. She had eaten more than she intended. They drove back to the motel, agreeing to meet outside in about fifteen minutes.

An almost full moon was rising over a nearby hill, giving plenty of light to see by. Stoke was outside first and waiting for Ari by the entrance of the motel. "Up or down the street?" Stoke asked. Both ways offered a country lane with modest sidewalks. There was little traffic.

"Let's try going up the street," Ari said, for no special reason. "If we don't like the view, we can go down the street later."

"Deal," said Stoke as they began their stroll. "But remember, I can't walk far these days."

As they walked, they made plans for visiting the various areas of interest the next day. Stoke was hoping for her company on some of his side trips. He was conscious of Ari's presence very close to him. He began to think it was his fatal charm, but then he noticed she wasn't wearing her glasses. *She's probably using me for a guide dog,* he thought to himself resignedly.

They had gone quite a way from the motel. Stoke loved to walk and was pleased that Ari seemed to enjoy it, too.

After a long silence, Ari said, "Stoke, I've enjoyed this day. And the food was really good. You know, I was afraid you were going to be a rather stuffy businessman."

At that moment, a car coming toward them suddenly veered onto the shoulder of the road, headed right for them. Ari reacted quickly and shoved Stoke away, while she jumped behind him. The car missed them both, slid a bit, and went back on the pavement as though nothing had happened. It continued at high speed down the road, getting away as fast as possible.

"What the hell was that all about?" said Stoke, as he picked himself up and unconsciously checked his sore leg for more damage. "That was about as close as I want to come to a guided missile!"

"I guess someone out there had a bit too much to drink," Ari said. "Are you all right?"

"Yes, I'm not hurt. How about you?"

"Pretty much undamaged, I guess," Ari said as she stood and wiped the hayseed off her dress.

"Thanks for saving my life, Ari. I owe you one. But I think something isn't quite right. Do you have any enemies here?"

"No, no one knows I'm here. It was an accident, Stoke. I'm not going to worry about it, unless *you* have enemies here."

"I have lots of enemies, but they don't know where I am. Anyway, don't stop there, Ari——what did you find out? You said you thought I might be a stuffy businessman… "

"Not too stuffy to have fun."

With that comment, the lights from the motel met them and they went in. Stoke said he would be eating breakfast in the motel about eight, if Ari were interested. She was, and they went to their rooms.

Stoke had forgotten to go over the rest of his copies with Ari or to re-read them himself. His broken leg ached, and he was tired from his hike through the cemetery and down the street after dinner. Sleep came quickly. He did not dream about his ancestors; he dreamed about Ari and how he was saving her from a hideous beast, and how grateful she was.

Chapter Six

Having had his first cup of coffee when Ari arrived for breakfast, Stoke was in a good humor and was well rested. "Good morning, cousin," he said to her as she came over to his table.

"Don't give me that cousin crap! Where's my coffee?" Ari said gruffly. Stoke choked on his last sip. He looked startled. Then she smiled. "I just wanted to see how you'd react. You can do that with family, you know."

Stoke looked relieved. "Uh, did you sleep all right?"

"Well, I didn't have any dreams of shootings or anything suspicious. So what you have isn't contagious."

"That's good. For a minute there, I was afraid you had a bad night."

Ari assured Stoke she had slept well. During breakfast they decided to leave right away for the library. But it wasn't open, so instead Stoke took Ari through the local cemetery. It was there Ari suggested that Stoke might look into some church cemeteries for Henry's grave.

It was about ten o'clock when they arrived at the center of town to meet May Havens. They had found a parking space in front of the library building. All three of them went in to the information area and were directed to the basement archives by a young man who had a southern accent that reminded Stoke of molasses. But the accent seemed to turn to acid when he told Stoke that most of the really useful information he wanted had been given to the State University many years ago.

May told Stoke that her husband, Greg, would be by soon to see if he could help them find anything useful.

Stoke waited while Ari began looking through the files for information on Bill Simkins. She took a stack of microfiche slides to a reader. Stoke waited. After fifteen minutes a different librarian walked up to him.

"Were you looking for Mr. Havens?"

"Yes, we were going to meet here, I believe."

A tall man of about forty with a head of red hair and a friendly grin was standing by the door, looking Stoke's way.

Stoke said to him, "I understand your wife volunteered your services. I really appreciate your help."

Shaking his hand, Greg said, "Glad to do it. I'm part of the Historical Society, too. Maybe someday you'll put us on the map with all your research."

As he and Stoke walked out the door, Stoke explained what he was doing. He asked if maybe Greg could direct him to the oldest Baptist church in the city that had a graveyard.

"That's easy," Greg replied. "There's only one like that."

Stoke drove his long Mercedes a few blocks and parked in front of a red brick building which had double doors in front, and a typical sign on its lawn telling about services. There was the ubiquitous cute slogan, too. This one said something like "Sermonettes lead to Christianettes." He imagined that the minister was long-winded.

They went behind the church to find the graveyard. Stoke and Greg drove the car up an almost invisible, overgrown lane. Then they got out and waded through tall bushes, vines and weeds. It was dark in the shade of the trees and bushes. Spiders had long ago put up their own fences of webs from tree to tree. Suddenly Stoke stumbled. He had found a headstone with his toe. Oblivious to the danger of snakes, he pulled weeds back from its face and saw a date of 1843. All it said was "Baby."

Soon one marker after another began to show in the morning shadows. Most were weathered limestone. They were dated from 1843. The oldest was 1905. Depressions in the ground showed where pine coffins had rotted away and earth had fallen into the cavity. This left no support for the headstones above the graves, so they fell over. Greg and Stoke found names like Carson, Woodson and Callender. But there was only one Vallandingham. Stoke could not connect the first name with any of the family.

As they were searching, they heard a gravelly voice behind them. It said, "Greg, that you?"

Greg shouted back, "Sure is, Charlie!"

A small man pushed his way through the tall weeds on his way toward them. When he got close enough, Greg said, "Stoke, this is Rev. Charles Allen. He's in charge here." He added, "Charlie, this is Stokely Towles from California."

Rev. Charles held out his hand to Stoke. "Always nice to meet folks from the Left Coast," he said with a big grin on his face. "What brings you here to our churchyard?"

Stoke explained that he was looking for a man, probably a Baptist, who might have been buried there in 1856.

"Well, let's do this the easy way," said the Reverend. He had a big voce for such a small man. "We have some records inside that go back maybe that far."

They both followed the minister into the church office. The minister hummed what sounded like an old hymn as he found an old ledger book in the bottom of a file cabinet. Then Stoke realized it was the Beatles tune, "Rita, the Pretty Meter Maid." After a few minutes the minister looked up. "Here it is. Did you say 1856? Yes, Henry Vallandingham was buried here on July 19, 1856. Wait, there's a note." He hummed a bit more. "It says, 'See 1887.'"

After a minute or two, Reverend Charlie said, "Aha! The body was moved to what looks like Scott County, Kentucky. He isn't here, boys."

"Do you know where he was buried when he *was* here?" asked Stoke.

With some rough directions to the area where Henry had originally been buried, Stoke and Craig spent more time in the mud and weeds. But they found no more Vallandinghams, and no Simkins, either.

Having spent a total of two hours in which they became covered with mud and weeds and perspiration, the two men straggled out of the dense brush back to the Mercedes. Greg was reluctant to get in, but Stoke said cleaning was part of the rental price. They were tired and Stoke felt frustrated. It was getting toward lunchtime, so the two of them drove back to town. When they got to the restaurant where they had agreed to meet, they didn't find Ari and May.

It was a half-hour later when the two women showed up, talking and laughing and having a great time. Stoke hadn't seen this side of Ari. He liked what he saw.

During lunch they traded information on how little the morning research had uncovered. Stoke shared his frustration, but Ari thought he was doing extremely well. Still, he was disappointed until Ari suggested he look at other courthouse records, in case something had been recorded before the murder. That was the bit of inspiration Stoke was looking for.

After lunch, May and Greg said they had to leave because they had businesses to run. Ari and Stoke thanked them several times, and got their telephone number in case they needed more expert advice. Then they, too, left. Ari went to the library again and Stoke went back to the courthouse.

The lady at the records department recognized Stoke. When he asked to see recorded deeds and any other materials that might have been recorded, she suggested mortgages. Armed with a pair of heavy ledgers, Stoke began a new search, starting at July 18, 1856, and working backwards. He found a mortgage agreement, which said, in effect, that Henry had bought a tavern in Levanger from a man named Limrick. Another man named Lightner lent Henry the money to buy the tavern. Henry then sold some of the tavern's contents. Henry and Alexander Noble, the man who later handled his estate, appeared to have previously borrowed money on this tavern, but their partnership was dissolved, and Noble was to have no more claim on the building at all. It was kind of messy.

Deed of Trust for Henry Bruce Vallandingham

Record Book Y p. 367—Crittenden County, Missouri

This deed of trust made and entered into this, the 8th day of May AD 1856, by and between Henry B. Vallandingham of the County of Crittenden in the State of Missouri of the first part and James S. Lightner as trustee for the uses and purposes hereinafter expressed of the second part, and Alexander Noble of the third part.

    Witnesseth that the party of the first part has this day for and in consideration of the sum of one dollar to him in hand paid by the said party of the second part as well as for the consideration hereinafter expressed bargained and sold and does by these presents bargain and sell to him the said party of the second part as Trustee for the use and benefit of the said party of the third part all of the furniture, bottles, glass, etc. in and about the house formerly known as the Edgar House belonging to William Limrick situated on north main street in the city of Levanger in said Crittenden County, Missouri, now occupied by the said parties of the first & third part, consisting in part of the following articles: Bar & counter, 2 dozen cane bottom chairs, 10 oak tables, 7 small tables, 109 yards oil cloth carpeting, 2 cooking stoves and pipes, 4 coal stoves and pipes, 7 lard lamps, 23 pictures, 21 common chairs, 25 yards rag carpet, 4 bedsteads & bedding, 2 lounges & mattresses, Bill of hardware worth about $20.00 & bill of ___ ware worth about $75.00, screens, 6 cane bottom chairs, 1 refrigerator, 6 six gallon Kegs, 3 looking glasses, 2 clocks, 5 waiters together with all other household and kitchen furniture and also bar glasses—decanters, bottle, spoons, etc, all wines, ale said liquors of all sorts in and about described said house and one cow and calf, to have and hold the above described property to him the said party of the second part and to his successors forever in trust for the following for the following purposes and this deed of trust is made upon this express condition that whereas the said party of the first part stands justly indebted to the said party of the second part in the full sum of six hundred dollars as is evidence of his certain six promissory notes of even date herewith all for the sum of One hundred dollars each, are to be due and payable one month after date, one to be due and payable two months after date, one to be due and payable three months after date, one to be due and payable four months after date, one to be due and payable five months five months after date and the other to be due and payable six months after aforesaid notes made negotiable and payable without defalcation or discount. Now, therefore should the party of the first part will and truly pay and discharge each and all of said notes when they severally become due and payable according to the times and effect thereto, together with all interest and costs thereon, then and in that case the deed of mortgage to be null and void, else to remain in full force and effect. And it is also fully understood that should the said party of the first part fail to pay off and discharge said notes as they generally become due and payable on whenever the said party of the first part shall fail or refuse to pay off and discharge either or any one of said notes when same shall become due and payable according to the tenor and effect thereof, then in that case the said party of the second part trustees as aforesaid shall have power and he is hereof fully authorized to sell said property or so much thereof as may be necessary at public sale before the court house door in this city of Levanger in said Crittenden County for cash in hand by first giving notice the time, the place and terms of each sale by at least at least four written or printed hand bills set up at four public place in Crittenden County at least fifteen days before the day of sale and appropriate the money arising from such sale first to the payment of the expenses of the trust and then to pay off and discharge the amount due the above described notes or such of them as may be then due and should there be a balance left from any one sale after paying off and discharging the notes then due, such balance shall be applied to the payment of the note or notes together with all interest thereon with expenses of this trust should anything remain in hands of such trustee the same shall be paid to said party of the first part.

In testimony whereof I hereto set my hand and seal this day and year first herein and above written   H. B. Vallandingham (seal)

State of Missouri
County of Crittenden

Be it remembered that H. B. Vallandingham who is personally known to the undersigned Justice of the Peace to be the same person whose name is subscribed to the written deed as party thereto this day appeared before me at the County of Crittenden aforesaid and acknowledged that he executed the said Deed voluntarily for the uses and purposes therein expressed witness my hand this 8th day May 1856.

Dan Veitch

The foregoing is the record of a Deed of Trust from H. B. Vallandingham to James S. Lightner for the benefit of Alexander Noble which was filed for Record May 8th 1856

Stoke carefully noted the names of Noble, Lightner and Limrick, in case he ran into them later.

It appeared that this was the tavern Henry mentioned in the letter to his daughter, saying he had bought out his partner (who was Noble). It was interesting to also note what was sold—all the items that made a saloon or a tavern what it was, the whiskey materials and the beds. *With Henry's wife upstairs, making clothes for the fine ladies of the area, there must have been a low tolerance for alcohol*, he thought. *Levanger's matrons would not go near a tavern.*

Then Stoke recalled a remark in the newspaper article about Henry's murder: "He was the keeper of one of those fashionable places which in polite parlance are called Restaurants." So he had gotten rid of the beds and the whiskey and made it into a fashionable place. He changed the name from a well-known tavern to a new word—Restaurant. *My, my,* thought Stoke, *A man who tosses out all the demon rum can't be all bad. I wonder what evil things he did beside chase around with someone's wife? And did he do that while his wife was around? Maybe that was a false charge. Whatever it was, it would have sent him "to the penitentiary for life."*

Stoke found no more entries in the records, so he made copies of the mortgage, and headed back to the main square where he had promised to meet Ari. He sat on a bench and pored over his documents. It was still early so he walked to the library to see if he could find anything else.

He went over to where Ari was reading her microfilmed articles. "Ari, I made one good discovery in the courthouse. Why don't you go ahead with your research? I'll run back to the motel and visit the Internet. Maybe we can meet tonight again at dinner."

Ari looked up from her reader. "Sure. That sounds good to me. I'll see you later," she said.

Back in the motel, Stoke unpacked his laptop computer, plugged it into the power supply, and then put his modem wire into the telephone jack. In a few minutes he was firing off a message to Lou Vanlandingham about his discoveries. Then he discovered a message from Lou saying the probate records had arrived, and that the dead man was H. B. Vallandingham, after all. Stoke already knew that, but he marveled at Lou's tenacity.

Stoke told Lou about the other records and thanked him for going to bat for him. He told about the trust deed and the names of the others mentioned in that legal document. He mentioned the churchyard and the missing grave, too. Writing all this information to Lou had the good effect of getting it organized in Stoke's mind.

In a few minutes, Lou was back on the Internet, asking if Stoke had located the tavern and knew what it looked like. It hadn't occurred to Stoke to locate the place. He was finding he had good help. But he didn't like feeling like an idiot all the time. This kind of research was something he wasn't used to.

That night at dinner, Stoke and Ari compared notes. Both had done fairly well that day. They felt like celebrating. Stoke wasn't shy about telling of his foibles and they had a good laugh. Ari said that maybe his dreams were a good sign that he was making progress. Stoke recalled the old Burma Shave signs along roadsides. They were set out in groups of five individual signs. Drivers enjoyed reading them to passengers as they drove down country roads. Stoke made one up on the spur of the moment:

Here lies Henry
Shot in the street
By a man
On whose wife
He was very sweet
BURMA SHAVE

Ari said, "Very funny. I've heard about the signs. And if you're going into poetry, don't give up your day job."

"Poetry takes my mind off the dreams. I'm uncomfortable with them. And that's mostly because other people would think I'm a wacko."

"I suppose if you hit me with the dream stories all at once, I might think you were a bit odd," Ari said. "But they've developed over the past few days in digestible lumps. I can live with that. Besides, they seem benign."

"I'm glad you think so."

"Look at it this way. Maybe you were here as a child. You may have heard all the stories before now. Probably some older relative told you all this stuff at one time or another."

Stoke nodded his head. "Yes, I suppose so. Then maybe the dreams are just my mind's way of letting me know that I know."

Having finished dinner, Stoke and Ari drove back to their motel. On the way, they stopped at a four-way stop sign. Stoke was driving. A car pulled up beside them on the passenger side and stopped, waiting to go through the intersection. Stoke noticed a movement in the car. As he turned to look, he saw Ari trying to scrunch down in her seat. A scruffy man was staring at her; he had a gun pointed right at her head.

Stoke slammed down on the accelerator and his car shot forward through the intersection. The other car turned right and disappeared rapidly down another road. Then he looked up to see a cop coming the other way.

The cop motioned from the front of his car for them to pull over, which they did. Soon the cop had made a 180-degree turn and was parked behind them at the curb. He got out and walked up behind Stoke with his holster unsnapped, ready for action.

"What was the problem back there? You don't look like a hot-rodder."

"Officer, the man in the car next to us had a gun pointed at us, and I tried to get out of his line of fire," Stoke said.

"It takes all kinds. May I see your driver's license, please?" The cop took it from Stoke and said, "Hmm....California. Mr. Towles, I suspect that you're too used to drive-by shootings on your freeways. That sort of thing doesn't happen in Missouri."

"Oh, it most assuredly happened, officer," Ari chimed in. "In fact, they did something to our car."

"What would that be, ma'am?" said the cop.

"There's a bullet hole in the window behind me," Ari replied.

"What?" said the cop, as he peered through the window to the other side of the car. "You say there's a hole in the window!"

"Yes, and there's glass on the seat," said Ari, getting more irritated. "Whatever caused it came from the outside."

"Did that happen here or in California?" asked the cop, unwilling to think Levanger, Missouri, had drive-by shootings, too.

"This is a rented car," said Stoke. "I doubt if it's ever been to California."

"Oh… Did you get his license number?" the cop asked quickly.

Ari and Stoke looked at each other. "No," Stoke said. "We were too busy dodging the bullet."

"Well, I guess he's gone now. You folks will have to come with me to the station so I can take your statements. I can't do it here. Follow me, please." With that, the cop went to his car and called the incident in. He pulled ahead of them and they followed three blocks to the sheriff's station.

The cop showed them where to park and kept them under surveillance until they had gotten into the sheriff's office building. Then he went with them to his sergeant's desk and introduced them to his boss, a Sergeant Andrews. He explained what he had seen and he left.

Sergeant Andrews took over the conversation about where Ari and Stoke had come from, why they were in Levanger and what they did for a living. Then he asked Stoke to go with a detective in another room while Ari stayed at his desk. The detective asked Stoke about his activities all over again. Then he began to talk about drugs. He was just getting warmed up when the sergeant came in and pulled him aside. They talked for a minute and then the detective left. The sergeant went over to Stoke, apologized, and thanked him for doing his service as a citizen. He was most polite.

Stoke went back into the sergeant's office to see Ari, looking pretty as ever, totally unfazed by the turmoil. The sergeant was very nice to her, and escorted them to the door, thanking them all the time.

As soon as they got outside, Stoke looked at Ari. "What did you say to those guys? That detective was just about to get his thumbscrews out when the sergeant came in and pulled him off. It was a good thing because all I had between me and a bad case of torture was a skinny lawyer in California."

"I told him I was with the federal government, working on a case."

"But Ari, why do they care about the Department of Transportation?"

"Whatever—it worked."

"And why did that guy have a gun on us in the first place? Was he connected to the guy who tried to run us down last night? Ari, is there something I ought to know?"

"Stoke... I can't tell you. Perhaps it would be better if we split up."

"Wow, and I thought my *dreams* were a problem. Whatever you're are doing, is it legal?"

Ari said it was. All of it. But it was not pleasant, and she was afraid he might get hurt. She said she had convinced the cops that the danger was over, but it wasn't. She was not able to say what she was doing, other than that she really was researching for her ancestors.

"Tell you what," Stoke said, "if you can take my crazy dreams, I can take your crazy schemes. Let's keep going, but stay in public places. What do you say?"

"All right, if you don't mind the danger. I need to spend a few more days in the area. I'd like to finish my research."

"You really are doing research?"

"Yes, well, I didn't get to do much these last two days. But as I have time, I plan to get more material for my book."

"Deal," said Stoke, as he looked up and down the street for strangers who might be after them. The trouble was that he was two thousand miles from home and everyone was a stranger.

After they left the sheriff's station, Stoke and Ari drove back to the motel. He went once more to his room to study the information he had obtained that day. He copied the address of the property that was mortgaged by Henry Vallandingham. It was "the house formerly known as the Edgar House belonging to William Limrick situated on north Main Street." *Piece of cake,* Stoke thought to himself

Chapter Seven

A BARGAIN IN LAND

One Hundred and Eighty acres of good land, with
plenty of fine Timber, Stone and Water, is offered
for sale on good terms. The property lies within
about two miles of Levanger and has some im-
provements. For terms, call on   .
WM. MUSGROVE, Agent

After meeting for breakfast the next morning, Stoke and Ari talked about their plans for the day. Stoke wanted to locate the Edgar House so he could take a picture of it. Ari had some official business to take care of, and afterwards she was going out into the county to locate a farm that perhaps belonged to Bill Simkins.

"So after lunch, I'm going out in the county to look for my ancestor's farm. Want to go?"

"Sure, I'll go. I'm running out of things to do," he told her.

"Then afterwards we can try to find a restaurant. Are you game, or do you have your other business to attend to?"

"I'm free for dinner," he told her, "but I may be too excited to eat."

"This means a lot to you, doesn't it, Stoke?"

"I guess it really does, but I don't really know why it's become such a stupid passion. Except that maybe the dreams will stop when I find Henry."

When they had finished breakfast, Stoke gathered up his papers and books and put them in the car. Ari went her own way and Stoke went to the library. The workers were getting used to seeing him and were also getting interested in his project.

"Good morning, Mr. Towles," a librarian said. "What can we get for you today?"

Stoke told them about the tavern and gave them the address. She looked at him for a minute and said, "Uh, the street names were changed about a hundred years ago." Then she thought a minute and said, "But let's look at some old maps." She got down the oldest city map they had and looked all over it for a Main Street. They didn't find one. The date on the map was 1865. Somehow the city had been rebuilt or the streets renamed for Southern army heroes about the time of the War. There was no record of an Edgar either. The librarian suggested that he look at the 1850 census to see if a man named Edgar lived near any larger building, or between two other folks who were better known. He would have to make that determination by the way the residences were listed on the census page. That made sense to Stoke.

Stoke could see from the map that the city seemed to have started at the edge of the Missouri River, and then worked its way back in a narrow strip that was only a few streets wide. But there was no Main Street. Since Henry's street was in existence in 1856, Stoke figured it was close to the water, one of the larger, early streets. But he didn't know whether it ran northeast and southwest with the Missouri River or perpendicular to it. He decided to drive around near the river area and look for two-story buildings that were about 150 years old (or at least, not obviously new).

So Stoke spent the morning just looking. For all he knew, the tavern could have been torn down many years ago, but he was just killing time while Ari was finishing her business. *So much for a piece of cake*, he thought.

That afternoon, Ari drove and Stoke navigated. After a few minutes they found themselves on small roads that barely provided two lanes. On old maps these were called turnpikes and there were occasional tollgates on them. But by this time, the tollgates were gone and the roads were paved. The roads weren't much wider, however.

After about an hour of driving up this road and down that road, Stoke asked Ari to slow down.

"Are we at old Bill's place?" Ari asked.

"There's good news and bad news. Which do you want first? I say that because you're going to get both."

"I want both," she said agreeably.

"The good news is that we're closer than we were. In fact, we're almost there. The bad news is we're being followed."

"How do you know that?" Ari asked anxiously.

"That we're close or that we're being followed?"

"That we're being followed," she said.

"Easy. We've been lost for fifteen minutes, doing all sorts of crazy things and there's been a dark green car behind us all the way. What do you think the chances are of two cars making the same back and forth motions on this godforsaken strip of asphalt in the middle of Missouri at this time of the afternoon?"

"Pretty slim. Does it look like the car at the intersection where the shot was fired?" she asked.

"It's a close match for that car," Stoke said.

Ari reached into her purse and pulled out a small telephone.

"Let's see if we can reach anybody from out here, Stoke. Would you dial the operator and see if we can get through to the sheriff."

Stoke looked at the number pad on the phone. He saw the inscription "Property of the U.S. Government" and then an ID number. He tried several times to connect with a local cell, but had no luck. The phone might as well have been dead.

Ari drove on down the road, looking for a farmhouse. She saw a small place a hundred yards ahead that appeared to have telephone lines leading up to it. She pulled into a dirt drive, got her purse and walked rapidly to the front door. She rapped loudly on the door but no one was home. She tried the knob. It turned. She walked in, with Stoke close behind her. She called out "Hello!" but there was no answer. Then she looked around the small two-room shack for a telephone. There was no phone.

They heard a car stop outside. It blocked theirs. Stoke looked out the window and saw three men advancing toward the house. Quickly, Ari took the telephone from Stoke's hand and went out on the porch in full view of the men. She made a big show of pulling out the antenna and of talking to someone.

She yelled loudly to empty house, "Where are we?" Then she talked more into the phone. She looked at the dark green car as if she were reading the license plate and continued talking, looking as if she were explaining something to an interested person on the other end of the call. Stoke knew she couldn't see the plates because she didn't have her glasses on.

The men saw what she was doing, stopped their advance to the house and went back to their car. Ari finished her imaginary call, confidently slid the antenna in, and sat down on the porch swing expectantly. The men drove off.

"Damn, you've got guts!" Stoke exclaimed as the men drove away. "I would have... well, I don't know what I would have done if you hadn't pulled that telephone routine on them."

"For starters, you could have whipped the .38 revolver out of my purse and pointed it at them."

"I didn't know you had a .38 in your purse," Stoke said incredulously. "From the looks of your purse, I thought it might be .44!"

"Believe me, I would have told you if my boss said I could," Ari replied earnestly.

"Well, well. Who were those guys, anyway?"

"I suspect they think I know something about them that's unpleasant," Ari said.

"Do you know anything about them that might be unpleasant?"

"I might, depending on their identities," Ari told him. "But I'm not sure who they work for."

"Maybe you're going to get shot just like my ancestor," Stoke said.

"Or hanged, just like mine. Frankly, I prefer a bullet to a rope, if it's well-placed."

"Can we get out of here before they realize those portable phones don't work this far out in the country?"

"You bet. I guess ole Bill will have to wait," Ari said as she started out the door to her car. They drove rapidly in the opposite direction from where the three men went, but that was no guarantee they wouldn't meet at a crossroad soon. Stoke kept a close watch. Every few miles he tried out the phone to see if he could make contact with the operator.

They were getting close to Levanger before the phone worked again. The other car was nowhere in sight. And it was getting too late to make any more trips.

"What do you think, Stoke, should I call the sheriff?"

"In your official position as an employee of the U.S. Government, do you think it would do any good?"

"Not a bit."

"Well, then, I vote for ignoring the matter and hoping they won't return. How do you vote?" Stoke asked.

"I'm for doing nothing at the moment. At least until I check out their license number."

"It looked kind of muddy to me. I couldn't make it out."

"I had the same problem," she said. "But when they drove away from us, I could see the back plate quite clearly."

"You don't miss much, do you? And you weren't wearing your glasses."

"I don't miss much with contact lenses. I'll let you know what we find out."

"Yes, I'd like to know what's going on. And if I ever come back here, I want to come back armed."

"Do you carry a gun?" she asked.

"No, I bring two associates who watch my back for me. They're my armor. Sometimes in my work I get into rough areas with rough people."

"Let's hope those folks won't be necessary."

"Do you think they'll just go away, Ari?"

"Not bloody likely. Had you thought that they could be connected with some kind of gang?"

"That crossed my mind. One of the people who lives here said the Klan is still active in this part of the world, and they are in the fancy hemp business."

Silence overtook them on the way back to their motel. Stoke looked up from the road to check Ari's profile from time to time. He was beginning to have a hard time keeping his mind on his business when she was so close to him. He also considered the pistol in her purse. He decided that if she were really a manager in the Department of

Transportation, he was the brother of the mother of a chimpanzee—an ordinary "monkey's uncle."

By the time Stoke and Ari got back to their motel, they had agreed to meet later that evening. Ari said she had "some business to conduct." Stoke thought that she probably had to talk to her office and develop a new strategy, since the old one was drawing too much attention. Ari seemed cool and unworried, but the appearance of the men in the dark green car was clearly unexpected. Stoke was worried for her, and himself, as well.

He went to his room with a copy of the current Kansas City paper. He could have looked at the news on his computer through the Internet, but the stories were too brief to meet Stoke's needs. Stretched out on the bed he tried to get caught up on local, national and international news. But he was restless and couldn't concentrate. He called Frank Kendall in Newport to see if there were any more developments in his proposed merger. Next, he tried to call Elizabeth and Marilee to see if they missed him, but all he got was their answering machine. The machine hadn't missed him at all, but he left a message anyway.

It was getting close to seven, so Stoke showered and shaved and put on some fresher clothes. The high humidity in Levanger had a way of taking creases out of everything but foreheads.

Because of national advertising, people in Levanger wore just about the same clothes as people in Los Angeles, except for the fabrics. In Levanger, the fabrics tended to be cotton to absorb moisture. Of course, some of the far-out people in Los Angeles tended to dress more extremely than those in Levanger. And there were more people at the extremes, so the general population seemed to think Los Angeles was vastly different from other places, but it really was just a bit more urban and less rural.

Dressed in slacks and a crisp short-sleeved sport shirt that quietly said "expensive and tasteful," Stoke went down to the lobby to meet Ari. She showed up a few minutes later, in the same clothes as before, looking somewhat frazzled and concerned.

"Bad news?" he asked.

"I have a telephone conference in two hours," Ari said with a note of exasperation in her voice.

"We'll have time to eat and get back, I suppose, depending where we go. Do you like Italian food?"

"Yes, I like most food too well. And if I keep eating so much of it, I'm going to need new suits and dresses."

"You seem to be doing quite well at the moment," observed Stoke as he admired her trim figure.

"At home I run a lot," she responded. "But here I don't have the time and I don't know where to run."

"I don't run anymore since I broke my leg. Maybe I'll be able to do it again some day. In the meantime, I fully expect to develop two chins, a pot belly and varicose veins."

"What about going bald?" Ari asked.

"Yeah, that, too."

"I don't think I'd like you that way, Stoke. Or has it already happened? Tell me, is the mustache a fake, too?"

"I'll have you know the hair is mine. The mustache is, too."

"Are you sure?" Ari said as she reached up and gently touched his mustache. She brushed against his lips with her fingers. Self-consciously, she drew her hand away, blushing.

Then she said rather quickly, "Since I have to get back, maybe we should go ahead and eat."

It was a small Italian restaurant, dark and cozy and cool. It sported the ubiquitous red checked tablecloth on each table, and a Chianti bottle with a candle stuck in it. There was a shaker bottle for red pepper and one for grated cheese, along with salt and regular pepper. The difference between this place and a thousand others across the country was that the food was quite good.

They compared genealogical notes as they ate. Ari seemed somewhat lost in thought. Then, as spumoni was put in front of them, Stoke broke a silence of several minutes.

"Can you tell me what's going on? In recent memory I can't recall a manager in the Department of Transportation needing to pack a pistol."

"Stoke, I'm not really in the Department of Transportation."

"Somehow, I'm not surprised."

"I didn't want to tell you this, but I suppose I owe you some explanation. I'm with the Drug Enforcement Agency. You know, the DEA.

Normally, I don't carry a weapon, but I'm on a special investigation and my boss thought it might be needed."

"How many drugs do they have in Levanger, Missouri, Ari? Hell, we had a hard time locating a copy machine. Do you think there are many drug users around?"

"Do you remember reading in the book about Owen County where it talked about the Civil War?" she asked.

"Sure. It said the area was full of Southern sympathizers and that troops trained in one of my ancestor's barns. There was a skirmish fought in Owenton in 1862."

"That's right. Do you know what both sides of the War needed to keep their armies going, beside food and ammunition?"

Stoke replied, "Wagons and horses and weapons. What do they have to do with your investigation? Do you check out Gatling gun smugglers these days?"

"No, but there was one more thing the troops needed that you haven't mentioned."

"Do you mean they were full of dope when they fought each other?"

"No, I don't," Ari said, somewhat exasperated.

Stoke thought and then said, "I give up. What was it?"

"Rope. You can't run a decent war without rope. Even in World War II, the armies used lots and lots of rope and that was almost one hundred years after the Civil War."

"Right," Stoke said. "People still use rope. Are you rounding up hardware store retailers and rodeo fans who are casual users of rope on weekends?"

"Something like that."

"Why?"

"There are all kinds of rope today. But one hundred and forty years ago people mostly used one kind," Ari said.

"Oh, you're talking about hemp, aren't you?"

"Yes, we're essentially talking about the weed called hemp from which ropes were made during the Civil War. It grows wild all over this part of Missouri and central Kentucky. Both armies planted it everywhere so they could harvest the hemp for ropes to move wagons and equipment."

"Did they know it was also marijuana?" Stoke asked.

"Oh, sure. At least some knew. But not all hemp is good smoking dope. It's what people know today that interests the DEA. Missouri is still heavily forested in places. Throughout the forests there are tons and tons of marijuana growing. It's been growing wild for at least a century. Some people have upgraded the plants, too."

"Well, if you're successful at stamping out that weed, perhaps you should start on dandelions next," he remarked.

"We're not so short-sighted that we think we can stop marijuana from growing in Missouri," she said. "But we believe we can discourage wholesalers from doing big business. We don't really care if a farmer smokes a joint from time to time."

"My dad used to say, 'Give a man enough rope and he will make a cigar for himself.' Dad was really naive." Then Stoke got curious. "How are they doing it?"

"Who?"

"The wholesalers. How are they moving the stuff?"

Ari leaned over and said quietly "When we think of drug transportation, we usually think of speedboats, fast cars and airplanes, but these people have a different twist. The Missouri River connects to the Mississippi, as you know. And barges come right into Crittenden County on the Missouri. The barges have access to all the cities on the Ohio and Mississippi Rivers and plenty on the Missouri River, too."

"Why didn't I think of that?" Stoke asked.

"You might if you needed to move a lot of illegal goods. During Prohibition whiskey traveled the same route. There were plenty of stills in Missouri. They had hills to hide in, limestone water, corn, sugar, wood to burn, and everything else they needed to make fairly good whiskey. They also had a good transportation system."

"So people are harvesting marijuana in large quantities and shipping it over water to other cities?" Stoke asked.

"Yes, it's big business in Missouri. Who'd ever think of checking river barges for drugs? You can hide a lot of pot in a small space and the owners of the barge lines don't even have to know about it."

Without thinking, Stoke reached over and picked up Ari's hand. It was small in his big grasp. She didn't pull away. He gripped her hand tighter and said, "Are you in danger?"

"Sometimes, but I'm trained to deal with it." Slowly she withdrew her hand.

"My concern, Stoke, is that *you* don't get hurt. You're just a bystander in all this, providing me with cover."

"Is that all I am?"

"No, and that makes me even more concerned."

"I hope so. Ari, what is your cover?"

"I've been telling people I'm a graduate student and that I'm doing research for a dissertation on the uses of vegetation during the Civil War. If I manage to get some family history done for my book, and I get it done at the government's expense, that's even better. People assume you're just a fellow researcher."

"Is that what those three men thought in that dark green car?"

"Possibly. They may have figured that they could scare me off. I suspect someone has told them I might accidentally stumble onto something and wreck their business."

"Okay, Jane Bond. Who are they?"

"There's one more thing about the operation we haven't discussed. People who ship marijuana out expect to get something in return. We don't know if it's money, coke, or what. If we knew more about this 'other side of the equation,' we could maybe figure out who some of the players are, and who is watching. Do you remember those four men in the Mexican restaurant? The ones who gave us a light for our candle?"

"Yes, vaguely. Are they part of the pot plot?"

"I've seen one of them before. I think he was with a dealer from New York. It was just coincidence that we sat next to him at the restaurant. And if he's the one I've heard about, he's very mysterious. Our group calls him 'The Gay Ghost.'"

"I wonder if he knows my grandmother. Well anyway, do you think he's a danger to us?"

"Watch that 'us' stuff, Stoke. And please, don't get protective. This is official business and people can get hurt. It's *my* battle. There is no need for you to get involved."

"Except that *you* are involved, and we are sort of 'partners' on an investigation of our own, and I have already agreed to be part of your cover."

Then Stoke added, "Uh, by the way, what you said about having no husband or 'significant other,' is it still true?"

"That part is true. I really don't have time for attachments."

"Good. Did you really lose a fiancée to a bullet from the FBI?"

"No. A drug dealer killed him. I just made up the story about the FBI."

"What happens now?" Stoke asked.

"I go back to my room and have a telephone meeting. I'll see you in the morning, I guess. If you want, we can continue our research together."

"I want."

Ari paid the check this time. Stoke figured she was on an expense account and he would he would end up paying the bill through his taxes. They went to the car and drove back to the motel without talking. Stoke tried to watch some TV. That didn't work. He got out his research notes and sorted through them several times. He called his secretary in California at her office. She went through his office mail for him and said there was a note from the National Archives saying they had nothing on Henry Vallandingham. They supplied a form for him to fill out so he could try again with more precise information.

After reading and digesting his latest notes, he began doing push-ups, the first he had tried since he broke his legs. Finally, he took a cold shower and went to bed.

Chapter Eight

NEGRO WOMAN FOR SALE

A very likely Negro Woman, 26 years old, who is a
good cook, washer, and house servant, is offered for
sale. Inquire at this office for particulars...

Just before dawn Stoke lay in his bed in a dreamy state. He saw his grandmother again and a small boy talking to her. They were in a large old-fashioned room. Stoke recognized a painting on the wall. It was now on his wall in Newport Beach. The room was dark, with just a little light illuminating the faces of the two people. It was sunlight, peering from behind heavy drapes. A ray touched the floor by their feet. The scene appeared to have been painted on black velvet.

"Grandma, did you see that man get shot?"

"No, I wasn't around then." As the boy talked with the frail old lady, she picked up a piece of paper and an old pen. She dipped the pen into ink and began to write. "Even my mother was just a small child, much smaller than you are."

"Don't you have any idea who shot him?"

"I do now. I see many things. But when I was younger I didn't know."

"Why did they want to kill someone?"

"They needed to let folks know not to mess with them. Remember that he was killed at noon on a busy street, so everybody could see." The old woman continued to write. Her pen made scratchy noises. As she turned, her sleeve caught the paper on which she was writing. It fell on the floor. It was upside down, but Stoke thought he saw a list of about six names, the first two of which were Woodson and Limrick.

The dream faded. Stoke gradually became aware of the sunlight in his room. He thought about the vivid dream as he shaved and dressed. He had felt warm and comfortable during the dream. He didn't want it to fade. He sensed a loss as it disappeared, wherever dreams go after they have been used once. He took a pencil, and even though feeling foolish, he wrote down everything he could remember, including the room details and the dark dress of his grandmother. He was beginning to accept the dreams as part of his research.

He went downstairs to have breakfast, hoping to see Ari, but she wasn't there. He had a cup of coffee while he looked at a local newspaper the motel supplied. Then he took his plate to the buffet counter and helped himself to eggs and strips of crisp bacon and hot sweet rolls. He sat down and slowly ate his breakfast, stalling for time so he could have something on his plate when Ari came in. He was beginning to get used to having this pretty girl across the breakfast table.

Ari did not show up, so Stoke went by the front desk on his way back to his room. He asked if she had gone out.

"Yes sir," the desk clerk replied. "Ms Edwards went out about 7:30 this morning with two men."

Stoke was puzzled about Ari's departure but knew she had business to attend to. It might include meetings with her Agency. So he went back to his room to get ready for another backbreaking day in front of the microfilm readers. He wasn't too worried about Ari, he decided. She was cool and somewhat prepared for danger. He wouldn't want to try to outsmart her himself, he thought.

After an hour at the library, Stoke noticed that some materials were missing. That is, some dated items were not in the series he was reviewing. Later he found that this was a problem of most genealogy researchers. He also noticed he was having a hard time concentrating on his work. He kept thinking about the men Ari had gone out with that morning. He was hoping they were Agency people and not the men who had been following them.

He got up every twenty or thirty minutes and paced back and forth, partly to ease the cramps in his back, and partly because he wanted to take some action about Ari. Pacing wouldn't do much for her, he knew, but it somehow eased the tension that was building up inside.

Stoke left the library and went out to lunch. On his way to a sandwich shop he went by the motel to see if Ari had returned. No one had seen her. He ate alone, alternately chewing on his food, the killing he'd read about and the disappearance of Ari. When he was through with the food, he went back to the library, so lost in thought he almost drove through a stop sign and two stoplights. He didn't make any friends on the road that day.

It took another two hours of searching before Stoke found yet another killing. This time, John Brown had attacked slave owners. It was the story he had heard about earlier.

Eight Men Brutally Murdered by the Abolitionists

The following letter was received by a messenger from Franklin Co., K.T., this morning that was written by the Commissioner of Franklin County. Eight men were known to be killed –three by the name of Doyle, three by the name of Sherman, a Mr. Whiteman and a Mr. Wilkerson. The messenger who brought the information to Franklin states that he had seen the party who were murdered—they were cut to pieces and horribly mangled. For every southern man thus butchered, a decade of these poltroons should bite the dust.

The gentlemen in the vicinity of these outrages were of the opinion that Governor Shannon was at the Shawnee Mission, and the letter containing the intelligence was sent by the sons of Mr. Wm. Muir of this county. They arrived at the residence of their father early this morning. The letter has been forwarded to Governor Shannon.

American Citizen
May 28, 1856
Levanger, Missouri

Stoke wondered if there were some connection between the murders of the John Brown victims and Henry Vallandingham. He did not *know* what it was, but a theory was beginning to form in the back of his mind. He noticed that the men were sliced and diced a few weeks before Henry wrote his letter.

Worn out, Stoke threw in the "researcher's towel" and decided to get back to his motel. He collected his notes and other materials and loaded them in the car. Driving back, he was much more careful of other drivers this time. As he started to ask the desk clerk about Ari, he was told there was a message for him. It read, "Stoke, save a place at dinner for me tonight." It was signed AE

Relieved that Ari was not in danger, Stoke went on to his room to shower and change his shirt. At six she called his room.

"Hey, sailor, will you buy a girl a mint julep?" Ari said when she heard Stoke's voice.

"I never touch the things," he said. "But I sure could go for a dish of grits and some fried chicken."

"You're the only man I know who insists on a good quality white wine with his grits! Don't you see a contradiction in those taste buds of yours?"

"Speaking of contradictions, what's a nice girl like you doing with a sailor like me?" Stoke replied.

"Research, or so I'm told," she said.

"I surrender. If we keep this up, I'll never get any dinner. And I'm hungry. I believe it's your choice tonight, so where do you want to go for your mint julep and pizza?"

"I'll meet you downstairs and we can talk about it. Can you be down in fifteen minutes?"

Ari met Stoke in the lobby. He admired her promptness. He also admired her short shorts, which gave him a clue that they were not destined for a swanky restaurant. She had great legs and for a minute he forgot about dinner. But only for a minute.

"I have an idea," she said. "Let's get some food at the local grocery store and take a picnic dinner out to the edge of town."

"Deal," Stoke replied.

Stoke and Ari took her car to a big grocery where they loaded potato salad, bread, mustard, sliced ham, fruit, cheese and a bottle of wine into their cart. They purchased paper plates and a paper tablecloth and plastic forks, knives and cups.

Having driven a few miles out of town to a smooth pasture, they pulled off the road. They went over to a clearing where Ari spread out a cloth and began to put food out in its middle. Suddenly, she stopped.

"Stoke, we're in trouble!"

"Are those guys back again?" Stoke asked seriously as he turned around fast, looking from tree to tree at the edge of the pasture.

"It's worse than that," Ari told him.

"Where's your purse?" he asked, thinking of the last time they had met up with the 'bad guys.'

"It won't do any good." Ari said. "What I need isn't in it."

"What do you need?"

"We forgot to buy a bottle opener at the grocery."

"That *is* serious," Stoke said with a lot of concern in his voice. "We may have to bust the neck off the bottle and take our chances with broken bits of glass. Of course, there may be another way."

"What's the other way?" she asked.

"You got your purse, I got my pocket." Stoke reached in his pocket and pulled out a Swiss Army Knife. "This little dude has saved me on many occasions."

"Do you go on many picnics?"

"No, this is the first in a long time. But once, when I was in India at a wine tasting party for Hindu nobles, I was the only person there with a bottle opener. We were able to have the party with my help. I was carried out of the tasting room on the shoulders of ten beautiful and grateful young women whose brothers were able to judge the finest wines in all Madras."

"You've never been in Madras, let alone India."

"Oh, would you believe a baseball game in Indianapolis on a hot day with no way to open beer bottles?"

She giggled. "I might, except that beer bottles have twist-off caps these days."

"Well, perhaps I may have enlarged on the truth a bit, but you will admit, won't you, that I've saved the day?"

"Yes, you did. But you were acting in your own self-interest."

Ari was getting the food ready as she talked and Stoke was wrestling with the bottle of wine in an attempt to get the cork out. He was getting red in the face, as the cork broke off and some remained in the bottle.

"Are we having trouble with the wine?" Ari asked with a grin.

"Yes, we are. The cork broke off. But if I get a stick, I can push the remainder of the cork down into the bottle, and we can kind of pour the wine around it."

Stoke searched around for a stick and selected a small branch from a tree. He stripped the bark and was successful with the cork. Then he poured the wine into two plastic cups.

"Come and get it," Ari said as she handed a plate to Stoke.

Stoke raised his cup. "Here's to the guy who invented short shorts."

"I'm glad that you approve. Is it the fabric you especially like?"

"The fabric is nice, but I am beginning to fancy the contents somewhat. And the perspective is great."

"Would you take that silly looking stick out of the wine and get serious for a minute?" Ari asked.

"What makes you think I'm not serious?"

"As far as I know, you're still on your wine tasting trip in India."

"Hey, I'm celebrating. It's a nice day. The temperature has dropped a few degrees, we have lots of fine food, and the company is pleasant. The trouble I expected has gone away."

"What trouble?"

"I was afraid something had happened to you this morning and I would have to do my research alone."

"Stoke, my boss came for me. That happens. There wasn't any trouble."

"Well, if we hadn't been followed by some tough-looking farmers, I would never have thought anything about it."

"I can take care of myself. I had to see my boss about taking care of you!"

"Ari, that *is* embarrassing! I can take care of *myself*. If there is trouble, I can bring in my friends from Los Angeles."

"You mean muscle work. I can imagine the people you would get."

"Hispanic musclemen can be very charming, young lady."

"I'm a cop, dammit! It doesn't pay to talk down to officers, you know!"

"All I know is that you make a great ham sandwich, officer. And I'm sorry I was worried about you. But I was."

Stoke looked at her as he spoke and saw a smile there. There was a silence. Ari picked up a cracker and offered it to him without saying anything. She didn't put it in his hand. She offered it to his mouth. Stoke took the cracker. As he ate, he reached for her hand and held it gently but firmly. Then he pulled her to him and kissed her on the mouth.

She pulled away for a minute, breathed deeply a couple of times, put her arms around Stoke's neck and kissed him back. They slowly leaned for the tablecloth and a more comfortable, horizontal position. Life was beginning to be quite pleasant for them until the intruder made herself known.

Ari discovered her first. She heard a heavy step, then looked up into the massive face of a large brown cow, and screamed. Not understanding the problem, Stoke rolled over and covered Ari with his body. Then he looked up and saw a pair of cow's feet. He pushed himself up into a sitting position and reached out to the muzzle of the cow.

"I guess this is about all the animal comfort I'm going to get this night," he said as he rubbed the snout of the friendly bovine, somewhat relieved. Ari was cowering behind him, looking for a way to run to the relative safety of the car.

"Watch where you step, if you make a dash for the car," he suggested as she ran. Then she slowed and stopped completely.

Ari returned, somewhat ashamed by her rapid departure. Stoke continued to pet the cow. He offered the huge animal some leftover salad that made him a friend for life. Ari edged closer. She asked if they might begin picking up the garbage from the "feast" and Stoke agreed that it was time. He wanted to stay and protect her some more, but didn't know how to get Ari to lie down again.

Slowly, and under the watchful, maternal eye of the cow, they picked up every last bit of their belongings. When they finished, they started for the car, thinking they were alone, except for Elsie, of course.

Back at their car, Ari and Stoke found a familiar green car blocking them. A harsh voice asked them, "Did you-all have a nice picnic?"

Stoke looked in the direction of the voice. He saw only trees. "The cattle enjoyed it more than we did. Are we on your land?"

Stepping from behind a tree, a man said, "This ain't my land. But this is my gun." He held out a large revolver and pointed it at them. A second man stepped out from behind a neighboring tree.

The two strangers were white, middle-aged, sturdy individuals wearing nondescript shirts and blue jeans. One was about six feet tall. The other was of average height. Something about them said "local talent" rather than "big city." As Stoke studied them, he realized he had seen them in Levanger and in the car that approached them when Ari used the telephone scam.

"What do you want?" Stoke said as he tried to get in front of Ari. He thought she might be able to get her gun out of her purse. But the men didn't like what he was doing.

"Stay where we can see you both," the tall man commanded. Stoke stood still.

"Is this a robbery?" Ari asked the men.

"For the moment," the man said, and added, "so gimme your purse." He handed the gun to his partner.

Ari handed him her purse.

"Don't want no more telephone calls," he said as he took her phone out of a side pocket. "What the hell you got in this thing, cannon balls?" he growled as he felt how heavy it still was. He opened the purse and brought out the .38 special revolver with the short barrel.

"Well, what do we have here?" He examined the gun and stuck it in his pocket.

"Now we got two good reasons for you-all to do exactly as we say." He rooted through the purse and found Ari's wallet, handkerchief, lipstick and more personal items. He dropped them on the ground, one at a time, except for the wallet. Ari's face grew very red.

"Well, well...this says you are Ari-something Edwards from Washington, DC. Are you really a student?"

"There's a college ID card in there if you can find it. I'm really a student."

The man looked further and found the card. "Why does a student need a gun? It looks like you'd rather have a pen or a book."

Stoke said, "The gun is mine. She was holding it for me."

Ari chimed in, "Yes, and you'll find a pen there, too."

The man looked at Stoke. "You-all let me have your wallet," he said menacingly. Stoke signed and handed it over.

The man went through it slowly and found a driver's license. "And you are Stokely S. Towles from California?"

"That's right. But who the hell are you to be asking these questions?"

"I'm the man with the gun. So don't get so damn smart!"

Stoke and Ari said nothing. The man thought a bit and asked, "What do you-all do for a livin', Towles?"

"I'm a business consultant in California."

"That so? So what are you-all doing in Crittenden County, Missouri?"

"Some of my ancestors lived here in 1856. I'm just doing some family research while I'm on vacation. Ms Edwards and I have some common interests, so we decided to meet here and do some research together."

"Research, my ass!" the man said. "I'm sure yore wife don't know about this Jew wom-man."

"You can research your own ass. I'm not married," Stoke told him.

"I'd rather research hers. But I don't have time. Now, Bert," he said to the other man, "get in our car and follow."

Then he looked at Stoke, "You two get into your own car and drive where I tell you. I'm going to be sittin' in the back seat, so do exactly what I say."

Ari said, "I need my purse."

"Oh, shit! Pick up your junk and do it quick."

Ari picked up the things thrown on the ground and stuffed them into her purse.

"I'll need my wallet," Stoke said with a straight face, "if I'm going to drive."

"We'll see about that later," the man responded.

Stoke got behind the wheel. Ari got in the passenger's side. The stranger got in behind them.

He said, "Drive!"

Stoke pulled onto the road and drove down a twisty, narrow lane. After about two miles, the man told him to slow down. Then he told Stoke to follow a winding dirt road that was barely wide enough for one car. When they came to a creek that ran across the road, Stoke slowed.

"Drive on through the crick," the man commanded. There were no houses anywhere in sight. Stoke drove slowly through the water and up the other side of the gully. The road led to an old house. It was a dilapidated farmhouse with the usual small outhouse in back. At one time both had been painted a white color, but now they were a uniform gray except where the paint hadn't peeled off. Siding was loose in spots and a TV antenna lazed at a crazy angle on the roof.

The man told them to get out of the car and walk with him to the old house. The second car drove in behind them.

Inside they found a "country slum" condition that self-respecting pigs would have forsaken. Even if they hadn't seen any slop on the floor, the air would have told them it was going to be an unpleasant stay.

"Don't you have something with a view?" Stoke asked with a grin.

"You-all have a roof over your heads, so consider yerselfs lucky," said the man. Bert watched over them with Ari's gun while the other man went out to his car for some rope. He came in and tied Stoke's hands behind his back, then Ari's. He pushed them to the floor and then tied Stoke's feet together. Then he tied Ari's feet.

"I sure would like some time alone with you, lady," he told her as he worked.

Stoke glared at him. There was nothing else he could do. When the man was finished, he admired his handiwork, tested the knots and then both men went outside. They shut and locked the front door from the outside. The door had a rather solid, dense sound, closing with a thud.

Silence hung around them like a soggy blanket. Stoke and Ari were almost completely submerged in darkness. After two minutes, they heard one of the cars drive away. They were silent for a while. Then when they didn't hear any more activity, Stoke turned to Ari and said in his best W.C. Field imitation, "Now, my little dove, I have you just the way I want you."

"Dammit, Stoke, stop making jokes. I feel horrible because I got you into this mess. And I don't know how I'm going to face my boss!"

"Hey, with any luck at all, you won't get out of here. Then you won't have to face him."

"Cut it out, Stoke. My people will find us eventually."

Stoke said, "So the cool Ms Edwards can't handle a simple problem like the old hands tied behind the back routine?"

"You know damn well I can't. Can you?"

"In times of trial you really get to know someone, don't you?"

"Stoke, that is not my problem at the moment. I'm a Federal Agent who got caught with her guard down. This is very embarrassing."

Stoke said, "You would have been caught with your pants down if that man had more time, don't you think?"

"No, I don't. He was definitely more interested in you than he was me. Better worry about your own pants. Now how in the world are we going to get out of this mess?"

What little light they had was gone. Stoke could hear Ari, but he could no longer see her.

"Believe it or not, Ari, there is a way I can get our feet untied."

"Well, do it!"

"First, I have to get my hands in front of me. When people tie your hands behind your back, they sometimes forget that you can get your butt and legs through the loop made by your arms. Try it."

Stoke lay on his side in the dark while he worked his hands around his legs. He grunted and talked to himself for a few minutes and said, "There! I've done it. What about you, Ari?"

"I need to lose a few pounds first."

"All right. Work your way over to me and I'll see if I can free your bonds."

"Free my bonds? Who are you, Abraham Lincoln?"

"Betty Friedan in deep disguise. I hope you're going to be very grateful when I get us out of this mess."

"Hah! You get me out of this mess or I'll arrest you for being in cahoots with those two men! That's what I'll do."

"How about a nice steak dinner tonight?"

"Well… maybe I can let you off with a warning this time."

Ari had worked herself over to Stoke and he was fumbling with the knots on her hands, while both of his were still tied. After a few more minutes and some continuing light banter, Ari's hands came free. Quickly she reached down and untied her feet.

"Okay, Stoke. I got loose. Move over here so I can untie your hands." Ari worked on his knots without much success. Then Stoke had an idea.

"I'll roll over. Reach into my pants pocket for my knife. I think it's still there." After some embarrassing groping, Ari found the knife, opened it and hacked on Stoke's ropes for a minute. At last, his hands were free. Then he took the knife from her and cut the ropes from his feet. Stoke got up and stood, waiting for the numbness to leave from where the tight ropes had cut off his circulation.

"How are we going to get out of this place?"

Ari remembered the locked door. Then she said, "Uh, Stoke, do you feel well enough to knock the door down?"

"I would if you were on one side and I were on the other. But since we're both on the same side, I'm not motivated enough. Maybe we should find another way. It seemed very solid."

Ari said, "You think we can find an easier way out? How're you going to manage that?"

"Do you remember the condition of the walls in here? I think the plasterboard is missing in a few spots. I might be able to kick out the siding from inside, and maybe you could slip through the studs and open the front door from the outside."

Stoke crawled to a wall and felt for a damaged place in the wallboard. After several minutes of fumbling in the dark, he found a big hole.

"Now let's see how sound the siding is." Lying on his back, he put his feet against the inside of the siding. He pushed. The boards gave some, but so did his sore leg. Then he drew his legs back and let go with a strong smashing blow that drove him back a foot, but also freed the siding from the studs.

Ari located him in the dark from the sound of his grunting and kicking. She crawled over to where Stoke was working and peered in the dark at the noise, hoping to see something. Suddenly they could see a low moon on the horizon through the smashed boards. Stoke pulled himself closer and raised his legs. He smashed out against the next higher boards until there was a hole between the studs large enough for Ari to squeeze through.

She slipped out into the night. She stopped and waited, looking for their captors. Finding no one, she walked to the front door. Releasing the lever on the lock that held them captive, she opened the door and said, "Is anybody home?"

Laughing, Stoke went out with Ari to the fresh air. He sat down on the front stoop and began rubbing his legs.

"When you get your legs straightened out, I need you for something."

"What is it?" Stoke asked.

"I believe I'm going to make a stop in that old outhouse, but I want you to check it first for snakes and spiders," she said. Quickly, he went to their car and located a small flashlight. Then he picked up a tree branch with leaves on it to use as a broom. After a thorough cleaning, he gave the "all clear" sign. Ari had her purse in hand as she took the light and went inside.

The first thing Ari saw as she left the outhouse was a bright automobile headlight. She ducked down, thinking their captors had returned. When her eyes became accustomed to the brightness, Ari saw only one car. Not entirely sure what had who was in the car, she waited until she saw Stoke in the glare, unconcernedly rolling down the window on the driver's side. He had turned on the car lights for her.

Ari called out, "Thanks for the light. Can you hot wire the car?"

She climbed in as Stoke turned the key on and started the engine.

"Where did you get a key?"

"Did you ever know the Boy Scout motto?" he asked.

"It's something about readiness," Ari responded.

"It's 'Be Prepared,'" Stoke said in his deepest radio announcer voice. "Before I was a Navy pilot, I was a Boy Scout. I always have an extra key. A Boy Scout never knows when some female is going to tell him to put out or get out, so he needs an extra key."

"Another one of your screwy stories!" sniffed Ari.

Then she added, "Well, how prepared are you if they come back? We'd better get out of here."

"Do you remember how we got here?" Stoke asked.

"No, I don't exactly. But we have the maps, don't we, the ones for our family history search?"

"I'm not sure if we have one for this part of the county. Anyway, a map might not be much help if we don't know where we are."

"Well, we need to get away." she said. "And there's only one road leading to this place, so let's follow it and look out for cars approaching us."

Stoke thought that was a good idea, so he headed out the way they came in. They again found the creek that crossed the road. He took some comfort in finding a familiar sight. But everything else looked different at night. After a few miles of driving at fifteen miles per hour, they came to a crossroad that was paved.

Stoke asked "Left or right? Your call."

Ari looked at the moon and said, "Does the moon still rise in the east?"

"Yes, you romantic fool, you."

"Well, I think the sun was at our backs for most of our trip this afternoon, so why not go west on our return trip?"

"All right, but there's a problem. See those headlights coming our way? Why not pull off the road and hide for a while?"

"Let's do it. Do you think they might be coming back?"

"I don't want to take a chance. It might be the bad guys or a sheriff's car or just a citizen. But it's coming fast, so let's make our move." Quickly, Stoke drove across the road and pulled off in a wide unpaved spot behind some trees. He turned the lights and engine off. They waited while their eyes became used to the darkness.

Suddenly over the top of a hill headlights glared at them from an oncoming car. It was a dark color, possibly green. Two men were seated in the front.

"Did you see them, Ari?"

"It could have been those men. Let's get out of here!"

Stoke drove the car out of their hiding spot and took off quickly in the direction from which the men had come.

"They'll find out we're gone and will come looking for us," Ari said.

"We'll get away," Stoke replied, "if we don't run out of gas first."

"How much gas do we have?"

"Less than a quarter of a tank."

They drove on in the night without speaking, as fast as the winding road would allow. Large bugs zoomed out of nowhere into their headlights and smashed on their windshield. Small animals looked at them from the roadside with eyes that shone like intense flashlights. Trees flashed by, some quite close. Leaves would occasionally slap against the car's surface. The gas gauge dropped ominously low. It began to show a red glow at the bottom, indicating that the last few drops were being squeezed out of the tank.

Stoke said, "Let's look for a side road where we can hide the car. When it's daylight, maybe we can find our way better. We can't afford to run out of gas on a main road."

"So true," Ari said with some strain in her voice. "Slow down and let's start looking."

It didn't take long. A dirt road showed up on the right hand side. They turned and followed it to another side road, then pulled a few feet up in it and stopped. Stoke turned off the engine.

"Do you snore in your sleep?" he asked her.

"Certainly not. Do you have any objectionable habits?"

"Not objectionable to me," he told her.

"Fine. Now that that's settled, you can take the couch and I will take the bed."

"Actually, you might consider putting your seat back to its reclining position or you might try the back seat."

"For the moment," she told him, "I'll stay right here. And where is the mosquito netting?"

"There isn't any. But don't worry, the big ones won't be able to get through window openings of less than a half inch."

Ari and Stoke were quiet for a few minutes. Constant chirping from millions of cicadas in nearby trees provided a steady background buzz that was almost deafening. Ari yawned.

"Ari?"

"Yes?"

"Why didn't those men find your badge when they went through your purse?"

"I left it at the motel. I should have left my gun there, too, I guess. Then I would still have it."

After a minute of reflection, Stoke said, "Those guys may not give it back without some discussion. Besides, they're probably on their way to West Virginia or wherever they came from."

More silence.

"Stoke?"

"Yes?"

"Thanks for getting me out of that mess tonight."

"I owed you one, remember? By the way, how did that man know you were Jewish?"

"Does it matter?" she asked him.

"Not to me. I'm only asking how he knew," Stoke told her.

"I'm not Jewish, so he couldn't have known. But sometimes bigots like that make me wish I were."

"Ari, sometimes I think you have an attitude."

Chapter Nine

Stoke didn't want to go to sleep for fear that the two men might come looking for them. But the drone of the cicadas was too much, and before dawn he slipped into unconsciousness. When he opened his eyes, the sun was in his face, coating it with a warm glow. Ari was beginning to stir.

"Good morning, Stoke," Ari said as she stretched and then opened the car door to look outside. Trees surrounded them. Cardinals, robins, mockingbirds and sparrows were commenting on the new day with a great deal of enthusiasm and excitement. A meadowlark sounded off in a field beyond the trees.

"Hi, Ari. You know… I've been thinking. We're on a road and roads usually lead to houses. Why don't we take a hike down this one to see if someone lives near us?"

"That sounds like a good idea. Let's go together. I have no idea where those two thugs are. They might come looking for us."

They started out the dirt road into the trees when Stoke spotted some wires. "Look, Ari! Those wires probably go to someone's home."

They walked on past the trees. Sure enough, at the top of a low hill, surrounded by a meadow of bluish-green grass, stood a modest white wood frame house. There were four wires leading to it from the trees. "They might have a telephone," Stoke said to no one in particular. It's eight o'clock, so they've probably been up for several hours. Let's go sell them some encyclopedias and a Bible or two."

124

They walked up to the door and knocked. Nothing happened except that the skimpy curtains at a nearby window moved a bit. Then the door opened. A young, pleasant looking black woman stood in the entrance, flanked by a boy of about five and a girl about nine years old.

The woman looked relieved when she saw Ari. She said with a pleasant accent, "What do you want?"

Ari stepped up and said, "Our car had trouble down the road. Do you have a telephone?" The woman nodded, stepped back and brought out a cordless telephone. She handed it to Ari, then closed the screen door.

Stoke said, "Do you have a telephone book?"

The woman disappeared for a minute, and returned with a Levanger directory in her hand. Stoke took it from her and began to look up the local AAA number. He read it to Ari. She punched the number in.

Stoke asked the woman, "Where are we?"

"You are on Longview Road," she told him, "15411."

Stoke told Ari, "15411 Longview Road." Then he asked for a glass of water for each of them.

"No water. The pump doesn't work," said the woman.

"What's wrong with it?" Stoke asked.

"I have a new switch but no one to put it in," she replied.

Ari was busy on the phone, so Stoke said, "I can replace switches. Let me look at it."

The woman thought a minute and then said, "Sure. It's out back." She stepped out the front door and took Stoke around the side of the house. Her two kids followed closely, occasionally looking back at Stoke to see what he was doing.

"Here's the switch," the woman told him. Then she pointed to a wall box that had an old switch hanging out of it. Someone had tried to replace it and had given up part way through the task.

"I'll need to turn off the electricity for a minute and then I'll need a screw driver, too."

"We have one," she said and scurried off. This time the kids stayed. Stoke looked at the girl and said, "What's your name?"

"Nancy," the girl said. "What's yours?" She had a deep Southern drawl.

Stoke told her, "My name is Stoke." Then turning to the boy, he said, "What's your name?"

"Herbert," the little fellow said.

"Good. Nancy and Herbert—-do you want to help me with the switch?"

"I'll help," said the girl. "We haven't had a drink of water for two days. I had to put Pepsi on my plants this morning."

As Stoke was contemplating the thought of Pepsi-Cola on his orchids, the woman came back with several screwdrivers. They were in varying sizes and states of repair. Stoke picked out one that might last long enough to do the job. "Is the electricity off?" he asked the woman.

"It's off now," she told him. Then she stood in a position where she could watch without being hit by a shower of sparks. Stoke handed all the other screwdrivers to the two kids. Then he unscrewed the three screws and their wires that took power to the pump and installed the new switch. He stuffed it and the wires back into the wall box. Then he installed the switch cover that he found nearby.

"Now turn on the power and try the pump," he said.

The woman hurried inside and turned on the electricity. She came back to the switch and, with a hesitant motion, flicked the lever. She seemed reluctant to try it, perhaps due to unpleasant experiences in the past. There was a hum from a small house a few feet away. A big smile spread over her face.

"Thank you very much!" she said to Stoke. "You won't believe what we had to do without water for two days!"

"Oh, I have an idea," Stoke told her. "Now how about that glass of water?"

Ari came around the side of the house as the glass appeared.

"There's only one clean glass," the woman said.

"We share," Ari said, taking it from her hand before Stoke could grab it. She drank the water and handed it to him, empty.

"We've been stuck in our car all night," she told the woman. "Do you have a bathroom?"

As Stoke looked on with an empty glass in his hand, the two women disappeared in the house. Ari called over her shoulder, "My people can't come for about an hour, so we'll have to take it easy for a while." Stoke was still staring at the empty glass.

A few minutes later, the two women came out of the house, chatting as if they had been friends for years. Nancy got a glass of water for Stoke, who was sitting down on the steps of the back porch.

"Do you have anything else that doesn't work?" he asked the woman. "We seem to have another forty-five minutes to spend with you. I'd like to pay for your hospitality."

"You can't pay for that. It's free," she said. "But a wire on the TV set sparks, if you have nothing to do."

Stoke rose and followed her into the house. It was the house of a person who didn't have many worldly possessions. However, what the woman did have was clean and neat. The TV was in a corner. There were some inexpensive toys spread around it. On the TV were a Bible and a partially completed crossword puzzle. A picture of a black Jesus was hung on the wall.

He didn't see anything wrong with the TV. "Well, I guess we'll have to ask St. Sony of Hitachi to fix this one," he said as he looked over the set. The woman picked up the set's cord and showed him a mangled plug.

"If this is the only problem, you're lucky," he told her. "We'll just need a replacement for the plug from a hardware store."

"There's a store near us," the woman said with a concerned look on her face. She wanted to get the set fixed. She was pointing in a direction west of them.

Ari said, "Stoke, when you fill our tank, you can get a plug. The kids say the store is close to a gas station. We were almost in a village and didn't know it."

Stoke looked at her with a leer. "You mean I slept with you all night when I didn't need to? That's a hell of a note. I could have been at our motel watching a baseball game or something."

"Well, I didn't know either," Ari said, "so count yourself lucky. No one else gets to do that." Then she said with some anxiety, "They got your wallet, Stoke! How will you pay for gas?" Ari was already rummaging through her purse.

"I may seem indigent to you, young lady, but I am not without resources. Everyone needs mad money, you know." He produced some twenties from his hip pocket.

The woman and her two children didn't know what to think about this conversation. She looked worried until she saw the smiles on their faces. She shrugged as if to say, "Who can account for the habits of these crazy white folks?"

Nancy looked pleadingly at Stoke. "Can you-all fix the TV?"

"I think so, Nancy. When the man comes with some gas for our car, maybe you and I can go get a part. You'll have to show me where the store is."

"Cool!" she exclaimed. She jumped straight into the air and clapped her small hands. Then she looked around sheepishly. "I get 'happiness fits' once in a while," she explained.

In a few minutes a car pulled up. Ari went out to meet it while Stoke entertained the kids. Ari came back to tell Stoke that she had to leave to go to work. Her office had sent someone to pick her up. She said she would report the details of their adventure to the sheriff. Stoke nodded and told her he would call her in the evening.

The service truck showed up on schedule with five gallons of gas. Stoke filled out the forms and started his car before the driver left. He thought it might cause the mother some worry if he took only Nancy with him to show the way, so he asked all of them to join him in a trip to the store and the gas station.

On the way he asked if they needed to stop anywhere else. Nancy had something dark in her small hand. She said, "Mistuh Stoke, what's this?" He looked, and there was his wallet! The two men either forgot it or just tossed it in the car so they wouldn't have to explain where they got it, in case they got caught. Stoke felt deeply relieved.

The mother shyly asked if he could let her go to the grocery. He stopped and waited while she went in. He stood outside, watching the other customers. On a hunch he looked in the store window at them and saw that the mother was paying for her small purchases with food stamps.

They went on to the hardware store where Stoke bought a replacement plug. It was almost lunchtime, so he asked if he could get them something to eat. The kids were so excited that Stoke knew he had asked the right question.

"Where's the best place to eat?"

The mother looked down at her dress to see if anything had improved its appearance in the last five minutes. Nothing had. She didn't say anything.

Stoke said, "The best place may be where Nancy and Herbert want to eat. Where is that?"

"Hardee's!" screamed Nancy.

The mother smiled. Stoke knew at least one person was going to be happy, whatever it was that Hardee's served.

"You sure you want to be seen with us?" the woman asked. "We aren't wearing our best clothes."

Stoke understood she was letting him off the "hook" if he did not want to be seen with them.

He smiled at her. "If anyone isn't good enough to eat with us, I will personally tell him."

They had a nice lunch of hamburgers and French fries. The kids took some food home. Stoke was able to fix the TV for them quickly. Before he left, Stoke hugged both kids and asked the woman her name.

"Helen Stillman," she told him, "Helen Wilson Stillman."

"Helen, that plug looked as if it was smashed by a hammer."

"My ex-husband did it before he left," she told him, "and he's not coming back."

Stoke paused to write down Helen's full name and address and the names of Herbert and Nancy. He told her he was leaving for the present, but would be back to talk with her once more or would call. Then he thanked her again for taking them in that morning.

"That woman, Miz Ari, she's not your wife, is she?" Helen asked.

"No, Helen. Ari is maybe a distant cousin. I just met her a few days ago. We're working on a family history project together. Her great-grandparents and my great-grandparents are both from the same county in Virginia. They had the same last name. We're trying to find out about them and some people that lived in this county in 1856."

Helen put a hand on her hip and looked right at Stoke. "Uh huh. Well, she's a cop."

"So she told me. But I'm not a cop. I'm a businessman from California."

"Uh huh. You won't find any problems here."

"No, I'm really not a cop. I'm taking a few days off from work to find my family's roots. I bet you could do the same thing if you had the time. Where is your family from?"

Helen thought a minute and decided it was better to talk about families than police business. "My folks are from this part of Missouri. They were slaves when *your* folks lived here." Then taking another stab, she blurted out, "Are you the good cop or the bad cop?"

"Neither one. Cops are in a different line of work. I'm a humble businessman. But if I'm making you nervous, I'll leave."

"Look, I'm sorry. It's just that some people have been trying to take the kids away from me because I don't have a job. But I'll get one, and then I can keep my children."

"That's heavy. I could ask some of my people to look at your work record, but they're in California. Would you want to live there?"

She said, "I don't want to seem ungrateful, but let me look around here first."

"You speak well. How are your clerical abilities?" Stoke asked her.

"I've had a couple of years at the University of Missouri," Helen replied. "I was going to major in English. I learned to do research well enough to get on the honor roll."

"Great. Let me know what happens. I don't promise anything, but occasionally I have openings. When I get back to California, give me a call." He handed Helen a business card. "Here's my card. Call me in about a week in California, if I haven't called you."

Helen looked as if he had requested her to call Mars.

"Oh, and make it a collect call. My secretary will accept the charges if you tell her who you are."

"Why are you doing all this?" Helen asked. "You know I can't repay you, and you don't talk like a man who will ask a woman for 'special' favors."

"I was born grateful, I guess. But you need to know I'm also a mean boss. I want people on my payroll who are so grateful they will work very, very hard. Then we all benefit. My company shares its profits."

Helen said, "I guess there's no use in tryin' to pay for the repair part, is there?"

"Not a chance in a million, Helen. But you already helped rescue us from a bad situation, so you've paid in full."

Stoke climbed into his car and waved as he drove back into Levanger. He was happy because he had solved two problems at almost no expense to anybody. He was heading for a shower and a change of clothes. Besides, he wasn't tied up in an old farmhouse anymore. It was going to be a good day.

There was a message for Stoke at the motel desk when he got back. It had been phoned in, and it said, "Call Lieutenant Kiefer of the Crittenden Sheriff's Office at 555-8900." As soon as Stoke got to his room, he had the phone in his hand and was dialing the number.

"Sheriff's Department," a tough-sounding woman said.

"My name is Stokely Towles. I just got a message to call Lieutenant Kiefer."

"Towles? Wait a minute. I'll switch you to the Lieutenant." There was a click and then a ring.

"Lieutenant Kiefer!" a woman's voice said.

"My Name is Towles. I got a message to call you."

"Oh, yes, Mr. Towles. There's been an accident. Miss Ariadne Edwards asked us to call. Do you know her?"

"Ari? Has she been hurt?" Stoke gripped the phone tightly and held his breath, waiting for the bad news which was sure to follow.

"She's in the hospital. But she's not in too bad a shape. There was an accident on the outer loop and it looks like someone drove her off the road. Her car was totaled. She asked to see you, so do you know where to find the hospital?"

Stoke said he didn't, and it took a few minutes for him to get the details. Then the officer let the other shoe drop.

"We'd like to talk to you sometime today. Can you drop by or do you want us to pick you up?" The "pick you up" question had overtones of officialness, so Stoke said he would come by to see the Lieutenant.

Running as fast as he could on a partially healed leg, he made a dash for his car and then tore out of the motel parking lot on his way to the hospital. It took only a few minutes before he was pulling into the parking lot of the emergency room. It was a typical hospital day. Stoke was just one more person among the many other worried-looking people in the lobby, trying to find what had happened to a family member or friend. The receptionist was directing people around the wards, but when she got Stoke's name, she made a telephone call and asked him to wait a minute. She said someone wanted to talk with him.

Three minutes later an older man appeared and asked for Stoke. He was dressed professionally in a dark suit. Stoke guessed him to be in his fifties because of his graying hair and the smattering of white in his mustache. He was slightly stooped, slender and generally in good physical shape. Stoke thought this man was probably a doctor and steeled himself for the worst.

"Mr. Towles, I am Special Agent Witherspoon of the FBI."

Stoke shook his hand, wondering what the hell was going on.

"Ms Edwards is here and she's in pretty good shape, considering the nature of the accident. I know you want to see her, but I would like to talk to you first."

Ignoring this, Stoke blurted out, "What's wrong with her?"

"She's just shaken up. The doctors are holding her for observation. She'll probably be out of here tomorrow. I understand you are her cousin?"

Relieved, Stoke got his thoughts in order. He said nothing.

"She's your relative?" prompted Witherspoon.

"Oh, yes. Distant cousin... on my mother's side."

"Mr. Towles, do you know what Ms Edwards was doing in this part of the country?"

"No, I don't. She told me she was researching her family tree and that she was with the government. We originally thought her ancestor killed mine in 1856. We were comparing notes."

"What do you do for a living, Mr. Towles?"

Stoke realized that the FBI knew all about him by this time. "I'm a businessman in Los Angles."

"Do you often visit your ancestral home?"

"No, this is not my ancestral home. My ancestor lived here only a short time before he was murdered. This is a vacation of sorts. I thought I would research my family since this is the only time I will have in the forseeable future."

The story sounded so dumb, it had the ring of truth to it. He wanted to convince Witherspoon he was not up to something illegal, or worse yet, working for another government agency.

"Is that all you were doing?"

"That's all I was doing. I don't know what Ari was up to, but I think she really irritated some people."

"What makes you think *she* irritated people and not you?" Witherspoon asked.

"She didn't irritate me at all. Just the opposite."

"No, I meant other people."

"Are you saying it's something *I* did that caused someone to run her off the road?"

"It could be."

"Well, I'm just researching a shooting that took place a hundred and forty years ago!" Stoke explained.

"Who did the shooting?"

"Well, it appears that it was a jealous husband, but there may have been a mixture of politics in the killing."

"Mr. Towles, be careful. I don't know who caused the problem, but there is some gang activity here and they seem to be in some kind of drug business. Perhaps they're irritated with something you've turned up. Ms Edwards has told me about some of the problems you've experienced. They sound as if they're related to gang activity. Now I believe you would like to see Ms Edwards. She is in Room 218. Take that elevator over there."

He was pointing to his left at a hallway. Stoke shook his hand and rapidly walked in that direction, wondering why Witherspoon called her Ms Edwards, and why he didn't mention what the federal government had to do with her accident. He thought they probably knew that Ari told him what she did for a living. After all, it was a government vehicle that was damaged.

Out of breath, Stoke tapped on the door of Room 218. A weak voice said for him to come in. He found a darkened room with a feminine shape huddled on her side in a metal hospital bed. There was only one bed in the room of standard hospital decor: steel furniture, stainless steel sink and hard, smooth surfaces on the floor and walls. *Just like the one I lived in a few months ago*, he thought.

"Ari?"

"Stoke?" a voice whispered weakly, "I didn't want you to see me like this. Then they gave me another shot of Demerol and I didn't give a damn anymore."

Stoke kissed Ari's cheek and picked up her hand.

"How long are you in for?"

"Maybe I can get out tomorrow. It looks like I'll be sore for a while, that's all."

"Can you tell me what happened?"

"Will you promise not to say anything about women drivers?"

"Of course, I won't. You never hear me make those kinds of generalizations, anyway."

"I'm just kidding."

"I'm glad you can still make jokes. So what did happen?"

"I had a meeting with my people, which you know if you got my note."

"I didn't get it," he told her.

"I thought I saw that old green car when I went to the meeting, but when I left I didn't see it. Then as I got onto the highway to come back to the motel, I saw it again."

"You sure it was the one that followed us?"

"Fairly sure. But there are a lot of dirty green cars around this part of the world. As I got up to speed the driver got closer. When we drove away from other traffic, he got right on top of my car and rammed it on the left side of my bumper. That pushed the front end of the car to the right and forced me off the road. I went off the highway and ran into a grove of trees. If I had forgotten to put on my seat belt, I might be dead now, instead of beat up."

"What can I do for you?"

"Right now you can get me a glass of water. Tomorrow you can pick me up when they release me."

"Do your people know what's been happening since you got here?"

"Yes, I had to tell them since I lost my gun. Now I've lost my car. I guess they're wondering what I'm going to lose next."

Stoke ignored that comment, not being able to add anything. "Do they have any opinions about what's going on? Do they think the people you're interested in are after you?"

"No, that's not their style. My boss seems to think *you* have stirred up something."

"Me? What could I have done? I'm not a danger to anyone."

"We're not so sure."

"Ari, do you remember getting their license number when they followed us one day?"

"Yes. There is no such license number. It was a fake."

"I guess there's no use in my asking if you saw that plate on the car that hit you, is there?"

"No point at all."

Ari was lost in thought until Stoke said, "By the way, why was Witherspoon, an FBI man, talking to me downstairs?"

She answered, "When the local cops pulled me out of my car and went through my purse, they saw my government ID and called the FBI. Then they asked me what I was doing in this area, and I guess they also talked to you."

"Do they know why you're here?"

"I asked them to call our area supervisor, so I don't know. But maybe they understood."

"Maybe they think you're looking into their backyards."

Ari coughed and recoiled from the pain of sore ribs. She again asked for water. Stoke put his hand under Ari's back and gently lifted her up while he put the glass to her lips. She drank some and then lay back, her eyes closed.

"Do you want to sleep now?"

"No, it's just the painkiller. It makes me groggy. I'd like it if you could stay with me for a few more minutes. Then it will be bath time. I would rather do that myself."

Stoke said with a very straight face, "I wouldn't leave you for anything, Ari. Can I get some soap and a washcloth now?"

"What kind of cousin are you?" she said. "If I wanted that kind of help, I would enlist the aid of an old maid aunt, not a stud from California."

"Is that what I am? Just a stud from California?"

"Yes, a stud with an airplane. So what are you going to do tomorrow?"

"I'm going to Kentucky before I go back to California. Maybe I can talk to more people and find out who knows about the killing."

There was silence in the dark hospital room. He looked at her. Her eyes were closed and she was breathing evenly. Taking out his pen, he wrote a note and placed it on the stand by her bed. It said, "Thanks for a great time. It's more fun than I remembered, sharing a bath with someone. The nurse liked it, too. Call me tomorrow for a ride or if you want to know where I put the soap."

Then Stoke drove slowly out of the parking lot, keeping one eye on the road and one eye on the rearview mirror to see if he were being followed. He saw an official-looking black car behind him, which contained Witherspoon. He waved and Witherspoon waved back. Stoke drove slower so the other driver would have no problem accompanying him.

When he got back to the motel, Witherspoon pulled in beside Stoke. He got out and walked to Stoke's car door.

"One more thing, Mr. Towles. Since you've had several encounters with your friends in the green car, it might be useful to talk to the sheriff of Crittenden County. He may or may not want to call in the State Police. But he may know the people who are involved. You can trust this sheriff, by the way. Our office has cleared him. I don't think he's in the Klan or any of the gangs. We'll be around, so call us if you have more troubles." He handed Stoke a business card and went back to his car. He waved and drove away.

Stoke remembered he had promised to see Lieutenant Kiefer, so without getting out of his car, he went to the sheriff's office building where he and Ari had gone when they were shot at. The Lieutenant recalled that visit when he found himself seated in her office.

"I'm told you've been here before, Mr. Towles."

"Yeah, two men took a shot at us. We'd never seen them before."

"Ms Edwards said it may have been the same car which ran her off the road. How did you irritate these people so thoroughly?"

"I have no idea, Lieutenant. At first I thought they were involved in one of Ms Edwards' projects, but now I'm not so sure."

"What are you doing here, Mr. Towles?"

"I broke a leg a month ago. Now I'm taking some time off, a time to heal."

"You can heal anyplace. Why here?"

He told her how he came to investigate an 1856 murder and the possible involvement of hostile political forces.

"And you're not with the U.S. Government in any capacity, are you?"

"Only as a dedicated taxpayer."

"Have you had any other problems?" she asked.

Stoke told her about the attempted kidnapping.

"Damn! I think we can rule out coincidence, can't we? I got an official enquiry about that, but it was outside our jurisdiction. It was in the next county. Did it ever occur to you that there was no fooling around by your ancestor? Maybe the outraged husband was a cover-up. Could be that some people want to keep it quiet."

"Who would care after a hundred and forty years? I bet they don't even know it happened."

"Well, I know it happened, and I believe trouble follows you around. How long are you two going to be in Levanger?"

"Only a day or two. But I plan to be back around Labor Day. Maybe I can convince Ms Edwards to come back with me."

"I'm not looking forward to your bringing more trouble to us," she said while making a note on her calendar. Then, "Thank you for coming in. I appreciated this little chat." She stood and Stoke took the hint to leave.

After dinner, Stoke went back to see Ari at the hospital. He found her much more alert, with hair combed and lipstick applied. She was sitting up in bed, reading the local newspaper. In it was an account of the accident.

As Stoke entered the room, Ari said, "Look at this! The newspaper didn't even check the facts of the accident before it printed them. It says there was a collision between two cars on the highway and a passenger in one car was hurt! I can't believe how screwed up they were!"

"Hello, Ari. How do you feel?"

"How could I feel good when they print such stuff?"

"Other than that, how do you feel?"

"Better. You didn't tell the newspaper this stuff, did you?"

"No, but maybe your friend Mr. Witherspoon did. If you're confused, think about the enemy. Anyway, I feel like I walked into the middle of a conversation."

Ari put down her paper and smiled one of her dazzling smiles at Stoke. "I'm sorry. I guess this sloppy piece of reporting irritated me. So, how're you?"

"I'm fine, but I really came to see if I could get you out of here."

"No, I promised I would stay overnight. They said something about a concussion. That's medical talk for a 'bump on the head.'"

He said, "Lieutenant Kiefer invited me down to the station to talk. I didn't say anything about you, but I suspect your cover is badly blown at this point. At least with the police."

"Well, maybe the bad guys haven't found out yet." Then she changed the subject.

"So, did you bring a deck of cards?"

"What did you have in mind, Ari? I don't know much about poker and I don't play with people who need credit."

"What do you mean?" Ari was indignant.

"Your hospital gown has no pockets."

Ari was puzzled. "So what does that mean?"

"You're in no position to cover your losses."

Ari pulled the sheet around her. "Yes, well we could watch TV. But there's not much on in the middle of Levanger, Missouri, on a Tuesday night," she told him.

Stoke put the back of his hand lightly against her cheek. Ari felt cool, not at all as if she had a fever. He left it there for a minute. She took his hand in hers and kissed it.

"Thank you for coming. I know you have other things to do right now."

"As a matter of fact, I have to make the rounds and kiss all the pretty girls in the place before lights out. Your room was first on my list."

"Why, thank you. I really ran my car off the road to get your attention, you know."

"You got it in a hurry. I was scared when I got the call."

"Who called you?"

"Lieutenant Kiefer from the local cop shop."

"How did he know I was in the hospital?"

"*She* found out from the State Police, who investigated the accident. They found a receipt from our motel in your purse and called the locals. I guess it was one of them who saw your ID and made a call to the local FB&I people. Do you remember them getting you out of the car?"

"It was actually no big deal. They had a problem getting the door open and they didn't want me to move at all. But the rest was standard procedure. They pulled me out and put me on a stretcher. I had my purse in my hand. I told them no one else was in the car. Then all I had to do was recite my Social Security number ten or fifteen times."

"Yeah, they do that to see if you're in shock."

"They carried me to the ambulance and drove me here. The only time I was disoriented was when I got the shots. The rest of the time I was kind of bored."

"What were you this afternoon when I came to see you?"

"Really out of it. But once I woke, I told them I didn't want any more medicine and they backed off. I couldn't think straight."

"You sound like yourself and look like yourself, so I guess you *are* yourself again. It's getting late, so I'll call you tomorrow to see when you want to go back. I guess you know I'm kind of spoiled now. I hate to eat dinner without you."

Stoke kissed her cheek, then squeezed her hand. He headed for the door, much relieved. He knew she would be back on her feet soon.

Ari smiled and said nothing.

Chapter Ten

$150 Reward

RANAWAY from the subscriber, 5 miles east of Dover, the 14th of April. He is about 21 or 22 years of age named Amos. He is about 5 feet 8 or 9 inches high with a scar on his forehead, and has lost one of his toes, has a slight limp on one leg, has a high brow and a flat nose, tolerably wide mouth, and always appears in good humor. Had on blue shirt when left, a black wool hat, brown jeans and casinet pants... JOHN M. DYCUS

Time was running out. Stoke had to return to California and he hadn't accomplished nearly as much as he planned. Early the next morning he called Ari in her room at the hospital.

"Hey, Miz Edwards, this is Stoke. How you doin' today?"

"I'm better. They're letting me out of here about noon. Can you come over?"

"You bet. I'll take you to your 'home away from home.' Then I'm going to Kentucky. Want to come with me?"

"I'm not up to it, but you go ahead."

It was noon when Stoke walked into Ari's hospital room. She was seated in the chair by her bed, dressed and ready to go.

"Do I carry you or what?" he asked, looking for a wheelchair.

"They're coming in with a wheelchair soon, just to get me off the premises, and then I can walk."

A wheelchair showed up in a few minutes. Stoke helped Ari into it. She signed some papers and an attendant took her outside the building to Stoke's car. At the car, Stoke tenderly put his arm behind Ari's back. As Ari stood slowly, the attendant took the wheelchair away.

"I'm walking. Slowly, but steadily." Stoke kept his arm around her protectively. She leaned on him for a minute, straightened her back and walked purposefully the next couple of feet to the car.

"What was that all about?"

"If the guy who hit me was watching, I want him to think I'm not hurt."

"Are you?"

"You bet," she said without hesitation.

"I thought so. Well, show time is over, so let's get back."

Stoke took Ari back to the motel and helped her into her room, where she headed for the softest chair in the place. He put her legs on another chair, but that left him no place to sit except for the bed.

"When are you leaving, Ari?"

"I have to wait for instructions, but I think it will be pretty soon."

"Then I think I'll have my plane pick me up tomorrow. Save me some time tonight."

"What for?"

"For discussion, drinks and plans for a meeting in the future. Or is that too risqué for you?" he said mockingly.

"Probably not enough risqué. Are you really going back?"

"Yeah, I have to. You sure you can't go over to Kentucky with me?"

"Can't," she told him sadly. "I have to work today and I don't feel much like moving around."

"All right. See you tonight."

Stoke got into his car and looked back as he drove out. Ari waved to him from the window of the motel.

Stoke went back to the sheriff's office to ask about the men who had been following them. Lieutenant Kiefer was out, but he found a sergeant who was willing to talk. Stoke offered to exchange a lunch for the man's time, so they went next door to a small café.

They sat down at a small table where they ordered sandwiches and coffee. Stoke made lots of small talk and asked questions about the main crop of the area, tobacco. It seemed the officer was aware the federal government was going to have to cut down on price supports and might even take a stand against the crop. He was indignant about the loss of income that would cause.

When the tirade was over, Stoke said, "Can you tell me anything about the locals who have been giving Ms Edwards and me such a hard time?"

"How do you know they are locals?" the officer challenged.

"They looked and talked like locals, and they knew the back roads quite well."

"You want to tell me what happened?" The officer took out a pencil and a pad of paper.

"I told the Lieutenant about this. But I think you should know what I know, even though it isn't much. It was two days ago in the afternoon, about four o'clock. I was having a picnic with Ms Edwards about six miles out on Highway 13. It was in a pasture. I don't know whose it was. We had eaten and cleaned up our mess when two men stepped out from behind trees and held a gun on us. They took our wallets and questioned us. Then they forced us into our car at gunpoint and made me drive to an old farmhouse. They left us tied up. We untied ourselves and drove back somewhere near Longview, just this side of Levanger."

"That's a hellava story! Is it true?"

"Every bit. Oh, the day before, they'd been following us all over the place. When they tried to stop us, my friend pulled out a portable telephone and acted as if she were calling you guys. That scared them off." Stoke did not mention Ari's gun. "And that isn't all. Yesterday it appears that the same car drove Ms Edwards off the road and almost killed her. I took her out of the hospital a few hours ago."

"What did they look like?"

"Middle-aged white males in blue jeans and work shirts. One of them was called Bert. He was dark haired and about five foot nine. The other one had gray hair and was about six feet tall, with a small scar on his right cheek."

The officer wrote it all down very carefully. "What did they take from your wallet?"

"Nothing. I found it later. I guess California ID and credit cards would be of little use around here, so they left them behind."

"May I see your ID please?" The officer had suddenly become very formal.

Stoke produced his California driver's license. The officer looked at him and then at his picture on the license. "Who's the other person you mentioned, the young lady?"

"She'll verify what I have told you. Her name is Ariadne Edwards and she lives in Washington, DC. I've known her for only a few days, and can't tell you much else about her. We're both here to do some research. She's a student and I'm a businessman."

"Washington, DC, huh?" The officer was thinking about something he wasn't going to talk about. "Well, okay, Mr. Towles. I got your story. I assume you'll be willing to identify the people if I find them."

"You bet!" Stoke said.

"I'll think it over. Maybe I should turn this over to the State Police. They do a lot of our detective work for us. Are you going to be around for a while?"

"No, sergeant. I'm going to Kentucky tomorrow and then back to California in a couple of days, but I'll be back in Levanger about Labor Day."

"That's not much help for us. If I find these guys, I can't hold them a month until you get back, you know."

"You nail, I'll return. Don't worry."

The officer thought a minute and said, "You realize there's still a Ku Klux Klan in these parts, don't you?"

"Do you think I've gotten them stirred up?"

"It's possible. By the way, I'm not in the Klan and I bust civilians who carry a gun in the city, so be sure you don't have one."

"Thanks for the warning, sergeant. I appreciate your fine efforts. And no, I don't have a gun. But I do have a business card with my phone number on it. I'd be happy to hear from you at any time. In fact, if you don't mind, I'll call you from time to time."

As Stoke got up to leave, the sergeant said, "Have a nice trip back," but his tone said, "and don't return too soon." Just as in the old movies, Levanger wasn't large enough for the sergeant and Stoke at the same time.

Stoke and Ari ate hamburgers in her car that night because she needed to work on a report of her activities, which cut short her time. Stoke had to pack his clothes and sort out his research into piles so he could be sure he'd left nothing behind. But he wanted to spend more time with Ari.

"You know," Stoke told her between French fries, "I'm going to miss you."

Ari looked at him. "When will I see you again?"

"My place or yours?" Stoke asked with a smile.

"Stoke, I told you I have to work tonight!"

"I meant," he artfully replied, "are you coming to California or am I coming to Washington?"

"When?"

"Any time soon. I can have my pilot pick you up."

"Don't forget that I'm a public servant. We can't accept gifts from people."

"Am I a suspect in an investigation?" Stoke asked.

"Not that I'm aware of. But it's not a good idea for agents to accept gifts. And really, I don't get a vacation for six more months."

"I'd like to know you better, Ari. I guess I could arrange a trip to Washington. Or I could come back here to Levanger if you're going to be here."

"I'll be going back to Washington soon. Who knows if I can come back here officially?"

"Does that mean your investigation in Missouri is over?"

"We've turned over our investigation to local people. But the case is far from closed. Someday we'll find out where all the drug money is going and to whom. But right now, we have to wait."

"Did you find out any more about the people who grabbed us?"

"Only that they seem to be locals. I think they were after you, Stoke, not me. Maybe someone told the Klan you were trying to get the goods on them."

"I've been thinking that, too. Maybe it's a good thing I'm leaving tomorrow. But I'll be back." Stoke was silent for a minute. Then he added, "Nevertheless, those men attacked a federal officer. Are you going after them?"

"If we find them, in the course of our investigation, we'll arrest them. But our primary goal is to trace flows of drug money, not kidnappers."

"So, when *are* you coming to California?" Stoke asked.

"So, when *are* you coming to Washington?" Ari replied.

"I guess it's a stand-off, Ari. I'll call you when I get back and we can discuss the arrangements later. But I'm going to be very unhappy if this is the last hamburger we share."

"I've enjoyed these past few days. But you've seen me on special duty away from home. And you're away from your business. We might be very different when we get back to our home bases. You *could* be a pre-occupied businessman who never takes vacations."

"I bet you're just as pretty in Washington as you are here," Stoke said as he touched her nose and stroked her cheek.

Ari blushed.

Stoke said, "That's a good color. Do you really think that I could forget you?" She was silent. He leaned forward and kissed her lightly on the cheek. When he straightened up, he saw that he had become too involved in the hamburger Ari was eating. It was in her hand and had become crushed against his chest. "Secret sauce" was now out in the open, covering a large section of his shirtfront.

Stoke looked down at his chest and examined the extent of the damage. "I'd do it again in a second," he said. "But frankly, Scarlet, I would prefer Grey Poupon next time."

Ari laughed. Using her paper napkin, she deftly wiped the gobs of sauce off Stoke's shirt. Then she looked up and kissed him firmly on the mouth. "I have a soft spot in my heart for big slobs," she told him.

"Then you're going to like me a lot."

After a few minutes, Stoke said, "Would it do any good to tell you that I'm going to get on a plane and it might crash and we might never see each other again?"

"It's not a good time for me, Stoke. Can we go back now, before I give in and lose what little respect my boss has for me?"

"Deal, Ari. I'll call you after I get back, and then maybe we can talk about who is going where. Would you put your home phone number on your business card? I hate to call you at the office."

Ari wrote on her business card and handed it to Stoke. He did the same for her.

"An answering service takes most of my messages," Stoke told her. "I'm giving you their number and a private number. I usually answer the private phone if I'm home."

"I'll try to remember all that," she said.

"I had hoped for candlelight and wine tonight, not dashboards and Pepsi. But remember, it was your choice."

"I had hoped for something better on our last night in Levanger, too, Stoke. However, duty calls, loudly and often. Can we get back now? I have to start my report and you have to change your shirt."

Ari picked up the messy papers and cups. Then they drove out of the parking lot towards the motel. She wanted to think about the report, but found herself thinking about Stoke instead.

"You're not making it easy to write reports, you know. I can't seem to put my mind on my work."

"Good," Stoke told her. "I'm happy to have made an impact, no matter how small."

"Well, you did. I'm trying to figure out a way to get the sauce out of your shirt. I feel partly responsible."

"Oh, I thought you were going to pieces because I was leaving," he said with a smirk.

"Well, that too. But I have a feeling we're going to meet again."

"Not on this trip. I'm leaving early in the morning. My plane gets in to Kansas City at five in the morning and I don't want to miss it."

"If you do, you can fire the pilot. But I'll probably still be working on that darn report."

They were back at the motel and parked by that time. Stoke went with Ari to her room. Just outside the door, he gathered her in his arms and pressed her closely to his chest. He held her so tightly that she couldn't move. But she didn't want to move anyway. He kissed her for a long time. Then he let go and walked to his room without turning back to look at her or say a word. He was thinking about that kiss. *In every romantic relationship there is one kiss that is outstanding. I think that was it. It doesn't get much better.* Then he felt the wet spot on his shirt. He was afraid the sauce had transferred to her blouse. *A nice Béarnaise would be easier to get out,* he mumbled to himself.

He packed and then called Ari for one last goodbye conversation. "Hey, why don't you give up that position with the government and let me hire you in California?"

"That's the most irritating thing you've ever said, Stokely Towles. I have a career with a prestigious government agency that makes a significant contribution to the welfare of us all. You're treating it as if it were just another job. I believe in what I'm doing, and I'm not just another industrial round peg in an industrial square hole that can be replaced at the whim of some executive!"

"Wow, Ari," Stoke said apologetically. "That sounds like a sales pitch for the DEA. I didn't intend to demean your job at all. But my company has important positions, too. And remember, industry pays the taxes that keep the government going. If there weren't any industry, there would be nothing to pay you people with."

"So now you're saying we're unproductive?" she replied hotly. "I want you to know we are one of the most effective government agencies. And I think you have a typical, uninformed view of government. You've never worked in government, have you?"

"No," he replied, "but the real question is, 'Have you government people ever earned a buck with a job in industry?' Do you know what it's like to be on your own without all the government protections surrounding you?"

"Have you ever been trapped in a back alley by a drug dealer?" she came back at him.

"I've been trapped in a dark alley by union thugs. Does that count?"

"It's not the same thing at all. But please, let's not end with an argument. Let's look forward to better times, okay?"

"Deal," Stoke told her and hung up the phone before anything worse could happen.

Ari put the phone down much more firmly. Stoke was very troubled. *How could this have happened?* he asked himself. All I wanted to do was offer her an alternative. Then he lay back on his bed with his arms behind his head to think about what had happened. It was all a little bit too fast for him. A piece of that puzzle was missing.

The next morning Stoke was at the airport at fifteen minutes past five. The sun was rising. His pilot had time to gas the plane and file a flight plan with the tower. He climbed in the two-engine jet behind the pilot and took off almost immediately. Stoke flew the plane while his pilot slept. But his mind was on Ariadne Edwards.

Two hours later, Stoke brought the plane to rest at Standiford Field in Louisville, Kentucky. Once again a car and driver were waiting for him. After the transfer of luggage, Stoke dismissed the driver and went east to Scott County. It was near Levanger, Kentucky, which was much larger than Levanger, Missouri. The city he had targeted was Georgetown, a college town where his mother was born. Remembering the Baptist church with Rev. Charlie, Stoke thought the body of Henry Vallandingham could be in the large cemetery in Georgetown. At least Georgetown was the county seat and the place to begin looking. He had been here many years ago at a family funeral, but he didn't recall whose.

About eighty miles from Louisville, through patches of gorgeous lush green woods and giant limestone cliffs along the road, Stoke found the pretty little town. Although it was a slightly familiar site, he knew he would need help if he were to find his way. At a gas station, he asked a man for instructions. The man looked like an old farmer, wearing bib overalls over a well-used dress shirt, sleeves rolled up. The man had been around somewhere for many years and should, Stoke thought, have much knowledge about the place.

"Hello," Stoke said. "I'm lost and wondered if you could help me find my destination."

"Where you goin'?"

"I hear there's a big cemetery in Georgetown. I need to visit it." It took a while to explain what he wanted, but Stoke was patient. The old man, whose name was Shasted, was hard of hearing.

Mr. Shasted made up for his hearing loss by staring intently at Stoke's lips as Stoke spoke to him. Such attention made Stoke nervous. Mr. Shasted finally understood and volunteered to go with Stoke to show him where the cemetery was. Stoke suggested they get some lunch first. Stoke learned to look directly at the old man when he wanted to say something to him.

"I thought you needed to pick muh brain," Mr. Shasted said.

"That can wait a few minutes, Mr. Shasted." He figured that Mr. Shasted had been six feet tall in his youth. But now he was bent over at a severe angle. Thin and wiry, Mr. Shasted had a twinkle in his eye when he smiled, which was often. It was almost as if Mr. Shasted, at eighty-seven, wasn't afraid of people or events anymore. He could smile and didn't give a damn if they didn't smile back. Of course, thought Stoke, he might be senile, too.

But Mr. Shasted wasn't senile. He was pretty sharp. And he could remember the past quite well, although yesterday was becoming a problem for him.

They sat down at a small table where they ordered sandwiches and coffee. Stoke made lots of small talk and asked questions about crops in the area. It seems Mr. Shasted was well versed about local produce. He told Stoke a lot more about corn and tobacco than he ever cared to know.

Mr. Shasted looked Stoke right in the eye and said, "We's talked about everything 'cept what you came for, haven't we?"

"Just about. Can we switch subjects for a moment?"

"That's what ah came for. What is it you want to know?"

"Mr. Shasted, I… "

"You kin call me Tom. My daddy was Mr. Shasted. He cared a lot about titles. Ah don't. What's in the cemetery that interests you so much? You don't look like no grievin' survivor."

"I am, in a way," Stoke told him. "Only, the death took place in 1856, in Missouri."

"Did you ever think you was in the wrong town? Or the wrong state? This here's Kentucky," the old man said teasingly.

"That's part of the mystery, Tom. The body was dug up and moved to Scott County."

"Yup, there usta be a lot of that at one time. Diggin' up people, I mean."

"It was my ancestor. He was blown away by a shotgun blast to the stomach and buried in Levanger, Missouri, in 1856. Then about 1887, he was moved to Scott County. I'm just starting here to look for his grave at the biggest cemetery."

"Sounds like 'tweren't much of a fight, then."

"No," Stoke said, "it was an ambush. And I'm not sure why he was killed. One story is that he was fooling around with somebody's wife. But that could have been a story to cover up political action. The city he was killed in was a place where feelings about slavery and freedom were running very high. Uh, you aren't in the Klan, are you, or were you?"

"No, ah ain't. Ah hated the bastuds fifty years ago and I still do."

"Are they still around?"

"Not in this county. They operate out of Rockport these days, same as a hunnert years ago. They prob'ly know you're here, nosing around."

"Well, they can breathe easier. I'm going to leave tomorrow."

"Who's your ancestor?" Shasted asked.

"A man named Henry Vallandingham."

"I heard some Vallandinghams were here at the beginnin' of the county. But they all left. Don't know nothin' about 'em, though."

With lunch finished, Stoke paid the bill. He and the old man walked over to Stoke's car. They drove a few blocks to Highway 25, and then went about a mile out on the highway until they came to some gates, where Shasted directed them to the right.

"Lookahere," Shasted said as they came to a sign.

Stoke braked and read a sign that said the cemetery was opened in 1860. It also said that any graves that had earlier dates were for people whose bodies were moved into the site.

"Now I need to do some paperwork if they have any records here," Stoke told Shasted. "So I guess I won't have to bother you anymore. I sure appreciate your leadership, Tom. Where can I take you now?"

"Nowhere. Ah live across the road."

"At least you can let me buy a drink, Tom."

"Cain't"

"Oh, I'm sorry. Doctor advise against spirits?"

"Nope. It's a dry county," explained Tom.

"Depends on who you know," said Stoke with a wink in his eye. "Why not look in the back seat and see what you can find?"

The old man turned and spotted a brown bag on the back seat. He handed it to Stoke. Stoke brought out a bottle of Jim Beam straight Bourbon.

"Tell you what," Stoke said with a sigh. "I can't drink and research old graves at the same time. Why don't you hold that bottle for me, and when I get back on my next trip, we can break it open. Of course, if there's an emergency in the meantime, and you need some for your cough or whatever, feel free to test the contents for its medicinal value."

Tom nodded, the gleam in his eye a little brighter. "That's mighty thoughty of ye. I'll hold on to the bottle all right, but ah might not be here when you get back. You might not have noticed, but ah'm not a teenager any more. There's a distinct possibility ah could be drafted into the army, or something more permanent might happen to me before you return!"

"Could be, Tom, so you do what you think best. But I expect to see you next time I come back. I can't thank you enough for your help today."

"Ah think you did already. You don't know how long this has been a dry county."

Stoke was laughing to himself as he went his way, partly because he enjoyed his time with Tom Shasted, and partly because he was ready to enjoy some serious research.

Parking his long black Mercedes in front of the office, Stoke got out and looked around the place. It was truly a beautiful, well-kept cemetery. It was also looking more and more familiar. For some unknown reason, he walked down a paved lane to a small obelisk. There he recognized the plot for the Grover family. He inspected the markers until he found Martha Ann's grave. She was his great-great-grandmother, and her maiden name was Vallandingham…

So Stoke looked around behind the Grover monument until he found a carved tree stump. That is, it was carved from stone. On it was the name "Armilda Vallandingham," and the dates 1809-1895. Next to it was part of the rest of the tree, obviously sawed from the stump, lying horizontally on the ground. And it said "Henry Bruce Vallandingham." The death date was July 18, 1856. It all fit together. The image of the tree said to Stoke, "Here is a life cut down before its time."

Stoke recalled that church records said Henry's body had been moved from Levanger, Missouri, in 1887. He subtracted Henry's death year 1856 from 1887, and realized that Armilda had waited thirty-one years to move Henry's body. He remembered that 1887 was the year her son-in-law, Asa Grover, had died. He was well-off, so money may have become available to make the move. Finally, it became possible for Armilda to be buried next to Henry.

The last name on Armilda's tombstone was still Vallandingham. She had never remarried. And she had erected a handsome monument to this man. This was not a woman shamed by her husband in a tawdry affair. This was a woman who longed to have him close to her once again. Maybe the Frenchman was wrong who said, "No man is a hero to his wife or his valet."

Stoke paused and looked at the graves for a long time. Then he went back for his camera and took a photograph of the stones.

On his way back to the car, a man came out of the office and spoke to Stoke. Something was familiar about him, so Stoke paused to tell him that he was taking pictures of the graves and that he hoped it was all right. The man was big, about six feet tall, and he had an eye patch on his left eye. But he didn't look like a pirate.

The man said it was fine to take pictures. He asked if Stoke were from around there, knowing he wasn't. That's just a way for some people to get to know others. Stoke said he was from Los Angeles and was investigating a very old murder. That got the other man really interested. He asked which graves he was photographing. Stoke told him about Henry Vallandingham and the man's good eye got very large.

"Heck," the man said, "Henry is my ancestor, too. Maybe we're cousins!" He stuck out his hand and introduced himself as Harley Grover. Stoke was stunned. He was indeed a cousin. He just hadn't seen Harley much in his lifetime. But he had heard plenty about him. Stoke told Harley about his mother and her connections to the Grovers and Vallandinghams. Then he told Harley about the murder in Missouri. Harley knew nothing about it, but he seemed delighted, because family history was one of his hobbies, too.

Harley invited Stoke in to the office to scan the records. Stoke looked very carefully to see if there was any note about when Henry's body was moved in, but he didn't find one. He would just have to accept what the Levanger church records showed. What he did see were notations by the Daughters of the American Revolution at certain entries indicating a historical interest in the name. There was one by Henry's name. This meant that there were Vallandinghams in the Revolutionary War. Then Stoke looked through the rest of the ledger and found James M. Walker and several of his children, including his great-grandmother, Stella Walker Pryor. James was the one who had been murdered in 1874 by the Klan in Owen County, Stoke recalled. His body had been moved in to this cemetery, also. And his wife, Alice Grover Walker, was a granddaughter of Henry Bruce Vallandingham, according to the old genealogy he had in his collection. *Getting murdered over civil rights issues seems to be a family trait*, he thought to himself.

Once he saw the Walker plot, Stoke recalled why the cemetery looked familiar. He had been here many years ago when his great-grandmother was buried.

Harley and Stoke went on to Harley's house, where Harley dug out paper after paper about the family. Stoke recalled his shoebox of materials and the old family Bible. Harley warned him about people's habit of sticking papers in the leaves of the Bible. He thought it might be full of treasures. Over a meal of soup and sandwiches Stoke promised to let him have copies if he found any.

When it was time to go back to Newport Beach, Stoke warmly thanked his host, who, it turned out, was a widower. He had been careful not to mention the eye-patch. But as he left, Harley said, "I've just had a cornea transplant and it's getting better. So the next time I see you, I won't have this thing on my face!"

It was with a great deal of sadness that Stoke said his farewells and headed back to Louisville for his plane.

John Wayne Airport in California. Stoke got out of the jet and took his luggage from the storage compartment. His pilot offered to do it, but Stoke told him he made too much money to be handling luggage. Almost immediately, his driver met him at the gate and they drove the few miles to Stoke's penthouse in nearby Newport.

Stoke used the car's phone to call several of his managers to discuss current business events. He was beginning to bring his mental focus to business once more.

When he got home, he called downstairs to Elizabeth and Marilee. There was no answer. There was no answering machine, either. Stoke looked through the mail that had been piling up for days. In it was an envelope from Elizabeth Cho. Hurriedly, he opened it. A plain sheet of paper contained a few handwritten lines. It said:

Dear Stoke,

It hurts to tell you that my brothers have found a husband for me. I could not dishonor them by refusing this nice man who will be a good father for Marilee. By the time you read this, I will be in Hong Kong. I am going to visit the home of this man, and I will not be back for several months. I know you will miss Marilee and she spends her days crying, but it is for the best. I knew this was going to happen when I came to see you. It was a "last fling" or whatever you people call it. I had no idea I would be so attracted to you.

Love,
Elizabeth Cho.

He felt a great sense of loss, mostly for Marilee. He was so upset that he almost missed another important letter. It was from his public library. It said it had received microfilms of the *Levanger American Citizen* newspaper for the years 1855 and 1856. He didn't know whether to laugh or cry.

For the next few weeks Stoke managed to keep himself busy with new projects. Working hard to forget the Cho family, he occasionally had pangs of regret. He was very fond of Elizabeth, but his feeling for Marilee was much deeper. He missed her funny little face and her brash ways and her fearless attitude toward him.

He was deeply involved with a new corporate merger. He had called Ari several times but had not found her at home. It was just as well because Stoke was too busy to set a time for a visit to Washington, and he didn't know if Ari could come to California.

Then one day his answering service said it had a message from a Mrs. Stillman in Levanger, Missouri. The message was, "I want to reconsider your offer. Would you please call me?" Stoke thought a while, then realized who Mrs. Stillman was. Helen Wilson was her maiden name. She was the woman whose TV he fixed. He recalled that he had offered her a job in LA.

Stoke called the number in Levanger. A woman answered. He said, "Mrs. Stillman, please. This is Stokely Towles in Los Angeles."

"Mr. Towles, this is Helen Stillman. Is your offer of an interview still open?"

Stoke thought about the soft southern voice and the tough-minded person behind it, and the two nice kids who had to put Pepsi on their plants the morning he was there. "Sure it is. What made you reconsider?"

"My husband is out of jail. He's tearin' up the place. I need to get out of here."

"I'm sorry to hear that. I'll have someone call you to arrange flight details. She will leave tickets for you at the counter of the airline. Are you coming out alone or are you bringing Herbert and Nancy?"

"I'll ask my cousin to keep the kids."

"That's good. Someone will pick you up at the Los Angeles International Airport when you arrive. Just look for a sign with your name on it as you get off the plane. Then she'll take you to a motel. I want you to call me when you get unpacked. Use the same telephone number you used earlier. My company will pick up the costs of the motel. The driver will hand you some expense money for incidentals. Please sign for it and keep receipts. Do you need any money before you leave?"

"No, thank you. That's more than I expected. Will I see you-all when I get to California, Mr. Towles?"

"Yes, I'm looking forward to taking you to dinner, so I can prepare you for the meetings you'll have with my people. They can be tough."

"That's wonderful, Mr. Towles. How can I thank you?"

"People in my organizations work like hell. You'll be able to repay me several times over in the first year if you get hired."

Chapter Eleven

FOR SALE

TWO valuable Negro girls, one thirteen and one
eleven years old are offered for sale by the undersigned.
T.H. ALLEN
my28tf

Busy preparing for a meeting with his Japanese bankers, Stoke's phone rang in his private office.

"Shoot!" he said into the telephone.

"Bang!" came the response. It was the receptionist and telephone operator.

"Hi, Marcie. What can I do for you?"

"You have a call from Mrs. Stillman on line eight. I hate to bother you, but you said to put her through if she called."

"Thanks, Marcie. Put her on."

There was a click followed by a nervous voice. "Mr. Towles?"

"That you, Helen?"

"Yes, you said to call you when I was unpacked."

"Great! Does that mean you're ready for dinner tonight?"

"I'll look at my social calendar, Mr. Towles, but I think that time is available. When do you want to go?"

"Well, it's five now. What about seven? I'll pick you up at your hotel."

"That would be fine. I'll look for you then."

"Helen, give me your room number and I'll call when I get there."

"It's 304. And thank you."

"That's all right, 304. See you at seven."

"My name is Helen, not 304."

"Bully for you, Helen. My name is Stoke, not Mr. Towles." He hung up the phone and went back to work on his financial plan.

At seven on the nose. Stoke arrived in his new Jaguar at Helen's hotel in Glendale. She had landed at Burbank Airport to be near one of Stoke's companies for her interviews. He called Helen from the lobby and told her he had arrived. As fast as it took to find the elevator, Helen rushed down so she wouldn't keep him waiting.

"Welcome to California," Stoke said as he held out a hand. Startled, Helen shook hands with him and managed a smile. She was very nervous.

Stoke sensed Helen's concern so he told her, "This is going to be a fun night for conversation and good food. I hope you're up to it."

"I hope you realize that I'm not dressed for California styles, just being a Missouri country girl."

"Now, don't worry about what you're wearing. We might be able to find a place in California that's dressy enough to accommodate us."

Helen was wearing a silky white blouse that had a slightly open collar. Her skirt was long and dark. A purse was hanging from her shoulder. She looked as if she had come out of an office to have a beer with her fellow employees. Stoke noticed that she had lost some weight. She was even more attractive than when he first saw her.

"First, Helen, how long has it been since you have eaten, and second, what kind of food do you like?"

"First, I ate on the plane six hours ago, and second, I don't do soul food, but I eat just about everything else."

Stoke liked her no-nonsense attitude.

"I know just the place," he said, "if you like Italian food."

"I like Italian food, but I don't know all the names."

They went out to the Jag. He helped her in. As they drove toward Pasadena, Stoke tried to draw her out with conversation to put her at ease.

"How do you like the hotel?"

"I've never been in such a nice place. I thought that since I was black, they might give me some hassle, but they didn't even look twice at me. I don't think they even looked once."

"I'm sure the men looked. But don't worry, my company is a big account for them. If we ask them to house a guest, they damn well better not give her any problems," he replied.

"I'm not so sure everybody feels that way," Helen said. She was taking in the palm trees and the buildings. Then she looked at the oddly colored lines down the large street. "Speaking of color, what are those funny looking lines for?"

Stoke said, "Those guide the floats on New Year's Day. This is the path they follow for the Rose Parade."

"Is it really here?" Helen said excitedly.

"Yep, and we're about at our restaurant." They went on down to Carmine's in nearby South Pasadena. They turned left from Fair Oaks and drove into a cul-de-sac. A young Hispanic man on each side of the car opened the doors. Stoke handed his key to the one on his side and said, "Gracias."

The man got in and drove the car away. Stoke took Helen by the arm and guided her through large iron gates to where there was an outside eating area.

He asked if Helen were agreeable to eating outside, which she was. The tables were mostly full of noisy people. Trees surrounded the tables and birds were happily cleaning up after everybody. Their table was not ready, so Stoke took Helen into the bar area to wait. As they sat down Stoke asked, "How do you like your Bourbon?"

"I don't," said Helen.

"I don't drink much of the stuff, either, so what will you have?"

"I've never tried Chardonnay. You know, that pale wine that skinny white women drink in TV commercials."

"It's kind of sour, so be prepared."

"I'd like to try it anyway."

Stoke ordered a bottle of the wine from a cute waitress.

Helen looked at him. "How come we're eating outside?"

"I like it outside. Would you rather move in?"

"You have friends here?" she asked.

"Oh, yeah, I know a few people, I guess. Why do you ask?"

"Well, it's one thing to eat with black people where no one knows you. But it's another thing to be with them where you might run into friends."

"None of my friends would be friends for long if they were that idiotic."

The wine came and they both tried it. Stoke watched to see if Helen's face reflected the dryness of the wine. It didn't.

Stoke saw what she was getting at. "Look, you aren't a criminal and you aren't so young that people will think I'm robbing a cradle, so I don't care. And most people around here don't care whom you eat with. We couldn't start a trend if we wanted to!"

"That's good to hear," she said, but not quite believing it.

"I think you had better know something about me and my company. I'm not concerned about race. I don't wear a phony ribbon on my lapel so people will know 'I care.' I asked you to come out here, partly because you impressed me, and partly because I want Nancy and Herbert to have a chance in life. They're great kids. I don't need another black female on my payroll to meet quotas. I have plenty of women and minorities on the payroll as it is."

"I'm sorry," she said in a small voice. "I guess my chip shows."

"That's all right. We needed to get that eight hundred pound gorilla out of the way. When you talk to my staff tomorrow, you'll see what I mean. Look, Helen, I know you're suspicious and you think I might take advantage of you because you're in a tight situation. And I will do just that; I will take advantage of you in a professional way if you come to work for us. But you'll love it or you'll fly back to Missouri. I already ordered an open return ticket you can use at any time."

Helen nodded and said nothing for a few minutes.

"Now I hope you're still hungry because the waiter is coming over here to show us to our table."

They sat down at a small table near the outside rail. It was getting dark and stars were beginning to show through the trees. Stoke said, "How did you like the Chardonnay?"

"You were right. It was sour. But I liked it."

"Will it make you be like the skinny women in the TV commercials?" he asked.

"I hope not. Who wants to look like a skinny white woman?"

"Not me, that's for sure," Stoke assured her. Then he explained the names of some of the dishes.

They gave the waiter their orders. Then after searching the wine list he suggested Chianti with dinner.

While they were waiting for a salad, Helen asked, "What is it I'm interviewing for?"

"There's an opening in customer service. Those are the people who deal directly with customers, usually on the telephone. Training for the job starts in the factory, though, working with the people who make up and ship out orders."

"What do you ship?" asked Helen, afraid she would have to move big boxes around.

"This company makes lenses for human eyes. People have them surgically implanted when their own lenses are damaged or when they have cataracts on them."

"Who is the customer?"

"That's a good question. A surgeon designs what he wants. He tells us how to grind the lens so it fits a person's eye perfectly. *He* actually makes the order. But patients have to use the lenses. A person might get one or two implanted. Usually they get one at a time and we must deliver them on time with perfect quality."

"But I can't talk to doctors about *lenses*. I don't know anything about them!" Helen was beginning to be afraid.

"I can't talk to them either on that subject. But if I wanted to take the training, I would be able to. It's a very narrow field, and from our viewpoint, not so tough to learn. Anyway, doctors usually send us forms with exact details on them, so don't worry about having to discuss diopters with them, whatever they are. Your first concern should be those people who are going to interview you."

"Aren't you interviewing me?"

"I'm doing what is called 'screening.' You just got a favorable review. But the next test is tougher. I don't force someone on any of my companies. They get to decide who it is they'll work with."

"Aren't you the boss? If you say, 'Hire Helen,' don't they have to do it?"

"In most companies that's the case. But in my companies a lot of people get to interview you, starting with the president. She's smart.

She'll send you to the people you'll work with. They get a vote, too. She makes sure the people who'll work with you can really get along with you and can get the best out of you. She abides by their hiring and firing decisions almost entirely."

"She?"

"Yes, the president is Marissa Rodriguez. Thirty years ago she was a shoeless girl in a border town in Mexico. Now she's a company president. She is a strong, smart person, and very tough. But her people have enormous confidence in her. She always wins."

"How long have you known her?"

"She was a clerk in a personnel office where I was doing some consulting, years ago. I noticed her and kept current on her activities until I needed her. She's been with us five years."

"I don't know if I can work for a woman."

"Your immediate boss may not be a woman. But you need to be more concerned about how well you work with all kinds of people, not just the ones you're used to. We have all kinds in this company."

"I've only had problems with white folks, mostly men. But what if they don't like me? Do I go back to Levanger?"

"Not necessarily. I have several other companies. You'll probably fit into one of them. But this group is the most experienced. I want you to train in it, so I can use you later in other companies." Stoke let that comment sink in. Then he added, "At no time am I making promises. I'm only talking about hopes for the future."

"What do you mean about using me in other companies?"

"I buy companies from time to time. When I do, I want *my* people in place right away. That means I take people who understand my way of doing things and who are successful in their present jobs. I ask them to reorganize the new company. They set it up and get it running our way. There is a core group of proud, experienced people in each of my companies. I won't tell you who they are, but if you come with us and succeed, you'll find out."

"Do I spy for you where I work?"

"Absolutely not. I don't spy. My people are free to yell at me any time they want. That way, I usually know what's going on in each company. I make myself available at each location every month just to talk with them. So far, I've had to go to them, rather than wait for them to come to me."

"Doesn't this bother the managers?"

"It took some time for them to get used to it. We put in a formal procedure so lower level people could register complaints to other levels and me. But people seldom use it. It's easier to catch me going by a work station where they can ask questions."

"Do I have to join a union and pay dues?"

"We don't have unions. If the people want one, that's their decision. But so far, they haven't wanted one. Nobody has asked for one since the companies were started. It's probably the pay system that keeps their minds on other things."

"That's great. Do you make us all rich?"

"I don't make anyone rich. If you make a lot of money it's because of *your* efforts, not mine. We have a profit-sharing system that's partly based on how long you've been with the company, and partly based on your contribution in the previous year. The company administers the time portion, but your fellow workers get a voice in deciding how much you contributed. That way, you can't make out by playing up to the boss. In fact, you'll probably lose money if you smile too often. People in my companies go around with worried looks. They're concerned about letting each other down."

"I want this job. What do I have to do to get it?"

"Well, you can begin by enjoying your dinner and getting a good night's sleep. You'll need it, since my people love to find my mistakes. They're going to put you through a wringer tomorrow. Of course, they seldom are able to prove me wrong. That's something in your favor."

Chapter Twelve

ASSIGNEE'S NOTICE

The undersigned, Assignee of the lands, tenements, chattels and effects of Frederick Myers, will on the 10th day of November A.D. 1856, at the law office of Sawyer and Sharp, in the city of Levanger, in Crittenden County, Missouri, proceed publicly to adjust and allow demands against the estate and effects of said Myers, when and where all creditors of said Myers, and others interested, can attend.

jy9tf   W. SHIELDS, Assignee

At home the next night, Stoke answered his phone.

"Yes?"

The voice on the other end said without introduction, "That person you sent us yesterday. . ."

"Helen. What about her?"

"We want her. Please don't send Helen to the competition." The caller was referring to another of Stoke's businesses.

"You get first choice. Did she handle herself well? She was nervous as hell when I brought her out here. And then when she figured out she wasn't going to be the only minority, she really got flustered."

"She was uptight, but she kept her dignity. All votes were favorable."

Stoke said with irony, "Good. You guys better agree with me if you want to keep the boss happy."

"Screw you, chief, sir. Just don't forget that it's the productive employee's right to tell the boss to go crap in his hat."

163

"Thank you for that reminder. And keep me informed about Helen's progress. I want her back in college next year. Do whatever you need to move her out here and get her located near your plant. She has two great kids. I'd like to see them in good schools."

"Right, Stoke, and thanks for sending her to us. How did you find her?"

"I was checking on an old murder in Missouri when I got into trouble and she helped me out. Seems she was in trouble, too."

"I see. I hope you understand that you really don't have to mess up your hat if you don't want to."

"Fair enough, Marissa. Thanks for the call. And I don't own a hat."

While Stoke still had his phone in hand, he screwed up his courage and called Washington, DC, to see if Ari were still up. It was midnight in Washington. The phone rang several times, and then a sleepy voice said, "Hello?"

"Oh, oh. Did I wake you up?"

"Yes, but since it's you, Fred, I guess I don't mind."

"Fred? Who's Fred?"

"Gotcha, Stokely Towles! I haven't the faintest idea who Fred is. But *I* want to know who 'Marilee' is."

Stoke suddenly realized why Ari was irritated with him on their last night in Levanger.

"How did you find out about Marilee?" Stoke asked incredulously.

"You left a rather touching note to her in my papers."

"So that's what happened to my note! You might as well know the rest. Marilee is my dream girl. But I didn't want you to find out about her just yet."

"The note sounded as if you were serious about her, Stoke. Is she Chinese? I noticed her name was Cho."

"Yes, and my heart is broken because she's gone back to Hong Kong and I'm afraid I'll never see her again."

"How serious are you about Marilee Cho?"

"I'm very serious about her and I miss her a lot."

"But are you through with her?" Ari said with some concern in her voice.

"Never! And I hope to see her again before she grows up."

"Grows up? How old is Marilee?"

"She's about nine and a half, maybe three-quarters. She lived downstairs. When I broke my leg, she would come up and help me get around the apartment."

"Oh, I thought she was a current girlfriend! I never asked you about that, just assumed you were free to date. Are you?"

"Am I what?"

"Free to date, silly!"

"Are you?"

"You know damn well I am. Washington is so full of available females that most of us don't get a chance."

"Look, Ari, I miss you and I never want to argue about the private and government sectors again. You're much more important to me that a winning argument about economics."

"Hey, what do you mean by 'winning'? You lost the argument as I recall!"

"Yes, that's right. I'll concede that point. Let's not talk about it, shall we? No one can really win if we can't be together. So when can we get together?"

"The government you make fun of, through its great largesse, is donating a couple of days to certain employees around Labor Day. I'm one of those it can do without for two days plus the weekend."

"Great! Do we have a truce?"

"Houston, we have declared a truce," she said.

"What if I pick you up at Reagan Airport and take you with me back to Missouri?"

"I'd love it!"

"What about 'government people accepting gifts of value from the general public?'"

"Oh, Stoke, I just said that because I wasn't sure what I wanted to do about you. But I've had time to think about how dull it is in Washington and I've decided to hitch a ride or two before I die."

"You made a wise choice, young lady. Look for me on Friday night. We'll zip into Levanger so we can have four days to investigate all sorts of things. I'll reserve your 'usual' room at the motel. Will that be all right with you?"

"That would be great! But don't forget that libraries will be closed. We'll have to do our literary research on Tuesday, before our vacation is over."

"We'll think of *something* to do until Tuesday."

"I'm sure we will. Before you go, Stoke, what happened to Helen Stillman and those two nice kids?"

"It's funny you mentioned them. I just had a conversation about them a minute ago. What made you ask?"

"Helen called last week and said she was having trouble with her ex-husband. She wanted to call you but was afraid. I told her you would be fair and probably would give her a chance."

"I think we just hired Helen. She's here now and will be moving the kids out here soon. My people liked her."

"You really are a good guy, Stoke."

"Hey, if she doesn't produce, I'll fire her butt back to Missouri."

"I'm sorry. I'll never call you a good guy again!"

"See that you don't. It's very embarrassing."

It wasn't long until Labor Day. Stoke figured there was enough time to close out most of his current business deals so he, too, could take a vacation. In the meantime he would be able to spend some time on microfilms of the 1856 newspapers from Levanger, Missouri.

The dreams had tapered off. Stoke's business deals seemed to have crowded them out. He hadn't focused his attention on the data he had gathered, so he wasn't thinking about Henry. Perhaps that was the reason the dreams went away. At least he hoped the dreams had gone away.

Although Stoke would never admit it to anyone, the dreams were unnerving. It wasn't because they were repetitive; it was because the dreams were so vivid. It was as if they were underlined in his memory. He wanted to know more about the mystery of the death of Henry, but he didn't care to use that particular method. Paper and printer's ink would have been fine with him. They were not quite so dramatic and involving.

He called his secretary and asked her to rent two microfilm readers and have them delivered to his office. He planned to take them home that night and borrow his friend, Frank Kendall, so both of them could look through the papers for clues about the murder. He thought that the murder didn't necessarily happen in isolation, that there might be activities that led up to it. There had been only one microfilm, so Stoke had it copied the week before. He had to return the original but he could keep his copy. His secretary was used to such odd requests and had several sources that might be able to help. Sure enough, two readers were delivered to the office at 4:59 that evening.

Frank came to dinner. If he cooked the meal, or if they ate at a restaurant, most of the evening would be gone. Frank picked up a simple meal and brought it with him, so they could eat and work at the same time. Then they realized that wasn't such a good idea because they might get food on the microfilms, so instead they planned their approaches while they ate. Frank was to look at the advertisements while Stoke was to look at the articles. They would work through the period of six months before the murder to six months after the murder.

They went to work. Stoke gave Frank a list of names of people he might be interested in. These he had collected during his stay in Levanger while going through the library and other papers. He didn't want to say he had dreamed some of them up, but that's what happened. The names were Woodson, Limrick, Lightner, Noble, Myers and Veitch; these were the people who had some contact with Vallandingham. Frank and Stoke agreed that as they found something that might be helpful, they would note the date and the general contents of the items. and the number on the counter of the reader. Later they would get the item photocopied.

The first item Stoke found was the viewpoint of the editor of the *American-Citizen* newspaper, William Musgrove. He called his enterprise, a "Native American Newspaper." First issued on September 4, 1855, its aim was to present the *pro-slavery* position of the South from the standpoint of white people, born in America. There were one thousand subscribers *in advance* of publication, which gives an idea of the popularity of such a position in such a small town (and the unpopularity of any opposed to slavery). The same edition reported there were only 3,000 people in the town. The editor seemed to feel that not only was the South being out-voted, it was also being out-shouted. He desired to bring balance to the slavery question. Stoke noted his find and said to himself, *Maybe Henry was on the wrong side of the slavery question. Maybe some of the terrible things he was known to have done had to do with slavery.*

Some of the articles had to do with the Kansas Territory becoming a slave state. If that happened there would be two senators and several congressmen in Washington who would vote with Missouri and the South. Such an event would even up some of the balance of power in the federal government. To lose Kansas was unthinkable—it would start a chain of events in which one Southern state after another would lose its right to maintain slavery as it saw fit. Slavery, as a long-accepted, Constitutional institution, would be lost to pressure from the northeastern elites.

Later, Stoke found the Missouri laws governing slavery that were being imposed on the territory of Kansas. These included prison terms for even discussing the freeing of slaves and the death penalty for actually freeing slaves or helping free them. He was finding that much of the paper was devoted to these kinds of issues. Then he found the first story about the killing of slavery owners by a man named John Brown. Brown had hacked the men to death with his sword.

Eight Men Brutally Murdered by the Abolitionists

The following letter was received by a messenger from Franklin Co., K.T., this morning that was written by the Commissioner of Franklin County. Eight men were known to be killed –three by the name of Doyle, three by the name of Sherman, a Mr. Whiteman and a Mr. Wilkerson. The messenger who brought the information to Franklin states that he had seen the party who were murdered—they were cut to pieces and horribly mangled. For every southern man thus butchered, a decade of these poltroons should bite the dust.

The gentlemen in the vicinity of these outrages were of the opinion that Governor Shannon was at the Shawnee Mission, and the letter containing the intelligence was sent by the sons of Mr. Wm. Muir of this county. They arrived at the residence of their father early this morning. The letter has been forwarded to Governor Shannon.

Eventually, Stoke came across the death of Henry. He knew that story well enough. In the next week's issue, he found a curious story. It was about a meeting of anti-slavery people known as "Free-Soilers" that was to be held. But no one went. The author of the article seemed to be chuckling about the failure of people to attend.

Great "Freedom" Excitement in Levanger

A meeting to devise measures for furnishing "material aid for bleeding Kansas" (or, in other words, to raise the "needful" for an Abolition electioneering fraud, under false pretenses) was held at Levanger on Monday evening, Rev. Charles Hudson presiding. It had been called by notice given from the pulpits of various churches on the Sunday previous... At the appointed hour, nobody was present... unless the Rev. Mr. Hudson bestirs himself, and poneys over two or three hundred dollars to start a subscription paper, his chances for a Black Republican Gubernatorial nomination will be but slim.

Then it hit Stoke: *If Henry's very public murder were a warning, no wonder people stayed away from the next Free-Soiler meeting!* Now he began in earnest to read his findings in terms of Henry as a leader in the anti-slavery movement. Killing a follower wouldn't have made as much of a statement. Perhaps, the crimes he was accused of were crimes of complicity in the freeing of slaves. Henry may have been a Free-Soiler in an adamantly pro-slavery area. Then maybe the charge of adultery was drummed up. That's what some people had suggested to Stoke in Levanger! The adultery charge was to explain to a jury that Henry was a bad guy and deserved death. Perhaps they couldn't prove the freeing-slaves charge at all, but they knew he was part of it. They knew if they could kill Henry and frighten the others who were with him, they could quiet the opposition to slavery in that area of the State.

"Frank, what're you finding?"

"You'd be amazed. I found those names you gave me all right and more. The same folks seemed to control the power base of Levanger. I mean, there was a Crittenden Emigration Society, which consisted of William Shields and Dan. A. Veitch, among others. They were dedicated to helping settlers get set up in Kansas as long as those settlers were favorable to slavery."

"You mean those men were in an organization *together*?" Stoke asked with some surprise. "Well, I guess that's not so unusual since Veitch was the Justice of the Peace who released Fred Meyers, Henry's killer; and Shields was the sales agent for Meyer's goods.

"Yes, and look here," Kendall added, "each advertisement has a code at the bottom which tells when the ad was placed. We might be able to determine something from it. Here's an ad, which puts up for sale all the worldly goods of Frederick Myers, the man who shot Vallandingham. The agent is W. Shields of the Emigration Society. The date on the ad is July 9, 1856. When was Henry murdered?"

Stoke thought a minute and said, "July 18, 1856."

"There you have it," Kendall said. "Myers puts up for sale all his possessions and nine days later he kills Henry, *knowing* he's going to leave the area for good!"

Stoke added, "The news article about the murder says Myers was to wait around until a circuit court could have a hearing. It looks like everyone knew that Myers was leaving town permanently." Then he added, "Wait a minute, I found something about the circuit court and its cases in September with a Judge Hicks presiding… there it is. Lots of cases, but Myers isn't mentioned. I guess he got out of town and there was no case against him. I bet that when Vietch, the Justice of the Peace, let Myers go to wait for the higher court, he knew Myers would not return even then. It's beginning to look like there was some kind of plot by these men to pay Myers off and get rid of him. I wonder if he lived to actually go somewhere else?"

Frank commented, "Probably they could justify killing Vallandingham if he were guilty of some bad crime and should be hanged anyway. Kind of the way vigilante mobs work, isn't it?"

"Yes, but there's one more thing," Stoke said thoughtfully. "There's a line in the article about how people looked at the murder. It said, 'public sentiment is so much divided' over something to do with the shooting of Henry. Now what could divide public sentiment that way?"

"Maybe some folks thought that killing was too severe for fooling around with a guy's wife," Frank said.

"Or it may be that people knew Henry was involved in the freedom movement and they didn't want someone on their side getting killed over it," Stoke theorized. "I really doubt that public sentiment was strongly for adultery."

Then Frank showed Stoke an ad that would have been in a "personal" section if the paper had one. "Stoke, look at this!" He held out an ad that said:

Independence, Dec. 6 — 8 P.M.

To W. Shields – Limrick and Lightner are here from Lawrence, where they slept night before last.

Six hundred Abolitionists in arms there – one thousand men at Jones' camp. All a mistake about the Governor receiving orders for troops. The matter expected to be settled tomorrow or the next day. Tell the volunteers to come on.

S. H. Woodson

"Well, I'll be... Frank, remember how Limrick and Lightner were involved with Henry Vallandingham's mortgage? Do you suppose they were spying on the Abolitionists? A lot of people were killed in Lawrence, Kansas, over the slavery issue. This date is just before the famous raid on Lawrence."

"Well, they were businessmen. That would be a good excuse to go visiting towns such as Lawrence. It's a nice cover. But why put such an ad in the paper? Why not just send a private message?"

Stoke said, "The message wasn't really for W. Shields. It was for everyone who read the paper. It was a call to arms!"

Both men were quiet for a minute, thinking about the call to invade Lawrence, Kansas. It was a historic message.

Then Stoke asked, "Did you find out anything about Shields?"

"Sure, he was a merchant in Levanger. He had lots of ads in the newspaper. Here's one:"

THOS. W. SHIELDS ....St Louis
W. M. Shields .... Levanger

(Successors to YONTI & SHEILDS)

CO-PARTNERSHIP

The undersigned have this day formed a co-partnership, for the purpose of doing a general wholesale Boot and shoe business under the name and style of THOMAS W. SHIELDS & CO., at the stand formerly occupied by Yonti and Shields.
Nov 18, 1855

Later, Frank said, "Stoke look at this!" He was pointing to an ad that said two little girls, aged 10 and 11, were for sale. "Can you imagine two frightened little girls, wondering who was going to buy them and what was going to happen to them? I can understand why Henry would be against slavery!"

It was late and they were both tired, so Stoke and Frank decided to call it quits.

A faint noise startled them. Stoke and Frank looked at each other, not saying a word. It was at the front door. It happened again. Stoke walked quietly over to the door and peeked through the peephole. He saw nothing. He peered at the video screen positioned in his hallway. It showed nothing. He started to walk away. Then he heard it again.

Stoke motioned for Frank to come near the door. He opened a locked desk and pulled out a revolver. Handing the gun to Frank, he grasped the door and pulled as Frank leveled the weapon. In Frank's sights was a small girl.

"Marilee!" Stoke exclaimed in surprise. "What are you doing here?" He gathered her up into to his arms and carried her into the house. Frank shut the door behind them and sheepishly put the gun back into the desk.

"Oh, Stoke," Marilee sobbed, "something awful has happened! Momma left me with Uncle Zhao. Then he left and never came back!"

"How long have you been alone?" Stoke asked, trying to quiet her down with hugs and pats.

"He went out two days ago," she sobbed, "and I've been in his house alone. I walked all the way here."

"Have you had anything to eat?" Frank asked, knowing that would be his problem if he were left alone two days.

Marilee told him, "Not very much and I'm tired. What has happened to Uncle Zhao?"

"I haven't heard anything, Marilee. But maybe we can find out. Now calm down a bit and let's see about finding you something to eat."

Frank suggested, "Maybe Marilee would like to go to the bathroom, too."

She nodded and scampered off to "her" bathroom, the one she used when she ran the household. After about fifteen minutes she reappeared with a washed face and without all the sobbing that marked her entrance. She was still very subdued.

Frank and Stoke had rustled up an appetizing plate of food for Marilee, much more than two nine year-old girls could ever eat. There was a glass of milk for her, too. They watched, kind of hovered around her, as she gobbled down most of the food.

Marilee looked at the big men in her most winning way and said, "Could I have some ice cream, please?"

Without protest, Stoke filled up a bowl of vanilla for her and gave her a spoon. Marilee was able to forget her troubles for a time. It was about midnight, so Stoke gave her another of his tee shirts for a night-gown, turned on some night-lights and sent her off to bed. Frank decided he was tired as well and went home.

In the early hours of the morning, Stoke's research triggered another dream. He was in that state when a person is beginning to come out of a deep sleep. He seemed to recall those dreams best.

Stoke was Levanger, Missouri. Shadows were short. It seemed to be about noon. There were people in the background, but he was focused on a pleasant looking, middle-aged man walking up the street toward him. A man stepped out from behind a tree in the path of the first man. His hand was behind the tree and his back was toward Stoke. The hand, which was out of the first man's sight, was holding a dou-ble-barreled shotgun. Stoke tried to yell a warning but no sound came from his throat.

The first man said, "Hello, Fred," and he smiled. Fred didn't say anything. He just brought the gun out in the open, leveled it at the first man and pulled the trigger. One barrel went off, and the first man was knocked backwards to the ground, his hands holding what was left of his stomach. Blood streamed out of the man onto the street. Fred looked on silently for a moment to see if another barrel were needed. He must have decided not, because he lowered the barrel of the shotgun as people began to approach. No one wanted to get too close because they were afraid of the man with the gun, so the man on the ground bled to death. It didn't take long.

The shooting startled women and children. Adults ran into stores, pulling their children with them to dodge bullets and to avoid being witnesses. The body lay still in the street, entirely safe from further harm. Citizens, however, were still in danger.

Quiet took over the scene. A breeze blew a few brown leaves from an oak tree toward the body. They came to rest against the dead man's leg. A large brown shorthaired dog, frightened by the noise, celebrated the silence by coming out from under a porch at a nearby house. He went to the tree and lifted his leg, but he kept his eyes on the body. Carefully he walked to the inert form. He sniffed a few times, shook his head as if to say he didn't know who it was, and wandered off to find more interesting things to do.

Chapter Thirteen

CRITTENDEN EMIGRATION SOCIETY

This Society is now fully organized and prepared to assist all deserving and necessitous persons wishing to settle Kansas and who are favorable to the establishment of slavery in that Territory. Assistance will be made either in money, stock, or provisions. The amount of aid and the mode of procedure to obtain the same will be made known on application to either of the following
MANAGERS:

William H. Russell,	**Edward Winsor**
Martin Slaughter,	William Shields
Geo. W. Baker,	O. Anderson

Nathan Corder,
MARTIN SLAUGHTER, Pres't.
Dan. A. Veitch, Sec'y. m7m3

Stoke got up and took a long, warm shower. Images from the dream lingered in every corner of his mind. He knew by now the story of Henry Vallandingham had become an obsession. But he was also becoming aware that the end of the story might be in sight. He wondered if the final chapter would bring him any relief.

Then he realized he was not alone in the house. He remembered that Marilee had shown up in the night. He had to notify someone in case her family was looking for her. He thought about it for a minute and then dialed a number from his coat pocket diary. It was after eight o'clock.

"Chief Manson," a voice said on the other end of the phone. He was chief of police for Newport and a friend of Stoke's.

"Stokely Towles, Armin."

"Oh, hi, Stoke. What's happening?"

"I need to report a missing person," Stoke told him.

"Well, I guess I can handle that. Occasionally the officers let me do a few things. Now who's missing and why're you telling me about it?"

"If I wanted a cop, I would have called one, Armin. I need advice."

"Okay, Stoke, I was afraid it wouldn't be easy. Now again, who's missing?"

"She's not missing, she's with me. I don't want the police spending hours looking for someone who's at my house," Stoke told him.

"A female managed to stray into your place? What's her name?"

"Marilee Cho. She's a nine year-old Chinese girl who came here last night at midnight. I let her stay over. She's the daughter of a neighbor. She helped me when I broke my leg. She and her mother lived one floor under me and they were up here several times in the past few months. Her mother was a widow and she went to Hong Kong when her family found a new husband for her. She left Marilee with her brother or her husband's brother. Something happened to the brother and Marilee was left alone for two days. She came here because she was hungry. And she needed to see someone who would help her."

"I'll call it in. Now, Stoke, do you know the uncle's name?"

"Marilee says 'Uncle Zhao'. That's all I know about him. I suspect he lives around here or Marilee would not have been able to find this place."

"So I'll ask around if there have been any problems concerning a man named Zhao. Where will you be later on today?"

"Marilee and I will be at my office. I'll ask one of the secretaries to take her to a store so she can buy some new clothes. She's beginning to smell a bit rank."

"I got lots of daughters, Stoke. A bath usually corrects that problem. I'll call you at your office if anything develops."

"Thanks, Armin. But you don't have to call. I know you have lots of other duties. One of your senior officers will be fine."

"Ho, ho, Towles. My people are far too busy pleasing the mayor to spend their time with you. I'll handle this personally. By the way, if Marilee doesn't get back to her family, I'll have to send over a social worker to make sure you're not abusing the child."

"I'm the one getting all the abuse, Armin. Who'll protect me?"

Armin chuckled and hung up the phone.

It was getting late. "Come on, madam," he called to Marilee. "It's time to get out of that bed. We have things to do."

"It's summer. What do we have to do today?" Marilee grumbled.

"I have to work. But we'll want to eat something first. I know a great restaurant that caters to us young people. You'll love it."

"I'll get something from the kitchen. Can't you just come to get me later?" Marilee grumped once again.

"'Fraid not. That was your problem before. Someone went off and left you behind. I can't let that happen again."

So Stoke and Marilee went out to breakfast and on to work at Stoke's office. It was late enough in the morning that Stoke was able to get one of the women to take a credit card and a willing Marilee to a nearby mall for clothes.

"Don't get Marilee what she wants. Get her what she *needs*," were Stoke's parting words. Of course, his aide was quite willing to spoil a "lost" little girl for a day and paid no attention to Stoke at all. She and Marilee happily headed for the nearest purveyor of young lady's garments.

It wasn't until much later that afternoon that Marilee showed up in Stoke's office, laden with many packages of socks, underwear, jeans, sneakers, sweaters, pajamas and even a coat. It was too much for a small girl to carry so Stoke had to help her.

And then the police chief called. He said there had been a killing and that a man named something like Zhao Cho was the victim. He didn't know if the killing were deliberate. Since no one claimed the body, it looked like Stoke was stuck with Marilee. In the meantime a detective had visited Zhao's business, where no one knew anything— in English *or* Mandarin. According to the "rules," a social worker would have to talk with Marilee and Stoke to see if the welfare department should take over Marilee's custody, or whether Stoke would be appointed temporary custodian.

Stoke said he would call his attorney who would call someone at State Welfare headquarters to take care of the matter or delay it for a couple of weeks until Marilee's mother got back. In the meantime Stoke would ask someone in the U. S. State Department to locate

Mrs. Cho, or whatever her new name was, so she could be told about her brother-in-law, and that Marilee was safe.

Stoke made his calls and wondered if he should tell Marilee about her uncle. He decided not. But he did ask about how she was to get in touch with her mother in case of trouble.

"Momma said to ask Uncle Zhao because he had the telephone numbers and addresses," Marilee said. So Stoke passed that information along to the police, hoping they could find the dead man's living quarters, and then could read Chinese characters when they did.

Then Stoke sat back with some of his and Frank's notes on the Missouri killing. He sipped his coffee and thought about the dream he had that morning. And he thought about the actions of the men who were so opposed to freedom that they would kill another man just to intimidate people. He realized that enough of those people could bring about a war, which is what they did.

The Civil War wasn't all about slavery. Some people in the South just didn't want a bunch of New England do-gooders telling them how to live. After all, there were people in the Northeast who also had people in bondage—their factory workers. They paid them just enough to subsist and worked them to death, including little boys and girls. Stoke thought about people's need to judge others, especially for what they were guilty of.

Stoke decided what he was going to do. He called his security director, Rodrigo Ramirez, on the phone. "Ay, Amigo! Are we still safe?"

"Yeah, Stoke. We're so safe it's dull as hell around here. How about stirrin' up something?"

"You got it, but not around here. Can you and Diego take a plane ride for me over the weekend?"

"You're the boss… "

"No, really, Rodrigo… if you're busy with your family, you don't have to go."

"What if I take my wife with me?"

"Yeah, you and Diego can both do that. Have you ever been to Missouri?"

"Yeah, chief, when I was in the Air Force a few years ago. Is that where we're going?"

"Not too far from Kansas City. I'll ask Marcie to get some tickets for you. She'll leave them at the ticket window."

"One more thing… "

"What's that?"

"When can we come back, señor?"

"Tuesday of next week. Can you handle that?"

"I guess so. What do we need?"

"Swimming trunks and a sharp eye. You're going to rent a car and keep an eye on my back. Use your regular tool kit. Oh, oh… I guess that means you'll have to use a company plane. You can't take a 'tool kit' on a commercial airline plane."

"Ah, some action! Who's out to get you?" Rodrigo asked.

"You still got a heavy tan?" Stoke evaded.

"Hey, I was born with this gorgeous coppery color!"

"Well, it may be the Ku Klux Klan. They aren't going to like you any more than they like me, so I guess you'll have to watch your own butt as well as mine."

"Mine's prettier," Rodrigo said.

"There's no explaining taste, is there?" Stoke replied, and then told Rodrigo what to expect and what materials he would need.

A few days later, Stoke asked Marilee if she would like to go flying around the country. "You bet!" she said, so Stoke explained that they would go to Washington, DC, to pick up someone, and then go to a place called Missouri for several days. He got out a map and showed her just where they would be. Marilee used a small suitcase of Stoke's to pack her new clothes and some of her games and books. Then they took off for Washington, DC.

Six hours after takeoff, they landed at Reagan Airport and taxied over to the general aviation docking area. Stoke got out to stretch his legs. He headed for Ari at the gate and the pilot taxied the plane to the gas pump for more fuel. Ari was waiting for them with a floral-patterned flight bag, one of the new kind with wheels.

Stoke hugged Ari and kissed her and then kissed her again. She smelled good, looked good, and felt warm and soft. Ari said, "What if I put my suitcase down and we do it again?"

"Oh, sorry. It's just that I've been locked up with a gentleman pilot and a young lady for six hours and crave the company of a grown female."

"Well, there's a lot of them here tonight. Which one do you want?"

"Oh... I'll take you," he said and took the suitcase out of her hand. They talked while they waited for the plane to get back. Then they climbed into the executive jet and sat back for the trip to Kansas City. Stoke introduced Ari to the pilot and helped her into her seat so she could get buckled in. Then he climbed in next to the pilot.

"Why don't you ride with me?" she asked.

"You're government property—-much too valuable to trust with only one pilot. So I'm going to be the co-pilot on this trip. It's safer this way."

"Well, I protest!"

"But I went to a lot of trouble to get you some company!" Stoke explained.

Ari turned around and saw Marilee, who had been hunkered down in her seat. "You must be the famous Marilee I've heard so much about," Ari said.

Marilee was suddenly shy and only grinned a bit. "Well, come up here and tell me what you've been doing," Ari said as Marilee edged forward into the seat next to her. A few minutes after take-off Stoke turned around and saw that Marilee and Ari were deep into conversation, as if they were old friends. He recalled how Ari and Helen Wilson became friends quickly, so he was not surprised.

It took only about four hours before the plane landed in Kansas City. Marilee entertained herself by lying on the floor and drawing some of her three-dimensional views of things. She was forced to stop for a few minutes to put on a seat belt during the landing. When they got out of the plane, Stoke's car and driver were waiting. Soon they were headed east on the way to the motel where Stoke and Ari had stayed before.

Ari and Stoke got connecting rooms with a small bed for Marilee in Ari's room. They had their luggage sent up while they went to the lounge. They relaxed with a round of Sprite in Marilee's honor. This was their first opportunity to talk face-to-face in several weeks. As they talked Stoke looked again at Ari to see if she were as pretty as he remembered. She was.

It was an hour later for Ari than for Stoke and she tried to hide her yawn. She said she hoped Stoke didn't think she was bored. He understood and suggested they turn in. Those were his words. He very carefully did not say "go to bed." He didn't know what Ari had in mind and he didn't want to pressure her.

Ari looked at him squarely and said, "Marilee and I will turn in. If I can't sleep, I may give you a call." Without another word, Ari got up and told Marilee that she would read her a story, since it was getting close to her bedtime.

Stoke signed the check for the drinks and went to his room and unpacked. In about twenty minutes he went out to the motel ice machine for a bucket of ice. Then he took the ice to his room and waited. He got a bottle of wine from the self-service bar in the room. It was a while before Ari decided that Marilee was really asleep. When she was sure, she opened the door between the rooms, dressed in a stylish blue robe and bare feet. Without a word, Stoke locked the door behind her. He smothered her face with kisses. Then he directed Ari to his table with its two chair. "Waitress, two glasses, please!"

Ari found two motel glasses in the bathroom while Stoke fought the cork out of the wine bottle. Then he put some ice cubes in each glass and poured wine over them. "It's okay. This is Sangria. You can't hurt it with ice," he told her. He held up his glass in a toasting position and said, "Here's to better times," and he thought about Sandy back in Newport.

Ari sipped her wine as they continued to catch up with each other. Stoke reached out to Ari, put a hand behind her head and pulled her to him for a deep, satisfying kiss. He was in no hurry and there was no reticence from Ari. They had a long weekend to get this kiss just right.

Soon he took Ari's glass and put it on the table. He pulled her from her chair into his lap. They hugged and kissed some more. Ari's robe fell open. Stoke was pleased to find she was wearing nothing underneath it. After Ari helped Stoke with his buttons, they found their way to the bed. It was not as big as a queen-sized bed, but on this night, it didn't matter. The two of them didn't take up much space.

Early in the morning Stoke became aware that he was not alone. He and Ari were wound up together, wrapped in each other's arms. He disentangled himself from her and stood to get rid of the numbness in his leg, which had peacefully gone off to sleep on its own, under the weight of Ari's leg.

He stared at her on the bed, her dark hair spread across the pillow looking very little like a cop. Rather, he thought she looked like a girl, very innocent and vulnerable in her sleep. He realized he loved her.

Ari slowly came awake and smiled. She called Stoke to the bed, then put her arms around him and said with a sneaky grin, "What shall we do today?"

"Well, when we get through here, I'd like to take you to a new picnic ground. Is that all right?"

"Oh, I might work up an appetite," she said. "Where are we going to get the food?"

"I had my friends gather some great Mexican goodies ahead of time. They'll leave them in our car."

"This is really great, Stoke! All this service and nothing we really have to do. I could get used to this. What if we made love in the middle of your picnic grounds? Would anybody care?"

"No. Only Marilee. And my people who are watching over us. They'd get a real kick out of it!"

"Rats! I forgot they would be that close. I guess we'll have to behave ourselves."

"There must be some way we can have fun with our clothes on, Ari."

Ari went back to her room to dress. Stoke put on some casual slacks and a short-sleeved shirt that had a muted crimson pattern and a soft silky finish. It was going to be a warm day. He called Diego and asked him to load up his car, then told him where they were going. Rodrigo and Diego and their wives had packed two lunches that day—one for Stoke's party and one for themselves.

At the car Stoke looked at Ari's outfit. She wore a white tee shirt with a softly rounded neck, flimsy tan short shorts, white socks and tennis shoes. Her black hair and tanned body looked great in contrast to the light clothes. Ari had put Marilee's hair into some kind of shape that cured its wildness. Marilee was also wearing shorts and a blue tee shirt with a design on it. Then he saw it wasn't a design but two words. In pink it said, "Pooh Bear."

He almost forgot to look around the area. When he did, he didn't see anyone watching them. He didn't see his two associates either. They were alone. So he put his arm behind Ari's back and kissed her. Ari was in a surrendering mood. Not to be outdone, Marilee moved closer. Stoke picked her up and planted a big wet one on her cheek.

When they got into the car, Ari said, "What was all that about?"

"Happiness over starting out on a nice day with two pretty girls. Also, I was stalling until my people got here."

"Dammit, Stoke! You could have left off the last part. See how far that gets you!"

"Yeah," echoed Marilee.

"Remember, young lady, I have the food. Be nice to me or you'll have to get out and walk—-before lunch is served."

"You drive a hard bargain."

"It's a 1999 Mercedes, I think."

"Sure, sure. Where are you taking me? I mean all of us."

"A little way out of Levanger on Route 13. On the left is a deserted house, once owned, I believe, by Henry and Armilda, my ancestors."

"How did you know that?"

"I'm an expert sleuth, young lady. I found it in the annals of the Levanger Library the last time we were here."

"Why do you want to see it?" Ari asked. "I thought your ancestors spent most of their time at the restaurant."

"I just want to take a close look. It might be the only time I ever get to see it."

They talked as they drove the two or so miles from Levanger. Before long, they pulled into a long gravel drive in front of a big old derelict that was once a rather fancy home for a big family. It was made partly of wood siding and partly of thick brick walls. The door was not open yet, so Stoke took Ari around to see what the yard was like. Hemp grew everywhere, like the weed it is. At least Stoke thought it was probably hemp and not high-grade pot. They continued to look around until Stoke found a shady spot under a walnut tree.

He put the basket down and began taking things out. "Is this place all right with you? I'd hate to see you girls leave me for a better spot."

"Sure. Hand me the tablecloth so I can spread it out." While they were spreading out the cloth, Ari added, "Do you really feel close to your ancestors?"

"I don't know what I feel, but I'm not coming back this way again. So I want to get a sense of the place to take back with me."

They unpacked the food, which looked unfamiliar to Ari. Stoke saw her looking at it strangely. "That's homemade Mexican cuisine. When you get to meet my compadres, be sure to thank them for it."

"Only if I like it," Ari said, not convinced that it was at all edible.

With the food spread out within easy reach, Stoke stretched out on his back and put his head in Ari's lap. "Peel me a grape," he commanded her.

"Would you settle for a glass of lemonade in your face?"

"Remember, it would get your shorts wet. And then you might have to take them off, right in front of my friends."

Marilee giggled.

"Where *are* those tough guys anyway?"

Stoke pointed to slight movement a hundred yards away on a small hill. "They're out there where they can see the whole area."

"*We* could use people like that. How did they do that without our seeing them?"

"I saw them. You were busy with the salsa at the time."

Taking turns feeding each other and laughing and generally cutting up, Stoke and Ari and Marilee ate almost all the food. Of course, ants were having a field day with the crumbs and mess the people made. A chipmunk hungrily watched from a distance.

"See, I said you could have fun in the great outdoors, didn't I? And you didn't believe me!"

"Not so loud!" Ari whispered. "I don't want your friends to hear us."

"Such false modesty. They've moved on anyway. Let's see if they've opened the door."

Standing up and wiping away the crumbs from their clothes to the delight of the insect world, Stoke and Ari held hands as they mounted the front steps of the long porch. The door was slightly ajar. Marilee came up behind them. The chipmunk ran over to their tablecloth for a quick nibble, his tail up high.

They went in. The air was musty and dark and very still. Rooms were bare of furniture. Wallpaper was loose in spots and hung down in cob-webbed folds in several places. A metal pot with green ivy trailing in it was sitting on a shelf. Something about it didn't look right. Stoke kept trying to figure out what it was.

Ari interrupted his train of thought. "Your folks sure lived in a spooky old house."

"Think of it one hundred and forty years ago, with lots of colors and warm furniture and little kids running around. Toss in the smell of a country ham and you got yourself a really homey place."

"I thought you said Henry and Armilda had only one daughter, who lived in Kentucky."

"I did say that," Stoke said. "But I'm sure lots of other families lived here afterwards."

"You never fail to amaze me, Stokely Towles. I didn't know you were so romantic or so imaginative."

"That's the way I see it. Only in my dreams there was no ivy on that shelf."

As they turned to look at the ivy, its leaves quivered and moved in the breeze. There wasn't any breeze in the room. The hair on Ari's arm stood straight up.

"Did you see that?" she said with amazement in her voice. "The ivy moved."

"How did it make you feel?" Stoke asked her.

"It scared me, that's how."

"It made me feel warm and very much at ease. It's a good feeling and I'm not scared at all. I felt as if I'd met an old friend."

"Well, maybe not a friend as much as a member of the family, Stoke. Isn't it possible that Henry and his wife spent many hours in this very room? They must feel pretty good about you by this time."

"I don't know if they're here. I just recall a welcome feeling as if I belonged"

"But I don't belong, I really don't," Ari chimed in.

Once again he put his arms around her shoulders and drew her to his chest. It was that time-honored gesture that said, "I'll take care of you." She snuggled closely in his arms.

Just then a very loud crash sounded from the top of the steps in the hallway. Marilee screamed.

Ari, the tough cop, burrowed her way further into Stoke's chest. Marilee grabbed them both. "What was that?"

"I sure don't know. Maybe I'm not welcome after all!"

"Aren't you going up to see what it was?"

"Aren't you coming with me?" The house was still reverberating from the noise.

"You go, they're your people!" Ari told him.

Marilee added, "Uh, I'm not so sure we should go alone. Let's get your guys to go with us."

"Stoke, I'm not going up there!"

"Just kidding, Ari. I'll go."

"Can't we leave now?" she asked him plaintively. "I bet Diego and Rodrigo would have a hard time defending us in a situation like this."

"Yes, they would. Still, I feel welcome here. Hmm, I wonder what it is I'm supposed to do?"

Stoke took Ari outside. As they walked out the door, he looked once again at the ivy on the wall. But now it was old and dried up, looking as if it had not been green for many years.

Stoke said under his breath, "I guess that proves it wasn't plastic!"

"What wasn't plastic?" Ari asked anxiously.

"Oh, nothing, Ari."

Then Stoke went back in and slowly walked up the stairs where the noise had come from.

Chapter Fourteen

CITY LIVERY STABLE

I would respectfully inform the citizens of Levanger
and the traveling public Generally that I have opened a
Livery Stable
Immediately back of the City Hotel, where I will be
pleased to attend to any and all people who will favor
me with their patronage. In a few weeks I will have a
large lot of fine Horses, Carriages, and Buggies.

Apr23tf   F. BOULDEN

Ari and Marilee sat in the shade of an old oak tree in the front yard while Stoke was inside the old house. They watched the chipmunk and his immediate family, along with his cousins and assorted friends, as they cleaned up their picnic area. The two bodyguards were out of sight. After five minutes, Ari walked back toward the house, wanting to go in and help Stoke, but not really sure it was safe inside. She waited by the front door. After another ten minutes she heard footsteps. Stoke came out, shaking his head.

"What's the matter? Are you okay?" she asked with a lot of concern in her voice.

"Nothing's wrong. I'm just telling myself that I've never seen the place before. Yet it seems familiar. I'm sure I was in a room that was in my dreams."

"What made all the noise?" Ari asked. "Did you see anything?"

"No. A big door at the head of the stairs had slammed shut. Probably a breeze. I just opened it and looked in. There were some

built-in shelves and a window seat. I believe that's where my grandmother was when I dreamed about the note she was writing, the one
with the names on it."

"But you aren't sure?"

"Not completely. It just seemed the same. But I found this on the
floor."

Stoke showed Ari a yellowed piece of paper with elegant handwrit-
ing on it. It had the names of Woodson, Limrick, Lightner and Veitch.
Ari shivered. He put his arm around her as they went to pick up the
picnic basket. A chipmunk saw them coming and got out of the basket just in time.

"Who are those people on the note?" Ari asked.

"From what I read, those are the men who were in cahoots to kill
Henry Vallandingham as a warning to others, so they'd stop meddling
in the slavery business. I'll just file it with my other papers. Maybe I
ought to frame it."

"What do we do now?" Ari asked with quiver in her voice.

"Let's just take the scenic tour on our way back to the motel and get
our minds off this stuff for a while."

With Marilee in hand, they returned to the car. Marilee sensed
something had changed. She said nothing, hoping to pick up a clue
when the adults began talking again. Stoke quietly drove towards the
Missouri River. On the way he turned into a kind of park just off the
main highway.

"What's this?" Ari asked him.

"It's just a park I saw the last time I was here. I thought I might like
to take a closer look."

It was densely packed with deep green trees and flowering bushes
and occasional clumps of black raspberries, illustrating the theorem in
physics, "Nature abhors a vacuum." Every square inch of land was
covered with some kind of plant. They could barely see that beyond
the closest trees lay a small meadow.

"I can see what kept drawing people further west from Virginia,"
she said. "This place just takes my breath."

"I never told anybody this, but all I ever wanted to do as a boy was
take a rifle and roam through the forests. School, civilization and family weren't as important to me as my time alone in the woods."

"Why didn't you follow that dream?"

"Poison ivy. And chiggers. I had to settle for occasional camping trips with my Boy Scout troop. Even then I came home covered with bites and itches."

"Now that's too bad. But if you'd become a hermit, think of all the disappointed women. Marilee, what would you think if Stoke were a pioneer and lived in the forest all the time?"

Marilee thought a minute and said, "It would be okay, as long as he would let me go with him. And just think—no school!"

"You'd miss too much if there were no school for you, Marilee," said Stoke. Then turning to Ari, he said, "There's not that many women, Ari, if that's your question. I've been too busy building a corporation that amounts to something."

They roamed the woods, holding hands and looking at wildflowers. Then a car door slammed. Two rough-looking men walked up to Ari and Stoke. Marilee was off to one side, picking flowers. The men stood in front of the couple with their thumbs stuck in their belts. They just looked, saying nothing. Ari and Stoke had never seen them before. They looked like a hundred others in the area, wearing the ubiquitous tee shirts and blue jeans. The older one, in his forties, was almost bald and unshaven. He was of medium height and quite stocky. The other was a little younger and taller, with stringy blond hair and a wispy mustache. He hadn't stood very close to his razor, either.

"So what's your problem?" Stoke said, staring straight at the older man. He could see one problem right away. The man had a tic that caused his right eye to wink slightly at rapid intervals. The action greatly diminished his tough guy image.

"We know you got our message," Tic-eye said, " but you continue to haing around. You must be lookin' fer trouble, ain't ya?"

"No, I'm not looking for trouble. I'm just researching my family history."

"Yore fambly's a bunch of jackasses!" Tic-eye said with a laugh.

"Oh, so we're related?" Stoke asked. "Which cousin are you?"

"Ah'm the cousin what's gonna' show you some manners, son. But don't worry, since it's all in the fambly, ah won't tell anybody. Whar's them two funny-looking niggers that's been followin' you around?"

"Oh, I think they left for Florida," Stoke told him. He felt Marilee put her arm around his leg.

Ari looked startled. She stared at Stoke as if to say, "Tell me it isn't true!" They were alone in woods. These two men seemed determined to inflict some damage on them.

"Damn, you-all's real purty," the younger man said to Ari as he made a grab for her. She didn't have time to get the gun out of her purse, so she backhanded the man across the face with the purse instead. The meeting of gun and jaw was announced with a loud dull thump. The man sat down, stunned.

Stoke doubled up his fist, but then looked at Tic-eye and found he was staring into the business end of a .38 Smith and Wesson revolver. Ari stood still, not wanting to upset the hand that held the gun. Everybody was silent for a minute.

Then a quiet voice from behind the trees said in a heavy Spanish accent, "Señor, if you want to see the sun rise in the morning, lower your arm slowly and drop the gun to the ground easy."

"Who th' fuck is that?" Tic-eye said, and half turned to see Diego, who stepped out from behind a giant poplar. He was holding a 30-30 rifle, leveled right at the chest of the gun holder.

"Where the hell did you come from? Yore suppost to be in Florida," Tic-eye said.

"Mazatlan, señor. But if you don't believe me, mi amigo over there will vouch for me." He pointed over to the far side of the clearing where Rodrigo was standing with a similar rifle. Not content to just hold a rifle, Rodrigo had applied a fake, terrible looking scar on his cheek. He was wearing an eye patch for added drama. With his Australian bush hat, he resembled a bloodthirsty pirate of two hundred years ago. The ensemble got Tic-eye's attention right away. His pistol fell to the ground.

Picking up on the costumes and fake accents of his friends, Stoke said sternly, "It's a good thing you two decided to cooperate. My men have been known to scalp their victims. Maybe I can convince them to just to shoot you."

Tic-eye and his companion stared at each other in terror. Diego hauled a big knife from his boot and began to feel the sharpness of its very keen edge. He thought for a minute and said, "Hell, thees bandito ain't got much hair to cut off. Somebody already got to heem."

Diego looked at the other "bandito" and said, "I weel have more fun with thees one."

Stoke said, "Now wait a minute, Señor Bruce. I know I promised you could have some fun with these bullies, but maybe they can tell us something." It was dead quiet in the woods.

"On the other hand," Stoke said dismissively, "maybe we should go for a walk. You men be sure to clean up after yourselves. I'll get the shovels out of our car for you. Don't leave a mess like you did last time. And put them over there," he pointed to the edge of the clearing. I don't think the local park service would appreciate a messy campsite. They might fine us for littering."

"Wait a minute!" the younger man said. "Maybe we can work something out!"

"No," Stoke said. "These caballeros haven't had any fun since they got out of prison. They need something to do. If I keep them from operating on you, they might come after me."

"Hold it, dammit!" yelled Tic-eye. "You can kill us but ya cain't stop the others. They're gonna get ya fer sure if you touch us."

"What others?" Stoke said as Diego pulled got a whetstone and smoothed out a few imaginary rough places on the edge of his knife.

"We're in the Ku Klux Klan and they's lots of us. You touch either of us and you'll never see California agin."

"Oh, I see. But if we let you go, you'll be really nice to us, won't you?"

Tic-eye thought a moment. "You let us go and we'll leave you alone."

"Why were you following us?" Ari asked, sensing that the men were about as ready to talk as they would ever be.

"Uh, we jist wanted to scare ya away. We know that the big guy was writin' bad things about us and we was trying to discourage him. But we got nothin against the two funny lookin' niggers. They prob'ly cain't even write." Tic-eye was motioning at Diego and Rodrigo.

"There has to be more than bad publicity at stake here," Stoke told the men.

"Yeah, well, we got a business on the side," Tic-eye said as he kept his good eye on the knife in Diego's hand.

"Does this business involve a modified form of hemp?" Ari demanded of him.

"Well, we make a few bucks, I guess, by harvestin' and shippin' the stuff," Tic-eye said in a very small voice.

"Who's your leader?" Ari asked.

"Ah ain't sayin'" Tic-eye said.

"Señor, eet ees good to take somethin' to the grave with you. It'll make you think you got away weeth a secret," Diego whispered, slipping into a heavier Spanish accent than ever. As he spoke Diego leaned down and breathed a heavy dose of garlic into Tic-eye's face. He took a step toward Tic-eye, his knife directed toward the man's crotch.

"Short Indians scalp mean," Diego muttered.

Stoke turned to Ari and said quietly, "Did you ever see such a performance? I didn't think Diego had it in him. He's Academy Award material."

"All right! Our leader's Bill Vance. Now will-ya let us go?"

"Who told you that we might be a threat to the Klan's business?" Ari asked.

"Billy Vance. He was the kid behind the soda fountain at the drugstore when you first got here, and he overheard you-all a'talkin.'"

"Well, well," said Stoke, "even the soda fountain has ears. Okay, Señor Bruce. I got what I wanted. Do you think you can postpone your fun for a few days?"

"Aw, patron, we got to go back home today and we ain't even got a ear to show for eet. You promised us some fun, you know." Diego seemed frustrated as he spoke.

"Yes, everybody knows that 'funny looking niggers' have to have some fun, but let's let these guys go, and maybe they'll let us alone for the next few days."

"Well, eef you say so." With that, Diego told the men to give him their pants. Reluctantly, they loosened their belts and handed over their jeans. Rodrigo took the jeans back in the woods, somewhere known only to him, and stuffed them in a rotten tree trunk. Meanwhile Diego kept a rifle pointed in their direction. Then Diego and Rodrigo backed away from the two villains, keeping their guns pointing in their general direction while they got into their car. Ari and Stoke had already gone.

Tears ran down Stoke's face as he laughed at Diego's performance. "He should get an Oscar. Can you believe it? He spent four years in college and never once took a drama course."

Ari wasn't laughing. She looked very stern. "Stokely Towles, I was afraid your people were really gone! Those bullies might have hurt us! And won't Diego resent being called Señor Bruce?"

"I have absolute confidence in my people, Ari. It was just a game to me."

Marilee said, "I was scared!" Ari hugged her. Stoke realized that his two favorite women were against him. He decided to change his tactics.

"Are they really going to leave today? If so, I want some of my people for back-up," Ari told him hotly.

"I don't think we'll need your enforcers. My team is still on the job."

"Just a minute!" Ari said. "Those men must know Mexican people when they see them. Why do they call them 'funny looking niggers?'"

"I suspect it's like chicken. You know, all kinds of meat are described as being like chicken, except... To these guys, everyone who's not white is more or less like a nigger. I don't even like the word."

Ari commented, "I don't either. Now all that excitement made me thirsty, so can we go get a soft drink?"

"Yeah!" Marilee said. "And ice cream!"

Driving back over the road to Levanger, Stoke and Ari didn't talk a lot. Stoke turned on the car radio as the setting sun drew long shadows of tree trunks that fell across the road. Diego and Rodrigo and their wives followed along behind. Ari began to loosen up a bit and smile at the plight of the two Klansmen. But it took a while before she managed the task. They were in a drugstore, finishing off their drinks when Ari said, "What are you *really* going to do tomorrow?"

"Oh, I want to take some more pictures of the buildings and things in Levanger. As I said, a lot of people will be out of town at the fair somebody is having across the river in Ray County. They won't be in the way. I'd rather not have people and their modern clothes and automobiles in my pictures. If you need to look into your research, go ahead and take the car."

"No, I want to go with you. Our vacation is about over and I, uh, we won't have much time together for a while. Maybe I can make notes or something as you take some pictures."

"Don't you want any more information on Bill Simkins?"

"Maybe just some photographs," she said. "Tell you what. I'll give you the number of the exposure and you can, maybe, make a small sketch of where I stood with the camera when I pushed the button. It helps to have records like that."

"Marilee's the artist," Stoke told Ari.

"I suppose we should also keep track of the f-stop and shutter speed you used."

"Good idea," he said. "I like having you around."

"So does the government and they pay me more than you do."

"Don't forget the fringe benefits," he told her.

"Yes, there's that," she said smiling.

Afterwards they went to the local shopping mall and spent an hour just window-shopping. Ari pointed out clothing and lamps and shoes and tables that she liked as they went past the highly decorated windows. It appeared she was interested in good-looking clothes and modern furniture. Stoke groaned inside, wondering what she would think about his collection of antiques and reproductions of early American furniture.

Eventually, Stoke's leg became tired and he suggested they turn in early. Ari said she had to stay near her cell phone. "Perhaps you could help me listen for its ring," she suggested. Stoke figured that something could be worked out. Marilee was yawning as Ari tucked her in and read another chapter of *Harry Potter*.

Second nights together are sometimes more difficult than first nights, thought Stoke. People don't know how much they can take for granted. One slip and you might hurt the other person's feelings and find yourself on the couch. He was careful with Ari, but he didn't need to be. She was warm and cuddly and very friendly. Stoke managed a good response despite his sore leg.

In the morning Stoke stayed in his room, and Ari went to hers to wake Marilee and get them both dressed for breakfast and the start of a beautiful new day. Ari was bright and fresh and cheerful when they met at breakfast. She reached across the table and rubbed the back of Stoke's hand. Then she leaned over and kissed him.

"What did you do that for?" Stoke asked in surprise.

"Well, I did it in honor of a handsome gentleman at the start of a pretty day," she said, mimicking Stoke from the previous day. "And," she went on, "I was trying to wipe off my excess lipstick."

"Touché'" Stoke replied.

Marilee got her first taste of grits. Stoke could tell it was not going to be a hit with the average Chinese person. The expression on Marilee's face was a bit like that on the Chinese lions that guard gates. But after eating a very filling breakfast of bacon and eggs, juice and coffee, they loaded their car with cameras and food, in case the restaurant people also had gone to the fair.

As they arrived in the center of town, they saw they were about the only people around. Stoke parked on a side street so his car wouldn't be in any of the photographs. They walked to the courthouse. They took pictures of the building, its columns and a small hotel across the street. Ari took some pictures of Stoke and he took some of her and Marilee. Marilee took some of them. It was a reminder that their vacation time was running out. They would soon be three thousand miles apart.

Having taken all the photos they wanted on that block, they wandered around to the old jail, which was now a historical site, and to the sheriff's office. There was a sign on the front of the building that said the sheriff was out for the day and people should call the State Police if they had really big problems.

Then Stoke noticed the town wasn't really empty after all. He began to see one or two men standing on street corners, watching what he and Ari were doing. Stoke and Ari wandered to the next block and the men followed. Ari sensed trouble coming. She and Marilee went into a drugstore to get some candy for Marilee and to find a telephone, in case they needed to make a quick call, but a sign on the phone said, "out of order." Ari began to feel trapped.

Just then a farmer stepped up to her and said some people wanted to speak with them outside. Ari motioned to Stoke, who was standing outside on the corner. He came into the store with her. The farmer left by the back door.

"Stoke, they want you to meet them out in the street!" Ari was becoming agitated.

"Do they look like they have guns?" Stoke said this with a measured calm in his voice.

"The man in here didn't have a gun. The rest of them may have guns, but I just don't know. What are we going to do? My cell phone isn't working!"

"I have just the plan. You walk out there, show them your badge and arrest them for something."

"Get serious, Stoke. I can't arrest them. There are too many. Anyway, they haven't broken any Federal laws that I know of. Besides, they want to see *you*. So while you're out there getting your butt shot off, I'm going to work my way back to the car with Marilee and call the State Police with your car phone."

"What if they try to stop you?"

"They'll probably be watching you, not me. If anyone gets in my way, I can always flash my badge and tell him I'm on U.S. Government business. That and my .38 may let me get past them.

"Right! I believe I've been getting ready for this all my life. It's what the dreams have been telling me, but I didn't understand. I'm going to walk out of this building to the middle of the street in front of the courthouse. Then I'm going to stand right where I think Henry was killed. And I'm going to turn around and tell those bastards to get screwed."

"They'll kill you if you do that!" she snapped.

"Maybe. Maybe not. But I'm tired of dodging silly people. I think they're fools and cowards. Now let me out of here before I really get scared." He kissed her and whispered, "Maybe Diego and Rodrigo will bail us out again."

Relieved somewhat at the thought of Diego and Rodrigo, Ari opened the door, careful to stand behind it so the men couldn't see where she and Marilee were. She wanted to keep them guessing as much as possible. The gang seemed to be holding most of the cards, so there was no use in letting them know where the aces were. Marilee sensed the danger. She hid behind Ari.

Stoke walked out slowly. He kept his eyes on the men as he found his way to the spot where his ancestor was shot down, "one hundred and forty-five years before. Then he stopped. The men just stared at him. No one spoke for a minute.

"All right, boys, I'm here. Now what the hell do you want?"

Walking up to Stoke, the leader, a tall, well-muscled man in his thirties with a scar across his right cheek, paused for a minute. He spat tobacco juice at Stoke's toes and said, "Look, asshole, we done had enough trouble with you and yore lady friend. We tole you to get out and you didn't do it. You've messed with us long enough. It's time you had a lesson in so-sy-a-tel skills."

The leader opened his denim jacket. A revolver was tucked in his belt. He reached for it and drew it out very deliberately.

Stoke kept his eyes on the man's face. "You're in the Klan, aren't you?"

"So what if I am?"

Stoke continued, "Do you know that you're standing on very special ground?"

"What kind of shee-it you talkin' about?"

"This is a special place," Stoke told the man. One hundred and forty-five years ago, one of the slave promoters in Levanger shot my ancestor here. Blew his stomach away with a shotgun. He fell where I'm standing now. So you see, I'm standing on kind of hallowed ground."

"If that's true, what you just said, then yore standing on ground where history is gonna repeat itself. You've had it coming for a long time. We been watching you for some time and giving you gentle hints, but they didn't do no good." The leader looked around for support from his men. They were grinning and drawing closer. He held the gun out in front of him.

"Shouldn't I turn around so you can shoot me in the back?" Stoke asked sarcastically.

"No, it don't matter where the bullets come from, if they got yore name on 'em."

"Well," Stoke said, "go ahead and shoot. You talk a hell of a good game but cowards and bullies are slow to act. Which one are you?"

"Well, you *are* a silly son of a bee-itch," the man told Stoke. "Gather 'round men, so no one can see anything."

Stoke, still staring him in the eyes, said, "Cowards and bullies and fools! There's no difference between you and Hitler. Just remember, Adolf, there's always an end to a war. And then there's a trial."

The leader said, "'Nuff shee-it. Screw with us and you won't live long. Good bye, asshole!" With that he raised his pistol to Stoke's head and pointed it between Stoke's eyes. Several of his men closed their eyes and ducked their heads in anticipation of the gun going off.

Stoke calmly said, "There's one more thing. Look at the roof behind you. I have some friends up there."

The leader licked his lips. "Screw you!" he said.

"Bill, there's two guys with rifles up there!" one of then told the leader excitedly. It was Tic-eye.

"They're not going to wait until you pull the trigger, you know," Stoke told him. "They would have taken your gun sooner, but they were making high-quality videotapes of your performance as a tough guy. If you'll look closer, you'll see the long distance lenses and microphones. You might just get an academy award for your acting, but an 'R' rating for your choice of words."

"Shee-it!" the leader said. He had been lowering his gun while Stoke talked to him. He turned and looked up on the wooden building across from the courthouse. Sure enough, there were Rodrigo and Diego, holding rifles and sighting down the barrels. Then Diego put down his rifle and picked up a video camera to show the men.

Stoke said, "A pleasant good day to you, gentlemen. You would be well advised to conduct your business at midnight when it's more of a challenge to make a good video. I also suggest that you might consider wearing hoods or something over your faces while you're shooting people. Until then, I'll see you in court. And by the way—-you'll be interested in knowing that Ms Edwards is a representative of the United States Government and she'll make a very good witness against you. The court is in that building right there," he said as he pointed to the old courthouse. Without looking back Stoke turned on his heel and walked back to the drugstore.

Ari stood at the slightly opened door with her pistol in her hand. She stepped aside as Stoke threw the door open and walked in. He sat down quickly and wiped his forehead with a paper towel. "Whew!" he said. "I don't want to do that again!"

"Do what?" she asked. "What went on out there? Are they coming in to get us?"

Stoke laughed. "We got 'em pinned down. They aren't going to bother anyone for a while. It seems they hate publicity. I told them you were a witness, so please act as if you're taking notes." Then he told Ari about Diego and Rodrigo on the roof of the old hotel and the conversation he had with the leader.

"Stoke, that was a brave thing to do! What if your friends hadn't shown up?"

"Wasn't bravery. I just reached a point where I didn't care anymore. They weren't going to shoot; they just wanted to scare us. Anyway, that's an important piece of turf out there in the street. I could no more back down to those bullies than I could fly."

"Maybe your ghosts can rest now. You've taken care of some bad guys, even though they aren't the right ones."

Stoke said, "I suppose so." Then thinking about her job, he said, "Speaking of winning, did you get through to the State troopers?"

"They're on their way," Ari replied.

"Let's go out and talk to them first. The gang will be thinking of a hundred reasons why they were holding a pistol on me. I want to get my licks in before they start."

The men in the gang were milling around, waiting for the next shoe to drop. Then they saw a police car and began to fade into the background. But a few were still there when the police approached.

It took a long time to explain to the two State troopers just what was going on. They were a bit more inclined to go along with the local people than they were with Stoke and Ari. Then Ari showed them her ID with the Drug Enforcement Agency. The cops suddenly showed an interest in the video. When they saw it, they called for backups because they could not arrest eight men at once.

The police demanded Stoke's video and the guns that Diego and Rodrigo used. Diego had made a copy, so he surrendered the tape and two wooden replicas of rifles that looked like real 30-30's from a distance. The original video was headed for the local news service. Stoke never asked Diego where the real rifles were hidden.

Chapter Fifteen

MUSICAL !

The undersigned, having located in the city of Levanger, offers his
services to the citizens of town and country as Tuner and Repairer
of **Pianos, Melodeons, Accordions,** and **Flutinas**. Having had
several years experience in tuning, he hopes to merit a liberal share
of your patronage from those who have pianos.
Pianos tuned by the year on reasonable terms. All work warranted
Well done or no charge. He is also desirous of forming one or two
SINGING CLASSES in this city...
G. A. A. RIGGS

Stoke and Ari and Marilee wearily climbed into the jet. He was
reluctantly taking Ari back to Washington. His vacation was over.
For once in his life, vacations seemed like a good idea to Stoke instead
of an unwanted interruption.

Marilee belted herself in and quickly dozed off to sleep. Stoke rode
beside Ari on the first leg of the trip, holding her hand most of the
way.

"I guess I can't get you to transfer to Los Angeles, can I?" he asked.

"Can you transfer out to Washington?"

"No. I can't move all my businesses. But I might be able to leave
them with good managers for a few weeks at a time," he told her.

"Well, you know my situation; the Agency says where I'm to be sta-
tioned. And you know how fast the Government works, don't you?
They'll only let me transfer if there's an opening, and if it pleases my
masters. Certainly there's enough business for us in California."

"I might get awfully lonely out in L.A," he said.

"I might get awfully lonely in Washington," she returned.

They were silent until the plane got into Reagan Airport. The plane taxied down the runway to its docking area.

"What happens if I don't like it in L.A.?" Ari asked.

"Maybe you can see your bosses about a transfer back."

"Then what happens to *us*?"

"All I can say is, try it and see," he told her.

"Will you come to see me while I figure out what to do?" she murmured, with her head on his shoulder.

"I plan to be in Washington a great deal in the future."

"To see me?"

"To see you."

"You aren't going to add anything such as, 'and to talk with my senator' or 'and to campaign for new labor legislation?'"

"Just to see you."

"Stoke, you really are getting serious."

Stoke got off the plane with Ari. He had already ordered a car and driver to take her home. It was a painful parting for them. He held Ari as long as he could, until the plane was refueled.

Stoke and Marilee headed for California, with Stoke allowing the pilot to sleep for a couple of hours while he flew the jet. Marilee didn't wake up until they were on the ground at John Wayne Airport in Orange County, California.

When they got back to Newport Beach, Stoke found that the State Department had located Elizabeth Cho, and that she was greatly relieved that Marilee was with him. Together Stoke and Marilee called the number she had left. Marilee got to talk with her mother for a half-hour. Then Stoke asked for a letter or a fax stating that he had permission to keep Marilee and to supply medical treatment or any other needs until Elizabeth returned.

That night Stoke slept well. He had a new dream. In it, he was standing alone beside a small dirt road, holding a handful of his research papers. A small group of people in old style clothing stood on the other side, looking at him and waving goodbye. Someone in the group looked like his grandmother in an old photo his mother had kept. They all seemed to know him quite well. A man stepped out of the group, facing Stoke. He looked just like the man in Stoke's dreams, who had been murdered in the street in Levanger. The man smiled and said something. There was no sound, but it looked like he said, "Thank you." Then he bowed, and turned and joined the others as they sauntered down the road. Stoke watched them go, feeling sad, as though he was never going to see these people again. But he felt as if a great weight had been lifted from his shoulders.

When Stoke got up the next morning, he knew the dreams were finally over.

Afterword

Five years after Henry was murdered, an even stranger event occurred. It was not discovered until after this novel was written.

In a book called *Levanger County, Missouri* there is a report about a Col. Charles Stiffel, who brought a Union Army regiment into Levanger, Missouri in July of 1861. The Colonel was a German-American leading a St. Louis regiment of German-American soldiers. In other words, he didn't know people in Levanger at all, nor did his mostly German-speaking troops. For a reason no one could discern, the soldiers took a dozen men prisoners. They were civilians. Col. Stiffel put them on a boat called 'White Cloud.' Apparently, it was easier to guard the men on water than it was on land.

For some strange reason, a guard by the name of Henry Hoefel of Company A took one of the prisoners out and shot him. He said the man was trying to escape. Then they let the rest of the prisoners go.

One of the most convenient excuses in the world for an official killing is, "My prisoner was trying to escape." The response has to be, "Escape what?" Why would a businessman, too old for the military, spend time and effort escaping from soldiers who made a routine pickup of civilians? They didn't know the man personally and hardly spoke his language. The Civil War had just begun. There was no record of atrocities against civilians. Many people did not even take the War seriously.

On the other hand, perhaps the story is exactly as presented. Maybe the dead man had reason to flee. If so, what was he doing that was so important?

The prisoner was James Lightner. He was the only one shot. Lightner was the man who had financial dealings with Henry Vallandingham, who seemed to be in the pro-slavery cabal that brought about the murder of Henry, and who spied on the Abolitionists in Lawrence, Kansas.

It is easy to suppose he was singled out for his part in the action against Henry Vallandingham and the people of Lawrence, Kansas in the years leading to the Civil War.

Perhaps Henry Vallandingham was connected with a powerful group from the East, such as the Boston Emigration Society. And then, when they had an opportunity, the group directed the Army to execute Lightner.

The death of this man is just one more mystery.

Fred Myers, the confessed killer of Henry Vallandingham, is another mystery. He was not on the 1860 census for Missouri. Perhaps he went to Kentucky and just disappeared. He was too old for military service. Kentucky was a neutral border state where a man could avoid most of the fighting. Whatever the case, there is no record that he showed up in circuit court in Missouri. It is possible he was killed just to shut him up. But since the people who used him didn't seem to want blood on their hands, they probably just made sure he had left Missouri.

One thing is not a mystery: Henry Bruce Vallandingham was a hero, not an embarrassment, to his wife and his daughter.